By JP Barnaby

Bane of Boston
A Heart for Robbie
Mastering the Ride
Papi
Saving Hannah

With Rowan Speedwell
ASTER
A Pocketful of Stardust

LITTLE BOY LOST
Enlightened
Abandoned
Vanished
Discovered
Escaped
Sacrificed

SURVIVOR STORIES
Aaron
Ben
Spencer
Anthony
Sophie

Published by DREAMSPINNER PRESS
www.dreamspinnerpress.com

By ROWAN SPEEDWELL

Finding Zach
The Florentine Treasure
Hopes and Fears
Kindred Hearts
Love, Like Water
Night and Day

With JP Barnaby
ASTER
A Pocketful of Stardust

Published by DREAMSPINNER PRESS
www.dreamspinnerpress.com

A Pocketful of Stardust

JP BARNABY
& ROWAN SPEEDWELL

DREAMSPINNER PRESS

Published by

DREAMSPINNER PRESS

5032 Capital Circle SW, Suite 2, PMB# 279, Tallahassee, FL 32305-7886 USA
www.dreamspinnerpress.com

A Pocketful of Stardust
© 2019 J.P. Barnaby and Rowan Speedwell

Cover Art
© 2019 Tiferet Design
http://www.tiferetdesign.com/
Cover content is for illustrative purposes only and any person depicted on the cover is a model.

Trade Paperback ISBN: 978-1-64405-467-3
Digital ISBN: 978-1-64405-466-6
Library of Congress Control Number: 2019932530
Trade Paperback published July 2019
v. 1.0

Printed in the United States of America

This paper meets the requirements of
ANSI/NISO Z39.48-1992 (Permanence of Paper).

CHAPTER ONE

NOAH SLID closer to the desk and added a digital rendering of the image upload screen before using a numbered list to outline the exact steps needed to perform that function. He painstakingly walked through each mouse click, each option selection, and each message the end user would see. The work was tedious, made more so because Production released the new software to Quality Assurance after deadline and QA released it to Noah's team after deadline. But it paid pretty well, which kept him in New York. The apartment he shared with Yeira was just a few blocks from the office. A few blocks that included coffee, sandwiches, and books—the trifecta for a happy life.

"How you doin', Noah? Are we going to make it?" Karen popped her head around the corner of his cube, naked panic clear on her face.

"I've just got the section on the last toolbar to go." Noah glanced at the low right-hand corner of the laptop screen to check the time. "Yeah, we'll make it. If...."

"If what?"

"If you order out lunch?" he asked with a hopeful grin.

"You got it. Pizza good, or something else?"

"After livin' in Georgia all my life, I'll never get enough New York pizza," he said with a forced twang. He'd started to lose the accent at NYU, but seven years in the city had nearly obliterated it.

"Keep working. I'll have Caleb order."

He turned back to the keyboard and moved to the next item on the checklist. When he'd left Aster, Georgia, for New York and an English degree, he'd been thinking more Capote or Ginsberg than Gates. He thought he'd be sitting in a café with his laptop, observing life, and writing the great American novel. Only he liked to eat and live indoors. So like most great novelists, he got a real job writing tech manuals and perpetually tinkered with the novel that lurked in the back of his desk drawer.

Noah had just added the last line for that section and clicked Save when his phone rang—not his office phone but his cell phone. The number on the screen had a 678 west Georgia area code, but he didn't recognize it. Glancing up to see Karen's office door closed, he slid his finger across the screen.

"Hello?"

"Noah?" a deeply Southern voice asked.

"Yes, this is Noah Hitchens."

"Noah, it's Mrs. Mackey. From next door to your daddy?"

Noah sat back in his ergonomically correct chair and dropped his pen on the pad. He'd never spoken to Mrs. Mackey on the phone. He'd played in her yard, eaten her famous peach cobbler, he'd even cut her grass, but they didn't really pick up the phone.

"Hi, Mrs. Mackey, of course I remember you. What's—"

"Noah, honey, I don't know how to tell you this, so I'm just gonna come right out and say it." Her voice held tears, he could hear them, and the phone grew hot in his hand.

He remained silent, and she continued.

"I went to take your daddy a cobbler. You know how he loves a good cobbler. Anyway, when I got to the house, Jake was a-howlin' like crazy an' no one answered the door. I decided to leave the cobbler on the counter, so I went in through the back and—" She stopped like the burden had become too much.

It took a long moment for Noah to find his voice. "Ma'am, did something happen to my dad? Is he in the hospital?"

"Oh, honey. I called an ambulance, but there wasn't anything they could do. They rushed him over to County, said it was a heart attack, but…. Noah, sweetheart, he didn't make it."

The world went cold.

"Noah?" Karen asked, and though he could feel the hand on his shoulder, everything felt very far away.

"Mrs. Mackey, you're saying… you're saying my dad died?"

"Noah, I'm so sorry. I asked Doc Simmons to let me call so you didn't have to hear it from a stranger," she said quietly, finality in her response.

"I—I don't…." There was nothing he could say. His mind went blank in an instant with a soft, insistent buzzing—bees filling his brain.

"I know, honey. I'm gonna call the Garners. They took care of my Frank, and they'll take good care of Charlie," she told him, and he recognized that take-charge quality in her voice that old Southern women got in an emergency.

"Okay, I… I'll be there as soon as I can." He dropped the phone on his desk without waiting for a response.

It couldn't be happening.

He told himself that as he left a note for his roommate, Yeira, then as he made his way into a cab and through LaGuardia. He told himself that as he rented a car at Hartsfield-Jackson. He told himself that until a quarter to eleven that evening, when he used his key to let himself into his father's silent house. His father had never wanted the key back, and Noah had never offered.

It was the absence of giant loping paws across the hardwood floor that caused him to slide down the front door and land on the mat. Mrs. Mackey must have taken Jake to her place, which meant his father was really gone. He hated that the playful pup wasn't there to dry the tears spilling down his face. Sobs rolled over him—terrible, frightening things that made it hard to breathe. His mother hadn't wanted him, and now his dad was gone. He was alone in the world.

Noah sat with his back propped against the front door, unable to move farther into the living room. The mantel clock stared him down from its perch above the fireplace. He'd given the clock to his father almost a year ago. They'd spent a quiet Christmas Eve in front of the fire, with cocoa and gingerbread cookies that Mrs. Mackey had brought over. They'd headed over to her place the following day, but for that moment, it remained just the two of them. He'd loved those times.

The room blurred, distorting around his tears. He saw his face staring back at him from every corner of the room. He aged progressively through the photographs littering the small space. Years flipped by like pages of a book—Little League, prom, high school and college graduations. Noah saw himself with his father on fishing trips, at backyard barbecues, and birthday parties—his entire life chronicled by a proud father.

The picture closest to him sat on the mahogany side table next to an ancient wingback chair his grandmother had given them when Noah was just a boy. It had been her mother's, passed down through the ages like a good peach pie recipe. In the photograph, he and his father were standing in the bookstore, near the electric fireplace that was unnecessary in the mild

Georgia winters. Ol' Charlie had loved the rustic, homey feel of it. He had read *A Christmas Carol* to Noah right there in the big chair by the fire after he'd closed up for the day. It was always his favorite. He was sitting in that chair in the picture, a five-year-old Noah on the ottoman beside him, and Noah noticed their resemblance for the first time. He'd gotten his black hair from his vixen mother, but his steel-gray eyes were all his father's. They had the same stocky build, the same awkward gait—the same easy smile. Even their glasses were similar—Buddy Holly squares.

It took a long time for Noah to pick himself up off the hardwood floor and shuffle into the kitchen, where he found a cold Coors in the old fridge. He cracked it open, desperate to take the edge off the day.

For nearly ten minutes, Noah tried to decide if he was hungry. His brain had shut off somewhere during the cab ride to LaGuardia and hadn't come back on. In the end, sleep won over food. Noah drained the last of his beer and tossed the empty toward the open garbage can near the back door. He snorted when it bounced off the edge and clattered to the floor. He could almost hear his father saying that Noah couldn't even buy luck.

When he reached down to pick up the can, a flash caught his eye, and he glanced under the lip of the cabinet near the sink. Light reflected off something half-hidden in shadow. Noah tossed the can into the garbage and picked up a pair of glasses from the base of the cabinets.

He held his father's glasses, one lens broken, turning them over in his hands. Then he stopped, his body cold.

It had happened right there. His father had died right there in the open space near the cabinets, right by the stove.

Noah dropped the glasses into the sink, and shards of plastic clattered across the stainless steel. He took the stairs two at a time as he tried to outrun the images of his father lying on the cold floor, the horror of Jake howling mournfully.

Noah slammed the door of his childhood bedroom and fished the Kleenex out of his pocket. He unwrapped the Xanax he'd taken from Yeira's cabinet to deal with the shock of the day. She used them for her nightmares; maybe he could too. Not bothering with the bathroom across the hall, he swallowed it dry and crawled into the full-size bed, pulling the Star Wars comforter over his head.

He closed his eyes and prayed for the quiet oblivion the drug would bring.

CHAPTER TWO

THE NEXT morning, the sun glared down at Noah through the half-open blinds under the watchful eye of The Boy Who Lived. *Have you seen this wizard?* It took a moment for him to remember that poster hung in his childhood bedroom, not in his New York apartment, and the previous day came rushing back like bad Chinese food. The room spun a bit as he lay there amid the childhood he'd spent in his father's house. Well, probably his house now.

He didn't want to get up. The drug lingered in his system, making him feel sleepy and stupid. He decided if he stayed in bed, his father wouldn't have died because right then there was nothing to make it true. If he refused to come out from under the covers, his dad would come in and say good morning.

Unfortunately he had to pee, which meant either getting out of bed or being wet, icky, and uncomfortable. He crossed his legs and weighed his options. Harry kept staring down at him, and Noah wondered if there was a bladder-relieving spell. His stomach had started to cramp.

The pressure got to him and he sighed, throwing the covers back and rolling out of bed. When his feet hit the worn carpeting, he realized he still had his shoes on. Tears came again, but he pushed them away and started to strip as he headed for the bathroom. He was down to his briefs when he opened the bedroom door.

"Sweet fucking Jesus!" he screamed as he nearly collided with Mrs. Mackey, who stood on the other side of the door, her fist poised to knock.

"Noah Hitchens!" she cried sharply, a hand flying to her heaving chest.

"I'm sorry, ma'am. You scared me," he said sheepishly, and then, remembering he was nearly naked, danced sideways and put the door between them. He peeked his head round to look at her.

"There's still no cause for language like that!" she cried and touched the cross round her thin, turkey-wattle neck.

"I'm sorry," he said again. "Uhm, can I help you?" His bladder screamed in response.

"Oh, sweet boy. I came to help you. I'm going to go downstairs and see what your… what's in the kitchen for breakfast. I'll have something made when you come down." She glanced down at the doorknob, which was right in front of his junk on the other side of the door, and raised an eyebrow before heading back for the stairs.

He didn't remember Mrs. Mackey letting herself into the house when he lived here. She and his father must have gotten closer after he left. Maybe his father was lonely. It hurt his heart to think about.

His bladder throbbed painfully at him, and he scurried across the hall.

Twenty minutes later Noah jogged downstairs in a pair of basketball shorts and a tight Aster High School band T-shirt. His father had never gotten around to cleaning out his room. Noah thought maybe, in his heart, the older man half wanted Noah to move back home. But the other half of his heart wanted Noah to be happy. When he walked into his father's kitchen, he felt like that gawky teenager again, shambling around life without a clue. He'd been caught out in his underwear a few times then too, awkwardly explaining to Principal Merriweather that Matt Handley had stolen his clothes… again.

Those were the memories Noah had of Aster, Georgia—fear and embarrassment.

"How about some pancakes?" Mrs. Mackey asked from the stove as she expertly flipped a couple of hotcakes on a large griddle.

"That sounds great, Mrs. Mackey. Thank you."

"Noah, you're a grown man now. Why don't you call me Edna?" She smiled, warm and indulgent. She had a kind face, older than when he'd last seen it at Christmas. When his mom took off, Mrs. Mackey—Edna—had adopted him and his dad, kind of like puppies. Her husband, Frank, had taught him how to fish. He loved this old lady.

"Yes, ma'am. Those pancakes smell awesome," he said, and she ruffled his hair.

"We've got a long day ahead of us, and a good breakfast will help."

The smile dropped from his face, and he couldn't stop himself from glancing at the floor where he'd found his father's glasses. She started to speak when something big crashed into the back door. Noah grinned as

Jake came bounding through the doggie flap and jumped half in his lap. Even at ten, Jake was still as exuberant as the coal-colored puppy they'd brought home.

"Hey, buddy," he said and rubbed the dog's head and neck. Black fur flew into the air like coal dust. Jake licked his hands and his arms and his face. "There's a good boy." The big old dog couldn't have been more excited to see him. He loved that about Jake. Then, almost as fast as he started, Jake stopped. He cocked his head like he'd just had some random thought or heard a noise. Then he took off up the stairs. Noah could hear his big paws clattering through the upstairs rooms.

Mrs. Mackey—Edna—set a plate of food in front of him, but he left it sitting while Jake raced back down the stairs and toured the living room. Then he came back into the kitchen. Slower. Quieter. He sat at Noah's feet and, with a look so somber it made Noah ache, asked a single question with his big brown eyes.

Where is he?

Noah abandoned his food and slid to the floor. Jake crawled into his lap, massive paws digging into his bare leg. He didn't care. Jake's head hit his shoulder and Noah wrapped trembling arms around the dog's body, rubbing him and taking comfort in his unconditional love. A tear slid down into the dog's fur.

"Honey, you need to eat. Jake'll be okay," Miss Edna said, her voice gentle. She set a plate of food at his father's spot at the table for her. Noah rubbed Jake again and kissed the top of his big black head.

"It's gonna be okay, boy, I promise," he whispered, more to himself than to the dog. He refused to think about the future. Right then he could only handle one hour at a time. Tomorrow he would worry about one day at a time.

"Noah, I called the Garners yesterday. They own that place over on Magnolia. They want you to come by today with your father's papers and make some decisions," Miss Edna said gently, like he might come off the rails if she spoke louder.

"I'm sure whatever you decided is fine." The sounds came out as one long, complete word. He shook his head slightly, trying to ward off the responsibilities that she wanted to foist onto him.

"Let's just find your daddy's papers first, okay? First things first," she said, her voice firm.

"Yes, ma'am." He nodded. Then he climbed back up into his seat like an adult and forced down a bite of the pancakes. They felt like sawdust in his mouth, but he was a good Southern boy. If someone put food in front of you, you ate it. Anything else would be an insult.

He finally got most of the pancakes down and declared that they were delicious, but he couldn't eat another bite. And they were, but his stomach roiled like snakes were fighting one another for the syrup.

"Okay," Miss Edna said, taking their plates to the sink. He noticed that she stepped around an area in the middle of the floor and didn't think too hard about why. "Why don't you start with the desk in the den?"

Noah knew an order when he heard one, so he stood up. Old Jake stood with him, and together they meandered to the den where his dad had kept a desk, a safe, and three full walls of bookshelves. They reminded Noah of his dad's bookstore. He'd spent half his life in that store, playing in the aisles. That was where his father had nurtured his love of reading.

Tears stung his eyes at the orderly perfection of the desktop that was the very definition of his father. *A place for everything and everything in its place*, his dad would say. Noah wasn't so conscientious, and his keys went missing about once a month. Last month they were in the refrigerator. An old laptop sat dark, quiet, and cold near the back edge, like it had been pushed out of the way and forgotten. A neat wooden cup of pens was positioned next to a cheap black blotter. All the pens were the same—style, size, and color.

The inbox on his left seemed out of place in the tidy space. It overflowed with opened, official-looking letters. Some of them had FINAL NOTICE stamped across the top. Perplexed, Noah picked them up and started to riffle through. They were bills. Some of them appeared to be up-to-date, like the electric and gas, but one looked almost like a legal document. He was no lawyer, but it might have been a foreclosure notice. Was Dad about to lose the house? The store?

"Noah, did you find anything?" Miss Edna called from the hallway, and he folded up the paper and stuffed it in his shorts pocket. He'd read it… after. Instead, he turned his attention back to the task at hand.

8

The desk had two bottom drawers that held hanging file folders. In true Charlie Hitchens fashion, his dad had labeled everything in neat block print: BILLS, RECEIPTS, JAKE, HOUSE. Noah flipped through each one until he came to a folder that had a neon tab and MY DEATH.

He sat on the hardwood floor, Jake's head in his lap, and opened the folder. Some of it he didn't recognize right away, but he figured out the will, bank accounts, and emergency contacts pretty easily. There was a note with his lawyer's number and his accountant's. The rest he had to read through. His father already had a plot at Sunny Lawns cemetery where Noah's grandparents were buried. He had a life insurance policy for ten thousand dollars near the front of the folder. It seemed everything Noah needed to bury his father lay in his hands. So simple.

"Noah, did you find anything?" Miss Edna asked again from the doorway. He held up the folder noiselessly. Jake didn't move or bother to look up; instead he snuggled closer to Noah.

She looked through and nodded.

"It was thoughtful of him to be so organized. Frank put me through hell trying to find everything when he passed. Bless his heart." She touched her cross again and then held out a hand to Noah. "We should get started."

He wasn't about to let the old lady heft him up, so he rolled onto his knees and Jake popped up next to him. Noah put a hand on his soft black fur and stopped.

"I don't want to leave him here by himself, where Dad—"

"Bring him along. Everyone loves old Jake, he's a good dog." She rubbed his head and he licked her palm. "Slobbery as he is." She laughed as she rubbed her hand over well-worn jeans.

"Yes, ma'am. I'm just going to run upstairs and change. My suitcase is in the living room. I… uhm, didn't take it up with me last night."

The compassion in her look hurt his eyes, so he turned and walked up the stairs without another word. Noah changed quickly into a pair of khaki shorts and a short-sleeved button-down shirt. He'd brought his only suit for… for later, so people would have to deal with him casual until then. Noah had no idea what the protocol was—he hadn't been to a funeral since his grandparents died when he was a kid—but he didn't feel like wearing grown-up clothes anyway.

The chirping of his phone caught him by surprise. It buzzed and sang across the top of the dresser next to an old remote-control jeep he hadn't touched in years. The phone clattered dangerously toward the edge, and Noah picked it up to look at the display. Karen's name appeared, and he realized with a hard slap of guilt that he'd forgotten to call and let her know what was going on.

He slid his finger across the screen and answered with a tired "Hi, Karen."

"Hey, Noah, how are you?" Her voice came across the waves agitated, but concerned, like she was looking over her shoulder while she talked.

"We're about to go to the funeral home and finalize the arrangements." He wanted to ask if everything was okay, but to be honest, he didn't actually care.

"I'm sorry." Her voice trailed off.

"I'll get through it." He fiddled with the control for the jeep. The little light didn't come on when he flipped the switch. Something in him cracked a little deeper. Broken. It was all broken.

"Any idea when you'll be heading back?"

"No. There's a lot to do here with the house and business, so it will take a bit. What's going on?" He flipped over the jeep and hit the power switch. That light came on and it lifted his spirits. He'd have to pick up batteries for the control.

"Noah, they sent us the wrong link. They needed to send us the stabilized release, but they sent us the link for the sandbox. Some of the documentation needs to be rewritten. They gave us two days," Karen said, the words tumbling one over the other. He could hear the panic between them.

He took a long, slow breath.

"Karen, I'm burying my father."

"Noah, I know, I'm sorry. I shouldn't have brought it up. I just wondered if you had your laptop, is all."

"No, Karen. It's on my desk." He set the jeep back down, resolute.

"A courier—"

"No. Are you kidding me? I get that Todd is your bowling buddy and all, but tell him to stop fucking day trading when he's supposed to be working. He's capable of doing the rewrites. I can't believe you'd consider putting this on me."

"I know, I—"

"I have to go. The funeral people are waiting." He didn't pause to let her say goodbye; he simply pulled the phone away from his ear and hit the End button. His hands tingled from anger and anxiety. It took a long slow breath, and then one more, before he could leave the room and jog back down the stairs. Noah didn't want Miss Edna to worry.

They both had enough to worry about.

CHAPTER THREE

"READY, SON?" Miss Edna asked and put a hand on his arm. It had been four days, but he didn't think he'd ever be ready to say goodbye to his father.

"No, but I guess hiding under my bed isn't really an option today." He turned to face her.

"And I don't think you're gonna fit anymore." She smiled, and that helped loosen the knot in his chest enough so he could breathe.

"Probably not, and Jake would just lie there and lick my face." Noah glanced past Miss Edna to the big lab lying on the rug in the hallway. The dog had flopped on his side, and he lay like a pile of rags, his furry face pointed toward them, lost haunted eyes watching. Noah wondered if the big guy understood that his favorite human had left him forever.

He followed Miss Edna downstairs, and Jake came trudging behind. He'd been so lethargic in the past two days that it had started to worry Noah.

"Okay, buddy, I'm gonna turn on the TV for you. We'll be back in a little while." Noah patted the couch and Jake climbed up onto the cushions. He didn't jump, he simply stepped. Miss Edna turned on a cooking show for him while Noah refilled the food dish the poor pup hadn't touched the day before.

He noticed Miss Edna didn't say Jake would be all right this time. Noah kissed the dog on the head and whispered for him to be a good boy, that he'd be right back, that he wasn't leaving. A tear slipped down his face and he wiped it away with the heel of his hand.

Neither of them would ever be okay again.

"I'm ready," Noah choked out and held the door open for Miss Edna as his father had taught him all his life. They took the rental this time; the woman could get in and out comfortably in her low heels. It was the first time he'd noticed her dress. It wasn't black but a deep navy that flattered her. She wore it with a pillbox hat.

"You look pretty, Miss Edna," he said as he settled behind the wheel and tried to remember where the parking brake was.

"Thank you, son." She didn't say anything more but gazed out the window. His father had been like a son to her, and her tired, drawn face held all of her words.

It took just two hours for them to bury his father. The funeral home, the procession, the graveside words, they all brought his world to an end. He wanted to go home, to curl up with Jake and cry alone in peace, but there were protocols. His father would expect him to be a gracious host.

Miss Edna's church ladies were in full flurry by the time they pulled up outside his father's house. Charlie would have been warmed by the turnout. Practically everyone in town had started to line their street, even people Noah didn't know. He helped his elderly shadow from the car, and together they came up the walk to the sounds of life and laughter Noah had not expected after such a somber affair. Even Jake had come out of his funk, though the fact that little Kimmy Conners, the six-year-old with pigtails from down the street, was feeding him bits of cold cuts off the meat tray probably helped. She giggled every time he licked her fingers.

Someone had opened up the windows, and Noah caught the smell of fresh burning leaves. You didn't get that much in New York, and he loved that smell; it always reminded him of fall in Aster with its hay rides and apple cider. He also smelled something sweet, peach cobbler maybe, as he headed into the kitchen to mountains of food on every available surface. A square sheet of plywood rested atop the stove for another makeshift buffet spot. Something akin to panic and anger welled up in him to see people standing in that spot by the stove. He wanted to yell at them that his father had lost his life right there where their dirty shoes scuffed over the tile. But he caught himself, because it was ridiculous.

It was so ridiculous.

The knot that had been tied around his lungs since he walked into the kitchen that first night loosened a little, and for the first time, he could breathe. It was just a room—nothing more. He took another deep breath and stepped out of the kitchen, bumping right into a short, round woman in a blinding yellow sundress. It was Noah's dad's neighbor from across the street, he thought; she'd moved in since Noah had gone to New York, so he didn't know her well.

"I'm sorry for your loss, Noah. Your father was a good man. He used to come over and help fix things after my Ralph had passed." Her soft gray eyes watered with sympathy, and she thrust yet another casserole dish at him. With the foil covering, he couldn't even begin to guess what it contained. When he took it, he felt the tape along the bottom, which would contain her name so he could return it after he'd washed the Corningware mountain.

"Thank you, ma'am."

"Call me, Sarah, Noah," she said with an earnest smile.

"Thank you, Miss Sarah."

Out of the corner of his eye, Noah caught a flash of auburn hair glinting in the late afternoon sun. He figured it was one of his Kentucky cousins who had come down for the funeral—they were the only ones he knew with such fiery locks. Then he saw the flash again and a pair of guarded hazel eyes, more green than brown, locked with his. No, he didn't know this guy. He'd have remembered seeing him. The encounter lasted no more than a second because the guy ducked his head and darted on, but the freckles spread across those smooth pale cheeks hit him like fire. He took a step forward, unsure what to do. It was a wake, for God's sake, he couldn't—

"Noah?"

The voice was vaguely familiar, deep and thick with an almost farcical Georgia drawl. Noah couldn't place it at first, but then the crowd around him thinned and a tall, heavyset man moved forward to grasp his hand in a punishing grip. "Uncle James?"

It had been years since he'd seen his mother's brother, and those years hadn't been kind. Oh, he was wearing an expensive suit—Noah's years in New York had left him familiar with designer wear. But his complexion was too ruddy, he was sweating even in the air-conditioning, and he wheezed a bit as he elbowed past one of the Edwards twins to get to Noah. "Good to see you, boy, even at a sad event as this. How you been?"

"Okay under the circumstances," Noah replied. "Um—can I get you a water or tea?"

"No, no, not at all. I can't stay long—your aunt Violet hates these things. Difficult woman, difficult woman."

Noah remembered his uncle's wife as a meek, indecisive woman whose main conversation was repeating whatever her husband had just said. He nodded as if in agreement. "Thanks for coming, anyway," he said. "I didn't see Aunt Violet...."

"Oh, she's in the kitchen. Brought you a casserole." He snorted. "Feed it to the dog—Vi's a lousy cook."

"I'm sure it's fine, sir."

His uncle snorted again. "Your freezer'll probably buckle under the weight of casseroles from all these biddies. They mostly came to see how bad your daddy left the house. Think a man alone can't manage."

"It's all fine."

"Charlie did okay for himself, domestically at least. Left his finances in somewhat of a mess, I hear,." Though the uncouth comment was completely out of place, James seemed quite pleased with himself. "Look." He reached into his inner suit jacket pocket and pulled out a business card. "When all this is over, give me a ring and we'll have lunch. Help you with the estate. Doing pretty well in real estate—I know the market around here. You're gonna sell the store, I can help you get the best price. I imagine you can't wait to get back to New York. Aster's a nice town, but sleepy. Not much here for a young firebrand like yourself. And you sure as shootin' don't need a white elephant like a bankrupt bookstore hangin' over your head, 'specially one where the last owner up and disappeared. Help you out—after all, you're family."

"Bankrupt? And wait, what do you mean disappeared?"

"Later, we can talk later. No one talks business at a funeral." He glanced around, not meeting Noah's gaze, and then started to turn.

"Um, fine. Thanks." Noah pocketed the card and shook his uncle's hand again.

He waited until his uncle had herded his aunt—who hadn't changed an iota since he'd seen her last—out the front door before wiping Uncle James's sweat from his palm.

If James knew about the bookstore, then other people did too. He'd talk to Miss Edna about it the next day. His uncle was right about one thing—a funeral was no place to discuss it. Maybe he would have lunch with James, see what his uncle had in mind.

"That man is very unpleasant."

He glanced over at Miss Edna in surprise. "Dad liked him. They were friends before Dad married Mom, and Uncle James was furious with her when she left. He always supported Dad."

"That's because he could always get more use out of your dad than his own deadbeat sister. But he's a rusty penny. Besides, if he wasn't here, word would get around, and James Montgomery lives and dies by his reputation. At least he thinks so. He's a legend in his own mind."

Noah chuckled. "Oh, Miss Edna."

She took another of the endless casseroles from his hand and bustled into the kitchen with it.

His mother. He hadn't thought about her in a long time. Thank God she hadn't shown up. Miss Edna might have taken a switch to her in the backyard. That sweet old lady had no love lost for the woman who had walked away from her only son. Noah felt the same way—he'd been so young when she'd left he didn't really remember her. She was just an unpleasant part of his past.

Another unpleasant part of his past was moving through the room toward him. Noah groaned internally. Matt Handley. Of course he'd still be around—his family owned the biggest bank in town, and knowing Matt, he was probably running it by now. He was still good-looking, and unlike Uncle James, his football physique hadn't decayed into flab.

If he hadn't been such an asshole, he would have been one of Noah's high school crushes. But after being shoved into one too many lockers, having his lunch stolen and Coke dumped on his homework, he'd lost any interest in the hometown football hero.

"Noah."

"Matt."

"Sorry to hear about your old man. Must be tough."

"Yeah. It's okay. How you doing?"

"Not bad. Work at the bank now, of course. You're in computers or something, I hear."

"Yeah."

"New York must be an exciting place after this sleepy little burg." He laughed. It irritated Noah.

"It has its moments."

"I have a fiancée. She lives in Atlanta, so I spend a lot of time in the city." The disdain in his voice told Noah more than he wanted to know about Matt. He might have his business here in Aster, but his opinion of the place hadn't changed in the years since Noah'd been gone. Never good enough for the scion of the Handleys. "You married yet?"

"No. Gay, remember?"

"Yeah, but you gays can get married now." Matt snorted in amusement. "Which would you be, I wonder? The man or the lady?"

Noah sighed. "Neither. Hey, there's cake on the sideboard. Why don't you help yourself? There's Miz Blackwell's chocolate cream cake."

"Oh man, that's the best. I might have to snag a piece, even if I have to work it off later." He eyed Noah's less-than-stellar physique. "I belong to a real nice gym in the city. It's a chain, so maybe there's one in New York."

Noah smiled with all his teeth. "Thanks. I'll let you know."

"By the way, you'd better come by the bank pretty soon. Your dad kind of left his finances a mess. You'll need to deal with it sooner rather than later."

Matt tapped his forehead and turned toward the sideboard. As soon as his attention wandered, Noah hustled out of the room, looking for someplace quiet to calm his incipient headache.

Well, that explained the notices. It hurt in a way he couldn't explain that his father hadn't confided in him that he was in trouble. Matt's jubilation about it just pissed him off more.

There wasn't a room on the first floor of the house that wasn't full of people, all dressed in their Sunday best. Noah moved through the knots of conversationalists, feeling like a ghost—when people spoke to him, he responded, though afterward he couldn't quite remember what he'd said. And though the knots parted as he moved through them, when he turned around again, they had closed up, like water flowing in to fill an empty space. He felt like that—like an empty space in the world.

His phone vibrated against his leg, and he slid it out of his pocket. It took just a second for his practiced fingers to pop open the text from his roommate, Yeira.

You doing okay?

17

Noah dropped onto a stair halfway up and thought about that for a very long moment.

I'm hanging in there, he replied because that was the best he had.

I tossed your leftover Chinese. It was starting to reek.

He snorted. It was just like Yeira to be practical when he wanted to be anything but.

I don't know when I'll be back, but I'll pay my half of the rent for next month right now so I don't forget. With everything going on, he would forget, and it was due next week. It took no time at all to bring up his banking app and send the payment, though he felt weird paying his rent at his father's memorial. He had an idea that he'd feel weird for a while.

Thanks, but I really just wanted to see how you were.

I brought one of your Xanax. Right now I wish it were a whole bottle.

I'd have given it to you. Sorry I wasn't here. He closed his eyes against the tears welling there. They'd become good friends since he'd moved in, and it always floored him how much she cared about people.

You couldn't have known. You were at work too. The show must go on.

I'm a junior reporter. It could go on without me.

I couldn't, he told her honestly.

You're going to be okay, honey. You'd be surprised what you could live through. I'm headed to the studio. Let me know if you need anything.

I will.

He drifted back into the kitchen, where Miss Edna was directing ladies on putting out cakes and lemonade and sweet tea on silver trays that must belong to her, because he couldn't remember his dad ever owning such things. Miss Norma, who played the piano at church, if Noah remembered correctly, handed him a sweet tea. "You look like you need it, sweet chile," she murmured.

"Thank you, ma'am." He took the glass, noting absently that her brown hand was thinner and the veins more prominent than he remembered. Surprised, he looked up at her face and realized she had gotten older. He glanced around the kitchen, recognizing almost all the ladies puttering around, and felt shocked and uncertain to see how old they had all gotten. Had it been that long since he'd gone to New York? He'd seen some of them on his visits home. Why had they all gotten so old so quickly? Or was it just that he was feeling his own mortality? His dad hadn't been that old when he'd died.

Noah wished suddenly that he hadn't gone to New York—that he'd stayed in Aster and worked with his dad in the store. He'd known that was what his dad had wanted, but he'd never said so. Never tried to change Noah's mind or pressure him into staying. He found his eyes suddenly full of tears and set the glass of tea down, unable to breathe.

Miss Edna took the glass and said, "Jake needs to go out."

He blinked at her. "Ma'am?"

"Take Jake for a walk. You've done your duty here. I'll see to the rest of it."

His eyes blurred again, and he said, "Thank you. You've done so much for us. I can't—"

"Hush, child—I know." She reached up and kissed his cheek. "Now go on. Jake's legs are crossin'."

With a sodden laugh, he went to get the leash.

Noah found Jake hiding out in the pantry, away from the crowds, but he leaped to his feet as Noah opened the door, and stood wagging his tail so hard he looked like he was going to take off like a helicopter. Noah slapped his thigh and the big dog followed him to the door. He found his dad's key ring on the hook by the door where he'd always kept it. It had an "I Heart NY" keychain Noah had sent him right after he'd moved there, though the tag had gotten worn and chipped over the years from unlocking the store.

Jake stopped in the back doorway, and Noah nearly tripped over him. The red-haired guy he had seen earlier sat alone on the back porch, gazing up into the night sky. Unlike in New York with its constant glow, you could actually see the stars in Aster. Noah looked up too. It was a clear night, and he wondered if his dad could see him through the absence of clouds.

The guy had a slim profile, with a shock of red hair that seemed black in the semidarkness. The hunch of his shoulders bothered Noah. It seemed he and the stranger both had the weight of the world on them. He wanted to sit down next to the guy and introduce himself, but Jake decided to lick the back of the guy's neck, just under his ear. It startled him so hard, he fell sideways off the steps and onto the unruly grass below.

"Jake! I'm so sorry," Noah called as he jumped from the stairs as he'd done a thousand times in his youth. Jake beat him to the punch and sat licking the guy's face with big slobbering kisses. To his surprise, the guy laughed, and the sound lifted him in a way Noah hadn't thought possible right then.

"S'okay," he said. "I love dogs." He continued to scratch Jake's ears until the big ol' guy gave up the ghost and threw himself onto his back in an obvious invitation. A smile lit up the guy's face, making it impossible for Noah to look away. He watched them for a long moment, smiling, until it started to feel awkward.

"I'm Noah." He gave a little half wave rather than trying to shake the guy's hand around Jake's assault.

"Kyle."

"Did you know my dad?" Noah sat on the edge of the porch.

"No, I'm here with my… Sarah from across the street."

Noah finally broke his gaze and found Jake wiggling back and forth in the grass under Kyle's pets.

"You're such a whore, Jake," Noah laughed, but the guy looked at him with strange intensity, almost anger. Then it was gone. He stood abruptly, a troubled expression still on his handsome face. Noah wanted to take it back, whatever he'd done wrong, so the guy would stay. For just a while, he hadn't felt alone.

"I should get back. Aunt Sarah's probably looking for me." He jogged around the back corner of the house and was gone before Noah could reply—before he could even get more than a name. Noah watched him go and the weight of the day crashed back onto him.

"What was that?" Noah asked Jake, but he simply lay in the grass waiting for someone, anyone, to rub that massive belly. Noah laughed and scratched his way from the neck down, making sure to miss the dog's frank and beans.

"Come on, buddy, let's go for a walk."

They wandered out of the yard and down streets gone unusually quiet. Noah wondered about that, then realized that half the town was in his house, eating cake and drinking tea. He turned down the side street that led to the business district, stopping on every block so Jake could claim another tree.

The keys rattled as he pulled them out of his pocket and used them on the front door of Stardust Books, Aster's only bookstore. The familiar sound of wind chimes tinkled cheerfully as it opened, but the shop was dark and smelled faintly dusty. Like old books. In the ambient light, Noah typed his birthday into the alarm keypad to stop the incessant beeping. It took him a minute to remember where the light switch was, but when he found it and flicked the lights on, he saw that the place was just as he remembered. Books had been piled everywhere in his dad's notion of organization: science fiction dumped on one table in weird stacks, with alien figurines and Star Wars characters climbing on them; the mystery books shelved backward, hiding their spines; the romance novels on a lace-covered table with a bouquet of silk flowers; a Stetson sitting on top of the shelf of Westerns. The "serious books" nook, floor-to-ceiling shelves filled with classics, held an oriental carpet and an electric fireplace next to the ancient leather chair and ottoman. A cabinet with an empty decanter set rounded out his dad's vision of a British men's club. Noah had spent a lot of time curled up in that chair, reading, while his dad tended the shop. Often—not just at Christmas—his dad would sit in that chair while Noah perched on the ottoman, both of them absorbed in whatever book they were into at the time.

He wondered what kind of books the red-haired guy liked to read. His dad always used that as a guide by which to measure people—the books they read. Noah would have been about twelve in his eyes, then, because he'd become a huge YA fan.

Toward the back was the kids' section. A model train track ran along the top of the shelves, and brightly colored books faced out so the kids could read the titles easily. Noah'd spent a lot of time there too. The shelf with the Harry Potter books had a set of wands in the display case, along with a bunch of other fantasy titles and a stuffed unicorn. That was new. There were kids' books on the shelves in front of the counter too, and a selection of greeting cards and stationery. The cash register was an antique, brass and tarnished, with keys that you had to really smack to get to work, and it didn't track your inventory the way new ones did. Noah supposed he'd probably have to replace it at some point—if he kept the store.

But that was crazy.

He stopped walking. It hadn't occurred to him until that moment—the bookstore was his.

But keep it? He didn't know anything about running a business. The idea of closing it, giving up on the store, kind of made him sick to his stomach. It was his dad's dream, not his, but saying goodbye to the store would be kind of like saying goodbye to his dad—again.

And he just couldn't imagine old Jake in his tiny apartment, on that tiny elevator, or padding through the crowded streets of Manhattan. What would a country dog do in the city?

He went and sat down in the leather club chair, and Jake came and lay at his feet, relaxing with a heavy dog sigh. "I dunno, Jake," he said, and Jake sighed again and rested his chin on Noah's foot. "I feel like I've been flapping in the breeze and just got cut loose. I don't know what to do. Do I want to stay here? My life's in New York. Yeah, I'm not exactly setting the world on fire, but I have friends and a job, and New York is so interesting. And busy. And so much is happening all the time. Nothing ever happens here. When someone talks about a sleepy little town, they're talking about here." He glanced around the tiny store, his eyes stinging with unshed tears. "How did he even stay in business?"

Jake lifted his head and looked at him. "You miss him too, don't you, Jake?"

The thick tail thumped once and Jake put his head down again. "Yeah, I know. Well, I guess I can't do anything right now, not till I talk to the lawyer and see what's going on. For all I know Dad left the store to Miss Edna." But he couldn't imagine the old woman faring any better at it than he would. He wouldn't know what was going on until he got access to his records. Dad always said there was no use borrowing trouble.

"But Jesus, Jake. I miss him."

Dogs weren't mind readers, but Jake seemed to know what Noah was thinking. Probably just responding to his tone of voice. But he whined in agreement.

A cold wet nose bumped up against his hand. Noah went down onto one knee and wrapped his arms around the big dog. He didn't say anything, and neither did Jake. They held on tight, buffeted by the swirling, storming seas of where life had taken them.

The door jingled, and Noah glanced up to see Fred, the mailman, standing there. "Hey, Noah. Been holdin' your mail. I was gonna drop it by the house, but saw the light on here, so I took a chance." He set a stack of envelopes and a thick package on the counter. "Looks like another book or three. Guess you need some, huh?" It was the same joke Fred had made with Charlie a thousand times over the years.

"Can't ever have too many books, Fred," Noah replied, just as his father used to.

Fred grinned but then sobered. "Sorry I couldn't get to the wake—I hadda get back to work after the funeral. He was a good man, Noah. He's gonna be missed. You gonna take over the store?"

"I don't know yet, Fred. I was pondering that very question."

"Think about it. Wouldn't be Aster without the Stardust."

"I will, Fred. Thanks."

The mailman nodded and, after greeting Jake, who'd padded over to get his usual pat on the head, wandered out the door. Noah got up and went to the counter, looking over the stack of envelopes. He'd have to go through them sooner or later, but for now he carried them and the package of books back to the office at the rear of the store.

It was really more of a kitchenette than an office; there was an apartment-sized fridge and a small bistro table with two chairs, and a bunch of cabinets. A counter-height stool sat in front of a computer setup on the counter; a green light blinked steadily on it. Still online, Noah supposed. He'd have to ask if the lawyer had the password so he could see if Charlie had fulfilled his promise to get the inventory uploaded. He added the pile of letters and the books to others on the counter and looked in the fridge, the way he automatically did when he'd come into the office before.

There they sat, the bottles of commercial sweet tea that Charlie had been addicted to. Miss Edna had always decried Charlie's habit, averring that the only good tea was homemade, but Charlie never had the patience for it. Other than those, the fridge was empty except for a black banana, which Noah plucked out of there and took out to the garbage.

When he came back in, Jake was growling at the door to the upstairs, the door Charlie never opened. He'd always told Noah there wasn't anything up there worth seeing, and even though Noah usually questioned everything, something about Charlie's voice when he said that had made him listen. He'd have to take a look up there, he supposed, but not now. He glanced down and saw Jake still staring at the door. "What is it, boy? There a mouse or something there?"

Jake looked up at him, then at the door, then shook his head, tags jingling, and went out into the store.

"Huh," Noah said. He looked at the door, then reached for the knob. It didn't turn, and none of the keys on the ring seemed to fit. But for some strange reason, he was okay with that. He didn't want to go up there. His spine tingled from Jake's growl, and a shiver raced over him like someone stepped on his grave.

He shook his head. He'd always had an imagination. Too bad he couldn't seem to harness it enough to get his great American novel written. Maybe he did need to stay here in sleepy Aster, running the bookstore and writing in the slow moments. Maybe a dull life was what he needed to focus on his writing. Hell, wasn't it Nathaniel Hawthorne who worked as a customs agent? Or was that Melville? He shrugged and thought about googling it; then he heard Jake's friendly bark and went back out into the shop.

"Miss Edna."

"I thought I'd find you here, sweetheart. Everyone's gone and it's safe to come home now. Doin' some remembering?"

"Yeah. It's a good place." He bent and rubbed Jake's ears. The tail was going two-forty again.

"It is. But remember, honey, your dad didn't want you to feel obliged to stay here. He knew you had dreams too. If you decide you don't want to carry on, he wouldn't be offended."

"Thanks, Miss Edna. I'll take that under advisement."

She laughed. "Fancy way of sayin' you'll think about it. Just remember, for all its faults, there are worse places to live than Aster."

He sobered and put a hand on her arm. "Did you know the bookstore was in trouble?"

She sighed and rested a small, wrinkled hand on Jake's head. He looked up at her expectantly and she rubbed his ears. "I knew something was wrong. He never told me specifically that it was the bookstore, but he'd been anxious these last few months."

"Why didn't he tell me? I could have come back. I could have helped out." Noah stepped back to let Miss Edna leave first, Jake at her side. He turned to set the alarm and lock up, and she waited for him to face her again.

"Maybe that's why he didn't tell you, Noah. He wanted you to live your life, not his. He said you'd found yourself in New York."

"That doesn't mean I wouldn't have come."

As he was walking home beside her, Jake gamboling like the puppy he used to be, Noah thought about it. Yeah, there were worse places. Aster was small and friendly, and there didn't seem to be a lot of crime. It had a charmed history—the town had been founded by former slaves, so it had been solidly integrated for generations. The worst that had happened to Noah, being gay, was Matt Handley and his cohorts, and they hadn't even been that violent, just harassing. The big oaks and elms that shaded the streets—even the main commercial streets—gave the town a relaxed, sleepy air, and the Victorian-styled streetlamps—new since last year—and the window boxes and plantings made it feel warm and welcoming.

Yeah. He could do worse than stay here.

But there was his job. And New York itself—busy, exciting, full of new things and new faces. Museums, libraries, Central Park, clubs, restaurants serving all kinds of weird, exotic ethnic food—the very rhythm of the traffic was like blood pumping through a living heart.

He could do worse than go back there too.

As they turned down the street they lived on, Miss Edna said softly, "Birds gotta fly, Noah. But sometimes—sometimes the nest calls them home. Take it under advisement."

He smiled at her. "Thank you, ma'am. I will."

Chapter Four

SATURDAY MORNING Noah worked at the counter on his father's computer, which, to Noah's horror, had no password. Bless his daddy's heart. They were coming up on the end of October in about a week and half. He needed to figure out what bills were due. Noah had flipped the sign to Closed, but the lights were on and the door unlocked. When he heard a tentative knock, Noah glanced up to see the young auburn-haired man standing there. He smiled and waved him in.

"Hi," the guy said shyly.

"Hey, come on in," he said, pushing a box over to the side so he could see the beautiful man a little better. Jake perked his head up at the newcomer, sniffing the air.

"Thanks. I saw the lights on."

"Were you just wandering by?" Noah smiled and pushed the computer away.

"I was asked to bring this over to you." He held out the package he'd carried over. "It's pound cake. Aunt... I mean, Sarah says you're probably sick of casseroles."

"That's nice of her. Please tell her thank you for me. I'll try and stop by later today to see her—it's been a while since I talked to anyone without a jillion people around." Noah set the package off to the side.

"Yeah, the... wake?" At Noah's nod, he went on. "It was really crowded. I've never been to a wake before."

"My dad was pretty popular."

"Yeah, Aunt... well, Sarah said he was a really nice man. I'm sorry I didn't get a chance to meet him. I've been here a couple of weeks, but I didn't get out much." Kyle glanced around at the books. Noah watched him quietly.

"So is she your aunt or not?"

"What?" Kyle's focus came back to him.

"Miss Sarah. You keep starting to call her aunt but then correcting yourself," Noah said.

"Well, she's sort of my aunt. Distantly. She said I could call her Sarah, but it seems kinda disrespectful. Where I grew up, we didn't call adults by their first names." Kyle shrugged. He put a hand on the back of his neck and looked up at Noah through his lashes. Something in Noah tugged at him, hard.

"Where did you grow up?"

It took Kyle a minute to answer, but then he said "out west" like he was trying to be deliberately vague.

Noah watched him play with a pen on the counter.

"We don't here much either, call elders by their first names. I mean, my dad was close with Miss Edna, but he never called her anything but Miss Edna. I called her Miz Mackey when I was a kid, but now that I'm grown-up"—he made air quotes—"I can call her Miss Edna. Why don't you call Miss Sarah that?"

"Call her Miss Edna? I don't think she'd like that." Kyle smiled shyly.

Noah laughed. The guy had a cute smile, shy as it was. He decided he liked Kyle.

"I like Miss Sarah." He met Noah's gaze again. There was something lurking in his soft green eyes, some kind of sadness or maybe fear, but Noah didn't press. Maybe if they became friends, he'd find out what it was.

"So. You want a glass of tea or something? Some of Miss Sarah's cake?"

"I... sure. Yes. I don't really have anywhere to be."

"Come on back, then. There's a fridge in the office." Noah grabbed the package and led the way back down a narrow corridor to a sunny office space. He'd set his personal laptop up on the counter there so he could sit on the barstool, though there was a big desk. It always just seemed to be... Dad's. Jake lay down on his bed in the corner. He must have come to work with his dad often, because he seemed to have a bed in every room. Noah opened the refrigerator. "Dad liked his sweet tea, so he always had it in here."

"I... um, if you're going to have some...."

"Are you kidding? Miss Sarah's pound cake is legendary. Or should I say 'legen—wait for it—dary'?"

Kyle cocked his head.

"It's from a TV show. Neil Patrick Harris is godlike."

"You shouldn't say that." Kyle looked appalled. "That's blasphemy."

Noah blinked rapidly. "I don't mean it literally. I don't worship him or anything—well, I kinda do, but not in a religious sense. I just really like him." He shot Kyle a grin, trying to dispel the awkwardness.

"Do you know him?"

"Me? Nah. I did see him in *Hedwig* on Broadway, which was awesome. But that was a couple of years ago."

"You've been to New York?"

"I live there. At least I think I do. I don't know yet what I'm going to do." He took a couple of paper plates down from one of the cabinets and a knife and forks from one of the drawers, then sliced pieces of the pound cake and plated them. They took them back out front to sit at the counter. Noah tossed a small cube to Jake, who snatched it up and followed.

"I used to live in Chicago. I liked it. But I had to leave—" Kyle stopped, looking distressed and maybe a little embarrassed. "I mean, I live here now." He shoved a bite of cake in his mouth.

"Because you're gay?" Noah asked, trying to sound offhand.

"No. I mean, not because… I don't…. How did you know?" Kyle stammered, his face flushing red below his crimson hairline.

"Guys don't smile at each other the way you smile at me," Noah said, bumping his shoulder. "It's okay, I'm gay too. And I like smiling at you that same way."

"Oh." Kyle couldn't seem to come up with anything else to say.

Noah sat down across from him and tried the cake as well. "She hasn't lost her touch. So you live here, with Miss Sarah—"

"Though I'm going to find a place to live as soon as I get a full-time job. Leroy over at the grocery store said he might be able to take me on when it gets closer to Thanksday."

"You mean Thanksgiving?"

Kyle blushed again, his fair skin going crimson. "Yes. Sorry. I don't know why I said that."

Noah shrugged. "It's cool—I knew what you meant. You want to work there?"

"I don't know—it would be okay, I guess. It's a job."

"I wish I could hire some help around here, but I can't afford it. And it's not helping having to keep it closed while I figure out what's going on. Dad was pretty organized, but he wasn't expecting to just drop...." Noah swallowed but managed a weak grin at Kyle.

"I'm sorry about your pa," Kyle said softly.

"Thanks."

A moment later the door chimes sounded, and Noah looked up.

It was Matt Handley. "Noah."

"Matt." Noah's voice was cool over Jake's low growl. "What can I do for you?"

"Just passing by. Thought I'd see if you were around."

"I am, but I'm kinda busy." He indicated the computer and stacks of books.

"Oh. So you're planning on staying?"

"I don't know yet," Noah said. "But it's stupid to not have a business open for as long as it's viable. I do have loan payments."

"True," Matt said. He laughed his fakey laugh. "Speaking of business—your daddy banked at First National Bank, did you know?"

"No, but I figured he did."

"He did. You need to come in in the next day or so. There's some matters we have to go over. Any time's fine—any time you can get away from your busy schedule, I mean." He laughed that fake laugh again.

"I'll be by. If there isn't anything else?"

"No, no. I'll see you in a day or so, then."

"Count on it."

"I'm a banker—we're always counting!"

Noah laughed, but it sounded as fake to his ears as Matt's. After the man had gone, Noah flipped the lock on the door and turned back toward the main part of the store. He'd had enough of visitors.

"You don't like him, do you?"

"Handley? No. I went to school with him. He's a jerk." Noah reached down and scratched Jake's ears.

"He certainly didn't smile the right way," Kyle observed and Noah laughed. He hadn't laughed so much since he left New York.

"No, he did not."

"I like your smile better."

"I like yours too." He returned to the counter, and they sat back down to finish their tea and cake.

Kyle left a little while later, and Noah locked up behind him, then went back to trying to make sense of Charlie's records. After an hour or so, he gave up and went home with Jake to the house that still echoed with his dad's laughter. He'd try again tomorrow. It was Sunday, and while he wasn't much of a churchgoer, it had always been the quietest day of the week, so maybe he'd get more work done. He had the appointment with the lawyer on Monday, and assuming he could find any ducks, he better get the little bastards to line up.

Tomorrow. He'd find something to help the store tomorrow.

CHAPTER FIVE

THE DOOR to the staircase loomed in front of Noah. He was five years old again, listening to his father telling him why he couldn't go up there. "It's dangerous," Dad had said in the serious voice that always meant Noah had to listen to him. "I don't even go up there—it's dirty and dusty and there are… spiders."

Noah hated spiders. Even twenty years later, he eyed the door dubiously, flashlight clutched in his hand. A Yale lock—but then again, so were most of the locks in the store. He searched through the key ring and finally found a key that fit. The one that did was the last on the ring. The lock was stiff, as if it hadn't been opened in years, which made Noah think that his dad really hadn't ever gone up there. Whatever "up there" was. But he wanted to make sure there wasn't anything in the attic he either needed to worry about or could sell to help out the store.

Finally he managed to work it into the lock and got it to turn. Then it was the door that resisted, the wood swollen against the frame. He yanked hard and almost lost his balance when it flew open with an acrid puff of age.

Stairs. Yup. Those were definitely stairs. Noah half wished he'd brought Jake, but it was Sunday and Miss Edna's time to socialize. She had taken Jake around with her to get him out with people because he'd been so listless.

He looked for a light switch and found one, but when he flicked it on, the bulb at the top of the stairs only lit for a moment before it popped and died. "Swell." He turned on the flashlight and shined it up into the darkness.

At least the handrail was sturdy—it didn't even wiggle when he put his weight on it—and the stairs seemed firm enough as he climbed to the top. That was good—he probably wouldn't have to factor in major structural repairs to the place, if he were to sell. He didn't see any indication of ceiling damage downstairs, so hopefully the floors up here were as good.

Noah found a short hallway at the top, with a window at the opposite end of the hall and two doors facing each other. Ancient metal slat blinds spotted with rust covered the window. When Noah pulled on the cord, it disintegrated in his hand and the blinds fell with a crash to the floor.

Noah jumped back, remembered the stairs behind him just in time, and grabbed the frame of the door on his right. The door swung open and Noah shrieked at the sight of a figure looming in the shadows. He prayed for a moment that God wouldn't let him die before he'd gotten a chance to know Kyle.

It didn't move. He stood there, staring at it. Waiting. When it didn't move, Noah took a step forward, then another. After a minute Noah's heart rate slowed and he realized it was a dressmaker's dummy wearing a vintage gown. Beyond the figure was a small living area, with a mouse-eaten love seat and a big old-fashioned radio on a stand. A floor lamp sat beside a wing chair, the leather of the chair cracked and split.

Weird. Aside from the killer dummy, it didn't seem so dangerous up here. The floors felt solid, and he didn't find any water damage. It smelled weird—mold maybe. The space probably just gave his father the creeps and he didn't want to admit it.

The door across the hall led to a kitchen. It felt like it sat over the larger part of the store below, because it was considerably bigger than the little sitting room. The appliances were antique, at least fifty years old, maybe older. The fridge even had the old-fashioned latch-type handle that was notorious for trapping kids years ago. Curious, he opened the fridge door to find it not only perfectly empty but immaculately clean, though there was a musty smell from it being closed up so long. Maybe someone would buy vintage appliances on eBay.

Same for the cabinets—the outsides were thick with dust, but the interiors were clean and as empty as the refrigerator. He liked the old red Formica table and matching chairs. The seats were as split as the leather wing chair, though.

A door behind the table led to a small, empty bedroom with a tiny window that had the same metal blinds as the hall window. The blinds were open, lighting the room enough that he didn't need the flashlight, though the room was gloomy. He didn't try the overhead fixture; the bare lightbulb in the socket looked like one of Edison's originals.

He'd have to do some serious updating if he stayed, maybe rent it out to help with the mortgage. Of course, it looked creepy now, and he could almost understand why his dad hadn't liked it, but that was because it was old, and the air was stale—and the feeling that he wasn't alone was just his imagination. Once he'd had the place painted and furnished, it would be fine and the creepy feeling would go away....

As he came out of the bedroom, he noticed another door to the right of the fridge. Behind it was another small bedroom with a slightly larger closet. Instead of the single door of the first bedroom's closet, this one had folding louvered doors. This room had a double window and plenty of light. He stepped into the closet, looking around. There were a couple of shelves built in on one side, and the brackets for a clothes rod, but they were both empty. Ah, there was the clothes rod, standing in a corner.

A recessed square covered the ceiling, probably a hatch to the attic, but he couldn't tell much without an overhead light fixture. Though he didn't see stairs or a ladder—just a simple latch.

He lifted the clothes rod and poked at the latch.

The door dropped open and something crashed onto Noah with a clatter, smelling of dust and must. It knocked him to the floor, half in, half out of the closet. He had a what-the-fuck moment, and then he realized what was staring him in the face.

A skull.

A human skull.

A white, bony, empty-eye-socket human skull.

Grinning at him.

He screamed and ran.

CHAPTER SIX

THAT EVENING, after he'd stopped shaking, Noah sat on the wicker chair on the back porch with his second beer, watching the lawn but seeing nothing. Someone had died in his father's store. That was why his dad didn't want to go into that room all those years. Did he know what was in there? Had he been involved? Questions chased conjecture around his head. Was it Jimmy Hoffa? Jesus, what the hell happened? Should he tell someone? Miss Edna? The police?

He grabbed his phone from his jeans pocket and dialed Yeira's number.

"Hey, Noah, how are you?" Her voice helped calm his anxiety.

"I'm a little freaked-out."

"Why?" She let the word trail out.

"So I was at the store earlier, and I went upstairs to see what was in the second-floor area. My dad never used it, not even for storage. I thought it was weird."

"Okay?"

"And when I got up there, I found…. Well, it could be like stage props or something, but I think it was a skeleton." He sounded ridiculous, but his shoulders finally relaxed from being able to say it out loud.

"Do you think your dad knew it was up there?" Her tone hadn't changed, like finding a body was a common occurrence. Maybe in her life it had become commonplace.

"No, but something about it made him uneasy, so he never went up there."

"Did the bones have any sinew on them? Like rubber bands between them?" He didn't want to think about how she knew that. As a Syrian refugee, she'd probably seen lots of dead bodies and such.

"I saw some, but mostly there was just rotted clothes."

"You need to call the police."

"Yeah, I figured. I'm going to go make sure my eyes weren't playing tricks on me, and then I'll call."

"Let me know how it goes." Ever the reporter.

Jake nudged his hand while he stared out at the old oak that overhung the garage and tried to figure things out.

"Hey, buddy." Noah rubbed the big dog's head automatically. It was muscle memory now. He didn't have a dog in New York, and he loved Jake's constant, warm affection. He could remember so many times when he'd come in to see the big guy lying on his father's feet as the man read the paper. Always the paper, even after Noah had gotten him an e-reader for his birthday a couple years before.

No, he refused to think his father had been involved in someone dying at that store. The image came back to him, haunting him as he washed up his dinner dishes. The bones had been clean underneath the mostly intact clothing, so they had to be pretty old. How long did it take for fabric to disintegrate? The dress on the mannequin had lasted, though in poor shape—was it newer than the bones or older? It had probably happened before his grandfather had even bought the store. Noah made a note to look up the last owner when he had time. He needed to go to the store, be responsible, and call the police. Gruesome as it sounded, he kind of welcomed the distraction. He had to meet with his father's lawyer the next day. Then he'd see how bad it really was.

He'd figure out everything else later.

Jake whined as he let him in the door. Bones and dogs didn't really make good company, and whoever was up in the attic didn't deserve to be gnawed on. Noah walked past the F-150 in the driveway. He supposed that with the truck, he didn't need the rental, but he couldn't make himself turn it in, though it was stupid to keep paying for it. If he took it to the airport, it would feel like his visit was permanent instead of wrapping things up before he went back.

He thought about going across and asking Kyle to come with him, but he was a big boy and needed to start handling things himself.

The streets were quiet. But then, in sleepy little Aster, they were usually quiet. Most folks worked during the day, and kids would be in school. He had the road to himself as he made his way back to the store, back to what waited. Assuming there really was a dead body and he hadn't imagined it. The past few days had been terrible, dealing with the grief and the stress of putting his father to rest. He had to have overreacted.

He wouldn't be surprised if the skull turned out to be a prop for the store, a *Hamlet* display or something. Noah needed to see it again before he decided what to do.

He used the I Heart New York keys again, slipping the front door key in almost noiselessly and turning the knob inch by inch, like he didn't want the body upstairs to hear him coming. He'd forgotten to set the alarm as he ran out like a frightened child, but the wind chimes gave him away anyway, and the tension in his body broke. His father had been the master of putting together a display; it had to be a prop. This wasn't a horror movie.

Noah twisted and turned through the aisles back to the staircase, back to the apartment, and back to the attic. There was a skull. He hadn't imagined it, and it wasn't a papier-mâché prop either. In fact, there was a whole skeleton, now lying a couple of feet away. It was posed on its side, resting on one elbow, with its other arm casually lying across its waist. It was fully dressed down to the shoes, but the fabric was moth-eaten. The bones were held together with what Noah realized must be old rotten tendons, all except the skull. It sat on the floor next to the skeleton. "Oh, what the fuck?" He didn't need this.

"Gracious, what language," someone said behind him.

He whipped his head around to see a man sitting cross-legged on the floor. He was wearing a vest and bow tie over a gingham button-down shirt and wool pants—the same clothes as were on the skeleton, but looking whole and new. His feet were encased in the same wingtip shoes, and he wore round, wire-rimmed glasses. His features were African American, but Noah couldn't tell what color his hair was because he was entirely gray. Clothes, skin, hair, eyes. Gray. And semitransparent. Translucent. Like a....

"What... the... hell?"

"Henry McDaniel, at your service." The figure rose to its feet. "I own this fine establishment. Which brings me to the question—what are you doing in my home, and where the deuce is my furniture?"

"Um. Actually, I own this place now, I guess. Because you... um... my family bought it back in the seventies.... Oh shit."

"Good grief, child. You have a mouth like a longshoreman." The man sighed. "I'm dead, aren't I?"

"Um… yeah. I guess so. If that's yours." Noah pointed over his shoulder at the skeleton. He'd gone past terror into a weird sort of calm, as if his brain had had all the weirdness it could take for a while and shut down his panic monitor.

"It's garbed in my clothing, so I expect it is." The man—ghost? Noah supposed so—shook his head. "I've been up in that attic a while, I guess. But still—you say you own my building now? How did you come to acquire it?"

"It was my father's. I told you—my grandfather bought it back in the seventies sometime, when my dad was younger." Noah cocked his head and regarded the man curiously. He supposed he should be more freaked-out about having a conversation with a ghost, but if there was an opposite to scary, it was Henry McDaniel. He looked more like an elderly schoolteacher than a haint.

"Grandpa had always wanted to run a bookstore, so when this place came up for sale, he jumped on it. When he left it to my dad, Aster was starting to go through gentrification and…."

"Gentrification? What's that?"

"Um. Where people start buying properties that are run-down or foreclosed on and fixing them up. To bring a neighborhood more upscale."

"Son, you're speaking English, but I'm having a hard time comprehending you."

So Noah sat on the floor in an empty room and explained gentrification to an elderly ghost. When he'd finished, Henry shook his head. "I heard of something called 'white flight' up in the North, but that seems to be the opposite of what happened here. So Aster is mostly white these days? No colored people?"

"What? Oh, yeah, it's still integrated. It's about half and half, I think. But there are more people moving in. It's getting trendy. I expect any day there'll be a Starbucks here."

"A Starbucks what?"

"Coffee shop."

Henry frowned. "What does coffee have to do with *Moby-Dick*?"

"What?"

"The character in *Moby-Dick*. Starbuck."

"Oh. I don't know. I've never read it."

Henry's eyes grew wide. "You've never read *Moby-Dick*? How can you run a bookstore without having read a classic like that?"

"I don't run it. It was my dad's, and well, we mostly covered contemporary authors in my classes. I did have to take a class on Shakespeare, but that was a disaster."

"Child, if I weren't already dead, you would have killed me right then. What was your high school thinking of, to not teach *Moby-Dick*?"

"Well, my high school didn't teach much of anything, but I do have a degree in English lit." Noah was starting to feel defensive as he sat on the cobwebbed floor discussing literature with a ghost. Which is a sentence he'd never even thought about saying. "We studied a lot of different writers, but mostly all contemporary. Or at least twentieth century."

Henry put his head in his hands and gave a long, shuddering sigh. "Joyce. Hemingway. Langston Hughes. At least tell me you've read those."

"Joyce who?" At Henry's moan, Noah laughed. "Just kidding. We did *Portrait of the Artist As a Young Man* and *Dubliners*."

"*Ulysses*?"

"The professor thought it was too obscure. Some of the students read it for extra credit, but they all said it was almost unintelligible."

"Child."

"Ghost."

Henry raised his head and chuckled. "You can call me Henry. And what's your name, child?"

"Noah. Noah Hitchens."

"Well, Noah Hitchens, under normal circumstances I probably would never have met you, so it remains to be seen if it's a pleasure. But I do appreciate your letting me out of that attic. It's an unpleasant place to spend eternity."

"Did you die up there?"

"I think I was dead before they put me up there. It's starting to come back, but I think it was a robbery—fools thought they'd find money in a bookstore, and when they didn't, they came up here looking for it. They found me. Whacked me on the head. I guess they got scared when they saw I was dead and stuffed me up in the attic."

"How'd they even know it was there? I mean, I wouldn't have seen it if I hadn't been standing right underneath it."

"I'd just finished taking down my Christmas decorations, so the attic door was open. They put me up there, slammed the door, and one of them said, 'And stay there!' so I did. Until you let me out."

"Wow. That's bogus."

Henry mouthed the words, frowning, then nodded. "Yes. As you said. 'Bogus.' I take it that's a term of disgust?"

"Yeah, I guess. Language has probably changed a lot since you... um...."

"Died. And while bits and pieces probably have changed, I doubt if it's significant. There are many words in English that date back centuries, if not millennia. English changes—but remains English."

"Yes, sir. But there are a lot of new things. They probably didn't have computers or the internet or anything in your day."

"Computers, yes, but they weren't for anything very practical. Basically for running calculations."

Noah took his phone out of his pocket. "This is a cell phone, and it has more computer power than the computers that sent Man to the moon."

"Man has been to the moon?"

"Yep. 1969. I can show you on the internet."

"What's the internet?"

"It's—well, it's a bunch of computers hooked together so that anyone can log into them and find information, or talk to people, or post pictures of cats, or pretty much do anything. News stories and stuff. You can look up pretty much anything on the internet."

Henry leaned over and looked at the phone curiously. "And all that's in there?"

Weirdly delighted that he knew something this dead man didn't, Noah said, "Yep, and it plays music too!" He queued up the last song he'd been listening to and hit Play. He'd been listening to oldies earlier while he'd walked over to the store and queued up the next song in line— U2's "Pride (In the Name of Love)."

The music started and Henry's eyes grew wide. "Good gracious. That sound is better than any record I ever heard."

"Yeah, U2 is pretty great—that's the band that's playing. They're from Ireland. This is a really good song too."

"It's… interesting," Henry said diplomatically. "Though I was referring to the sound, not the music itself…."

After a moment, though, he frowned. "Those words," he said. "'Free at last….' Some things are still fuzzy, but I remember hearing a speech that ended like that. 'Free at last, I'm free at last, oh Lord, thank God I'm free at last,' or something of that nature."

"Yeah, that's what it's referring to. Martin Luther King's 'I Have a Dream' speech."

"You know it?"

"God, yes, it's famous. Did you—were you there? In person?"

Henry nodded, but his face was troubled. "The song—it says that his life was taken…."

"Well, yeah. It's about his assassination…."

If a ghost could pale, Henry did. "Reverend King—assassinated? When?"

"1968, I think."

"Then… then the civil rights movement failed?"

"Jesus, no. His death was kind of a rallying cry for it. I mean, things still aren't perfect—we've got a long way to go for that, but we've made progress." Noah looked at Henry, still distraught, and grinned. "We had a black president."

"You are joshing me."

"Nope." Noah grinned so hard his cheeks hurt. "Duly elected—twice. A Harvard-educated lawyer."

"Noah… what *year* is it?"

"Today is October 21, 2018."

"Child," Henry said, "we need to talk."

"Sure. Think you can go downstairs? I'd like to get something to drink—and we kind of need to call the police."

"Police? What for?"

Noah jerked his thumb over his shoulder. "To report a murder."

NOAH HALF expected Henry's ghost to vanish once the police had taken his body away, but when he came back into the downstairs kitchenette, the ghost was sitting on one of the wooden chairs, looking through the papers on the table. "I can't seem to move much besides my bones," he said, "and I suppose that's because they're mine, but I seem to be able to shuffle paper. Takes an effort, though. My bones get off all right?"

"Yeah. The police are going to try to track down your daughter and let her know. She'll have to decide what to do with… you." Noah sat across from Henry. "The detective said it looked like your skull was cracked and that could have happened if you fell, but the coroner will know for sure. They think you had a heart attack or simply hit your head pretty hard. She said either one would have killed you."

"You didn't tell them someone hit me?"

"How would I have known that?" Noah put his hands on his hips.

"Fair point. Well, it's good to know I didn't suffer."

"It'll be a comfort to your daughter."

"If she's even still alive. She'd be in her eighties now." The sadness in his eyes was heartbreaking. "I think of her wondering, not knowing, for all those years. We were so close. Her mama died young, and for the longest time it was just me and her." He closed his eyes for a long moment. "I'd love to see her again. See how she grew up."

He glanced up at Noah with a faint smile. "Have you read *The Time Machine*?"

"No, but I've seen the movie. And I've read lots of time travel stories. It's kind of like that's what you are—a time traveler."

"Except I can't go back to where I came from."

"It's all right. You can stay here as long as you want."

"Thank you, child. It's most generous of you." Henry's smirk was transparent but still visible.

"And I'm sure they'll find your daughter. What was her name?"

"Berenice." He pronounced it with a French accent: *Behr-eh-nees*. "That was my *maman*'s middle name. Everyone called her Bernie, but I always called her Berenice. I don't know how they'll find her. It was so long ago."

"They'll search public records on the internet. It won't take long to find her. I could tell them her name, that would speed things up."

Henry snorted. "And they would wonder how you knew that."

"Hey, my granddad bought this place from her. For all anyone knows, he used to talk to me about it. Was she married?"

"Yes. Her husband died in Viet Nam." He separated the name into two, the way Noah's dad had. "That war is over by now, isn't it?"

"Oh yeah. The North won, but they're our friends now."

"Huh. Same thing happened with the Germans and the Japs after Dubya Dubya Two."

Noah winced. "The Japanese. We don't call them Japs. It's not polite."

Henry blinked. "Well. I guess there's quite a lot I need to get caught up with. Having a Negro president is only the start."

Noah flinched again.

"What now?"

"African American. Not Negro. Or… the other *n* word."

"Son, it's okay to swear like a sailor, but you have to be careful about what you call people?"

"Yes, sir. Swearing doesn't hurt anyone. But calling people names—it sucks."

"Well, that could have been worded more elegantly, but I get the picture."

"Right. Okay."

"These seem to be documents regarding the store. Are you managing it now?"

"My dad died and left it to me. I still have to talk to the lawyer about the estate and probate and all that stuff. Jeez, I don't know anything about that." Noah sighed. "But I think there are some financial issues. See anything in those papers that might give us a clue what to do to get this place back on its feet?"

"Just this." Henry slid a folder across the table toward Noah.

It was an application to add a coffee bar to the business. He found a letter attached from the state business department approving the application and then some other kinds of documents. They were dated some two weeks before his father's death. Both the application and the other documents gave the name of the store as Stardust Books, LLC.

"I didn't know he incorporated. I guess I'll have to talk to the lawyer to find out more about what that means."

"That isn't the point, Noah. He's gotten approval to add a coffee bar to the shop. That's extra income. Your father had already come up with a way to save the store."

"Oh. Oh!"

CHAPTER SEVEN

THE LAWYER'S office was in a high-rise near Midtown, and Noah was glad he'd taken MARTA in from College Park. The drive to the MARTA station took about an hour, but the ride on the transit line was faster than if he'd tried to drive downtown on a Monday in midday Atlanta traffic. And the stop was only a block or so from the office, so he didn't even have time to build up a sweat in his one suit jacket. He showed his ID to the guard in the lobby and took the elevator to the thirty-seventh floor.

His laptop case was doing double duty as a briefcase, and he dug through the stack of papers for the business card he'd found with his dad's stuff. The receptionist in the office took the card and picked up the phone. "Mr. Gorwin's two o'clock is here." To Noah she said, "Please take a seat. Mr. Gorwin will be out shortly."

He wandered over to the big window overlooking Piedmont Park and the botanical gardens. He was standing there when a voice said, "Pretty view. Too bad we rarely have time to enjoy it."

Noah turned to see a slightly rumpled middle-aged man giving him a wry smile. He held out his hand. "Mr. Gorwin?"

"Please. Call me Steve. Come on into the conference room here and let's get started. I'm sure you don't want to spend such a lovely afternoon in a boring old office." He led the way down a short hall to a room with an expensive-looking marble table and leather chairs. *Crap,* Noah thought in despair. *How much is* this *gonna cost me?*

His expression must have shown his thoughts, because the lawyer grinned. "Don't worry," he said in an exaggerated whisper, "this is all covered by your dad's retainer. Prepaid."

"Phew," Noah said.

This time the guy laughed out loud. "Yeah, I hear that a lot. Okay. Introductions. I'm Steve Gorwin—I'm a partner here even though my name's not on the door. We have about three hundred partners in this law firm, so not everyone gets that honor—the name would wrap around the

43

building a couple dozen times. I specialize in business succession and private client law, so I work a lot with small businesses like your dad's. I was really sorry to hear about his death—Charlie was a great guy. Smart man." He pulled out a chair and sat down.

Noah followed suit and took out the file folders he'd amassed from Charlie's desk. "He seemed pretty organized, but I was surprised when I saw he'd gone here for his will and stuff rather than just the lawyer in town he usually worked with."

"Ray Sanders is a good guy and a good lawyer. He referred Charlie to me because he doesn't handle a lot of corporate work, and he wanted to make sure Charlie had a good handle on his business succession plans."

"What does that mean, business succession?"

"It's what happens to a corporation when an officer or primary—in this case, your dad—dies while still managing the corporation. Rather than getting all tied up in probate, as it would be as a sole proprietorship, a company with a good plan transfers seamlessly to the other stockholders. The stock itself is stuck in probate, but the board can continue to run the business just as it had all along."

"There's a board for the bookstore?"

Steve chuckled. "There is. It's made up of the officers of the corporation and the majority stockholders. That would be your dad, who was president and treasurer, your neighbor Mrs. Mackey, who was secretary, and you, vice president. The terms of the succession plan make you president and treasurer, and Mrs. Mackey becomes vice president and secretary. That's based on a decision made at a board meeting from last December."

"Board meeting? I don't remember any board meeting…?"

"You talked to your dad about the store, didn't you?"

"Well, yeah. We always were doing that."

"And you've signed papers he asked you to, haven't you?" The lawyer was grinning like the whole thing amused him.

"I… remember signing… something?"

"Well, that's how you became vice president. And all that's required for a meeting is a quorum—in this case, two officers—and the filing of minutes by the secretary."

"I don't remember Mrs. Mackey being there or taking notes or anything."

"She didn't have to be. Your dad did. All she did was file them." Steve shrugged. "Charlie's idea of meetings was the Braves and beer."

"Wait—Steve. You're the guy Dad went to games with."

"Yep." This time the smile had a tinge of sadness. "Like I said, he was a great guy, even if he did hate old Smoltzie."

"He sure was. Okay. So what do I need to know?"

IT TOOK over an hour, but by the time they were done, Noah knew more about inheritance laws than he ever wanted to know. As Steve had said, the plan kept the store going while the rest of it was in probate. The house wasn't part of the corporation, but since his dad had no other heirs or potential heirs (Noah was relieved to find that his parents hadn't been married long enough and *had* been divorced long enough that his mother had no legal rights to any part of the estate), Noah wouldn't have any trouble living at the house. He just couldn't sell it until it had gone through probate.

So much for selling the house to get funds to keep the store going.

While it turned out that Steve was also a CPA, he wasn't the accountant who handled Charlie's business—that was a firm in Macon that Steve recommended Noah call—so he didn't have any information about the two loans Noah had found the paperwork for. He did say he'd look over it and see if there was anything Noah should know, so Noah gratefully handed the file to an assistant, who took it off for copying.

Other than Noah being an officer of a corporation he hadn't known existed, nothing in the files was an absolute surprise. As his dad's only living relative, he knew he would get everything Charlie had left, essentially. Steve read out a few minor bequests in the will, specific gifts to people like Miss Edna (a clock she'd particularly liked) and Fred the postman (a Zane Grey trilogy in hardcover), but other than that, everything came to Noah.

As they were wrapping up, Steve reminded Noah to call the accountant. "Though knowing Charlie, I doubt if he had them handle more than his taxes. He liked to keep his own books." Steve snorted. "Literally."

"Yeah, literally—he had them all in these big paper ledgers. It's gonna take me forever to transfer the data to the computer."

"I recommend doing a complete inventory before you talk to the accountants. It'll give you a feel for what assets you have. Are you planning on following in Charlie's footsteps?"

"I don't know yet. I'm still trying to figure out what I'm going to do."

Steve walked him out to the elevator lobby. "Well, when you know what your plans are, let me know. Maybe we can take in a Braves game in honor of your old man."

"Thanks. I will."

"Good. In the meantime, I'll go over those loan documents. It might be a couple of weeks before I get back to you on them, so you'll probably want to talk to the bank to get extensions on them for now, at least until we know what's going to be tied up in probate."

"I will."

"Okay." The elevator dinged and Steve shook his hand again. "Good luck, Noah. Call if you have any questions."

"Thanks, Steve."

CHAPTER EIGHT

NOAH DECIDED he might as well get the bank out of the way too while he was already looking like an adult. He needed to get the loan balances and see what kind of funds his father had for the business. If he were completely honest, he needed to see exactly how much trouble his father had been in. From Matt Handley's little jabs, it seemed like the scales weren't tipped in his favor. Deep in his heart he knew this was about more than just the state of the store, but it was about the state of his life. He'd need to know how far in the red his father was, to decide whether he'd stick it out and try to save the store or call James to cut and run.

Traffic from the station back to Aster slowed in the midafternoon exodus from the workday. He used the lack of movement to ask his phone when the bank closed. Six o'clock on Mondays. He'd have about half an hour—hopefully that was all he'd need. He hated Handley. The less they had to talk, the happier Noah would be. Plus, he wanted to get home to Jake, whose presence calmed him more than he could say.

As he navigated the rental down Aster's main drag toward the bank, he glanced at the bookstore and noticed a familiar shock of red hair. Kyle stood in front of the door, peering in through the glass. Noah slowed and pulled a not-so-legal U-turn to sidle up to the curb. He fumbled for a second with the unfamiliar window controls, but finally the glass slid down.

"Hey, Kyle!"

Kyle turned, and Noah watched the clouds in his expression roll back to let the sun shine through. His face turned from troubled to happy in a heartbeat.

"Hi, Noah. I came by to see… well, how are things going?" Kyle stuttered.

"Things are okay," Noah admitted. "I just came back from the lawyer."

"You needed a lawyer? Are you in some kind of trouble?" The clouds threatened to return, and the concern touched Noah.

"No, no, nothing like that. I met with the lawyer that handled my dad's business. But I guess I may be in trouble, I don't know. I haven't been to the bank yet."

"Why would you be in trouble with the bank?" Kyle asked, learning forward. Noah got the impression he wanted to say more but held back.

"My dad borrowed money from them, and I don't think he could pay it back," Noah admitted.

"So they would take the bookstore away from you, even though it's yours now?"

He wondered how Kyle knew so little of the world and how it worked.

"Yes."

"That's terrible. Can I help?"

Noah didn't see how he could, but his tone was so earnest. "I don't know. Me and—" He stopped short before saying "Henry" aloud. Noah didn't know why, but it felt like a secret. People would think he was nuts anyway if he started talking about his new ghost friend. "Me and you could take a look and see if there's anything worth selling in the basement."

Kyle didn't answer. He was looking behind the car. Noah glanced up and his mirrors were full of truck. Someone got out of it with the boom of a big door, and he heard his dad's name being called out. Noah climbed out of the car, leaving it parked on the curb.

"Hey, I'm Noah Hitchens. Charlie was my dad," he called to the ether, since he couldn't see the person yelling. Noah walked the length of the huge delivery truck and followed the words JAMESON SUPPLIES along the side.

"Was?" the voice asked Noah as he rounded the back. Two guys began hauling boxes from the trailer, making a stack taller than he was on the sidewalk. The blond looked too thin to heft those huge boxes, but the other guy was burly. He straightened a Braves hat over razed black hair.

The boxes couldn't be books; they were too big. What the hell?

"Well, we can't take returns. You'll have to call the sales office," Braves Hat said and tipped the boxes to slide a hand truck beneath them. "Where do you want 'em? We got more stops."

"Oh, sorry." Noah stopped examining the labels to grab his I Heart New York keychain from his jeans pocket and open the front door. They had to pull the top box off the stack to get it to fit, but the blond was apparently stronger than he looked. Noah directed them to an open area off the main room that his father had cleared of books and shelves. They dropped the boxes in the space and were back out the door before Noah could say boo.

"Hey, I've got to help Miss Sarah with the leaves, but I'll help you unpack those as soon as I have time. You have to set them up right or you'll break them," Kyle said, making Noah jump. He hadn't realized Kyle had followed him in.

"Wait, what?"

"Those machines, they're tricky."

"Machines?"

"Yeah, the coffee machines? I've got to go, Miss Sarah is waiting," Kyle said over his shoulder, and then he was gone. Noah stood alone amid mountains of boxes.

"What the hell just happened?" Noah wondered aloud.

"That language," Henry admonished, coming through the wall to his left. Noah staggered back and slammed his knee into the corner of a box. Okay, maybe not exactly alone.

"Damn it, don't do that!"

Henry chuckled. "How did it go with the lawyer?"

"Fine." Noah grabbed the phone out of his pocket. "Twenty to six. I can still make it."

"Make it where?" Henry called as Noah sprinted for the door.

"The bank!"

He climbed back into the rental as Aster's only squad car rolled up behind him.

"Sir!" a voice bellowed toward him, and Noah sighed. He leaned over to grab his registration before he remembered it was a rental. Crap. Now what did he do? He tilted to the side and pulled out his wallet as the cop reached his window, still down from his talk with Kyle.

"I'm sorry, Officer. We got a delivery and I didn't have time to move the car," Noah offered.

"A delivery? At the bookstore?" He leaned down and peered into the car. "Hey, Noah. I was sorry as hell to hear about your dad, son."

"Sir, can I get out?" Noah asked. In New York that could get you in a lot of trouble. The sun was setting behind the guy and he didn't want it in his eyes as he looked up.

"Yeah, come on out."

Noah got out of the car, acutely aware that he would no longer make it to the bank. When he glanced up at the guy, he was surprised to see a familiar face. It was older and the hair far more gray than brown, but the eyes were still the same.

"Hi, Officer Thompson," Noah said, almost in that singsong voice they'd used when he was Officer Friendly at school. He seemed to be in charge now, judging by the bars on his uniform.

"Son, you can call me Cooper. Everybody does. Well, unless you plan on gettin' in some trouble," Cooper said with a smile. The man had seemed like a grizzly when Noah sat in front of him as a freshman, face averted, and told him about the shit Handley and his friends had done. It seemed almost ironic that Handley held the key to his future now.

"Thanks, Cooper, and I'm sorry about the car. I was moving it when you came up." Noah leaned against the door.

"Don't worry about it. Just wanted to make sure everything was all right." Cooper wiped sweat off his brow in the early fall heat. "Not like folks round here give me a lotta trouble."

"Everything is fine, I guess. Except I missed getting to the bank."

"Sorry I slowed you down."

"Nah, I don't think I really wanted to go there tonight anyway." Noah shrugged and glanced down the block to the bank's sign, mostly hidden by foliage.

"Not in a hurry to see Handley again?" Cooper surmised, but Noah didn't see any hint of a smirk. In fact, the man's expression had softened.

"You remember that, huh?" Noah sighed.

"I remember everything," he mused, rolling back on the heels of his cheap shoes. "Most people grow up as they get older. Mature—"

"Stop being dicks?" Noah offered.

"Handley never left high school. His mama died when he was real young, and Daddy never made him grow up. He's kind of a bastard, the old man."

"I never knew that, but yeah—it's like being back in high school."

50

"Just watch out for that one, Noah. There's something off about him, and it's only gotten worse these last few years." The comment didn't seem offhand, but a genuine warning.

"I'll do that."

"Have a good night now." Cooper turned and headed back toward the cruiser.

"You too."

CHAPTER NINE

MATT HANDLEY was Aster's only loan officer, and Noah had half expected the guy to leave him sitting in the waiting area for an hour or so, just to show Noah who had the power. But on a slow Tuesday morning, he couldn't really manage it, and the office door opened almost immediately. That was not a good sign, nor was the smug smile that flickered on the banker's lips. "Noah! Glad you could make it. Come on in."

He gestured to a chair and settled himself behind the desk, pulling out a file folder and setting it on the surface. "Everything's online now, of course, but I printed out the documents we'll need to go over. As I mentioned, Charlie's finances were kind of in a mess. No surprise—I'm just amazed that he managed to keep that place going in these times. Amazon, you know."

"Yeah. I know."

The smug smile grew. "Oh, I imagine he had a little sideline in antiques—everyone down in that part of town is either an antiques dealer or a gallery owner. Barely making ends meet, all of them. So."

He flipped open the folder. "Charlie had two major loans out with this bank—a forty-two-thousand-dollar loan with the store as collateral, and an existing mortgage on the house on Oak Street. The original mortgage had been paid off, but about twenty years ago he refinanced it. The balance on the mortgage is a little over ten thousand. He's been keeping up with the interest payments, but there hasn't been any payment against the principal for a long time. The store loan is more recent, and he had been paying the set amount fairly regularly, but about three months before he died, he missed the payments. So the loan has gone into arrears, which makes it due now."

"Forty thousand dollars?" Noah felt a little sick.

The smile broadened. "Fifty-three thousand, eight hundred sixty-four dollars and eleven cents. Since he hasn't been paying on the principal for the mortgage, with his death, that loan has also gone into arrears."

"I don't have that kind of money."

"Well, no surprise. What about his life insurance? Investments?"

"If he had investments, wouldn't he have paid his loans off? I can't even sell the house until it goes through probate."

"That's true."

"His lawyer said something about the store being incorporated—does that have any bearing on the loan there?"

Matt shook his head. "The loan was a personal loan against the store building, which was Charlie's personal property. The business itself was incorporated, which lets you go on running the store, but the physical property was owned by Charlie."

"I get it." The nausea had slid all the way into numbness. "What are my options?"

"You could always apply for a replacement loan to cover the existing ones. Do you have a current assessment on the value of the house?"

"I... I don't know. Maybe?"

Matt snorted. "I doubt it. The loan was taken out twenty years ago. Unless he's filed a tax appeal recently, there wouldn't have been any reason to get it appraised. What's your FICO score?"

"My what?"

"Your credit rating. Do you have outstanding loans, that sort of thing?"

"Student loans, yeah."

Again, the faux-sympathetic shake of the head. "Student loans suck. The rules around them are vicious, and you can't even include them in bankruptcy. 401(k)?"

"Yeah, but I've only been at the company a few years, so I'm not even fully vested yet."

"So much for that. Look, I can do a review of your credit to see if you're even eligible for a covering loan. If not...." He shrugged. "The loans come due the first of December. I can maybe get Dad to stretch it out through the holidays, with the final due date the first of the year. But I'll definitely run some numbers and get back to you tomorrow. Look at it this way—in the grand scheme of things, fifty grand isn't that much money. The house and store are worth more than that. If we can get you covered in the meantime, once the estate's out of probate, you can sell both of them and recoup not only the loan, but probably your student loans as well, and go back to New York." He put a piece of paper in front of Noah. "This is authorization to run your credit and do an analysis of the collateral. I'll crunch the numbers and call you tomorrow."

Noah read over the form and signed it at the bottom. He didn't have much choice; no other bank would touch him with his credit and the loans already in default. "Thanks," he said.

Matt nodded. "Anything for an old school buddy."

"Really?" Noah couldn't help the sardonic tone.

Matt laughed. "Hey, it was all in fun. Just goofing around. Boys will be boys, right?"

"You know there's a whole lot of people who consider it assault."

"PC." Matt waved a hand dismissively. "Losers with no sense of humor and stuck-up dykes who couldn't get laid if they paid for it. Don't know what this world is coming to."

"Right." Now was not the time to get involved with an argument over politics. Noah needed Matt sympathetic—if he was at all and not jerking Noah's chain. Still, he couldn't take the risk. "Anyway, thanks for the help. That's my cell number, so you should be able to get ahold of me any time tomorrow."

"What did we do before them, huh?" Matt stood and shook Noah's hand. "I'll talk to you tomorrow."

"Yeah, thanks."

The walk back to the store, while only a couple of blocks, felt like eternity to Noah. Fifty thousand dollars. Fifty. Thousand. Dollars. Five-O. Grand. Where the fuck was he going to get that kind of money? Even if he could get an extension or a covering loan, he'd still have to pay it back. And the reason Charlie was in arrears in the first place was because he couldn't make the payments.

How was Noah going to do better?

"SO THAT'S the situation," Noah told Henry with a sigh. "I need to pay off the loan by the first of December—first of January if I'm lucky, not that it makes that much difference—and I don't have the money. As for the rest—the house is worth a bundle, according to my neighbor's daughter, who's a real estate agent, but it's part of the estate that's going into probate, so even if probate closes quickly, it'll still take longer than that to get it fixed up enough to put on the market. Then to find a buyer and do the closing… it'll take too much time. And there's no guarantee it'll sell high enough to pay off the existing mortgage and the loan for the store."

"Another loan…."

"They're looking, but my debt-to-income ratio may be too high— I've got no assets and a metric crap-ton of school loans. The only person I know with enough money to help is my uncle James, and I don't know that he'd be willing to. He seemed pretty adamant about me selling and going back to New York. I can borrow against my 401(k), but only to the tune of about ten grand, which is way short."

"What's a 401(k)?"

"A retirement fund. You contribute to it over the course of your working life, and hopefully your employer does too, so you have savings when you retire."

"You don't have a pension?"

Noah laughed bitterly. "No. Hardly anybody has pensions nowadays. It's all about the businesses and the stockholders. Don't get me started on that."

"Huh." Henry shook his head. "Might as well be a small businessman for all that. Never had a pension, and hardly anything in Social Security. I was planning on working till I died…. Guess I did at that!" His laughter was a low, rolling rumble that made Noah smile back at him.

"Guess you did."

"So, then, what are your assets?"

Noah shrugged. "The house and the store are in probate, but the books are part of the business, so I can work with those."

"I used to have a nice sideline in rare editions—there might still be some around. But even if we found them, by the time we got them advertised, got the orders in, and got the checks cashed, it'd be well past your deadline. Mail orders have long turnaround times, sometimes six to eight weeks, and that's after the order's made…."

Noah felt a spark of hope. "Not anymore. We should be able to find a website where we can sell them online and collect the money through

PayPal or something. We'd see a much faster return… and God knows I can get a website up pretty damn quick if I have to. I told Dad for years he should have had one."

"Whoa. Who's a PayPal and what's a website?"

Noah explained. Henry just sat shaking his head. "So you don't use the mail anymore for any of that?"

"No, a lot of times we use UPS or FedEx—those are package delivery services. They usually have next-day delivery."

"My goodness. Things happen very quickly these days."

"They sure do. And I don't even know where to start."

"Basics first. You need to know what you have before you know what you need."

"I don't even know where to start," Noah repeated mournfully. He gazed at the bookshelves. "There's got to be a million books here."

Henry snorted. "There are only a few thousand. Stardust was never a big store like Kroch's and Brentano's."

"There are boxes in the basement too."

"Which you'll get to. Now, the most valuable books are signed first editions. First editions of some books are valuable on their own, but we're mostly talkin' classics. A first-edition Steinbeck would be worth a bundle. A signed first-edition Steinbeck would be worth a fortune. But don't expect to find one here—they're rarer than hen's teeth, and your daddy would have had that up for auction long ago. Have you looked at the books in the cellar?"

"Yeah, to make sure they're in decent condition. They're in plastic bins and on shelves. Most of them are labeled with the name of an auction Dad went to a few years ago. Don't know why they're still down there."

"Good. We'll start with your daddy's records—if he was a decent businessman, and I think he must have been to keep the store goin' for all those years, he'll have kept good records."

"On paper." Noah sighed and led the way to the back office, where a half dozen big old ledgers lay on the worktable. "He'd only just started to get things computerized." He opened the first ledger. "Do we start with any particular one?"

"This one looks to be the oldest—it's from the 1970s." Henry shook his head. "To think of the 1970s as being old times…. Let's see what he's done here." The page ruffled under Henry's insubstantial finger. Well, good. Good."

"Good?"

"Yes. You're goin' to look at the right-hand column and eliminate any that are marked sold. When you find a blank, make a note of it."

"Title, author... edition?"

"Publisher too—it might be a first edition from a publisher who picked it up after the contract with the author ran out, in which case it won't be worth as much. Ignore the prices—they won't mean anything. If there's any indication where the book is, note that too. No sense spending time lookin' for something when you have a map at hand."

He didn't see a lot of blanks, and Noah wasn't sure whether to feel grateful. Some of the books were marked "disc," which he figured meant "discarded," but mostly they were sold. He set up a spreadsheet on his laptop and entered the notes there. Henry watched him a while, then shook his head and wandered off into the main part of the store.

It was dry, dull work, but a lot of writing tech documentation was too, so after a while he got into a sort of zen state: coasting his finger down the faded pages and stopping to enter data, then back to the coasting. It wasn't until his phone rang that he looked up and realized it had gone dark outside.

"Hello?"

"Hi, Noah," Karen said. The hairs on his arms bristled at how flat and stiff her voice sounded.

"Everything going okay?" He didn't really care, not when he felt so tired and everything was going wrong.

"No. Cheryl's baby came early and now she's out on maternity leave, and Jane just told me that she found a new job. Our department is falling apart."

A pang of guilt flashed across his gut, but he pushed it away. He had every right to take leave.

"Send me my laptop," Noah offered. He could work from the store. The Wi-Fi was good enough.

"That's not going to work. I need you here. Your time ended already, and I can't approve PTO for you with everything going to hell here," she said, and Noah could hear her typing in the background.

He looked up to see Henry watching him with cool, transparent eyes—no condemnation or acceptance in his expression.

"I can't come back right now, Karen. I'm still trying to close out my father's affairs. It's not something I can do from New York. He had a business." Noah picked at the ledger page he'd been reviewing, running his fingers along the indentations made by his grandfather's pen. This was his history—his legacy.

"Damn it, Noah. You've got the rest of the week. You have to be back by Monday or I can't help you."

The phone went dead in his hand.

"Sounds like you have a decision to make," Henry said and ran a finger down the page near his. A cool electricity crackled along the paper. "But no point in worrying until you hear from that banker about your credit. For now, let's find some of these books."

CHAPTER TEN

NOAH CLICKED off his cell phone and set it gently down beside the register, then put his head back and screamed. Henry flickered in and out of view, startled.

"I can't believe him!" Noah raged. He shoved the thick ledger across the counter in frustration. "He said I'm running out of time, and of course he 'can't help me'—that's bullshit. His family owns the frickin' bank. He could give me an extension, he just won't. He's been torturing me since we were teenagers."

"I take it that was the bank."

"Yeah. Fucking Matt Handley. Guess he wanted to round out his week with a laugh. Thank God he didn't know Karen tried to fire me yesterday. He probably would have called the loan for sport."

Henry said gently, "What did he tell you, son?"

"He said my credit is for shit and I have no other assets. He also said that because of my debt-to-income ratio, I can't even take a second mortgage on the house. Since I have a life in New York, the bank isn't willing to bet I'll stick it out and not let them foreclose. As if." Noah reached down and rubbed Jake. That always seemed to calm him, especially now that Jake seemed to be more comfortable around Henry.

"Well, I suppose we'd better sit down and figure out your options."

"Do I have any?" Noah sank down on the barstool behind the cash register. "I have a bookstore I don't know how to manage, a mile-high stack of coffee equipment I don't know how to use, oh, and I forgot to mention property taxes are due. On both the house and the store. So I need to come up with another three grand by the end of this month. My dad's only been gone a week and already I've screwed things up."

"Can you manage the taxes? That's the first priority." Henry floated at the end of the counter.

"Yeah. I have a little in the bank, and with what's left from Dad's life insurance, we'll manage that."

"Noah…."

"But that'll almost clean me out until I get paid, and given Karen's threat, that won't last very long."

"Noah...."

"I guess I could go over Karen's head and see if they'll let me telecommute for the rest of the year...."

"Noah...."

"What?"

Henry tilted his head toward the door. Kyle stood there, his eyes wide.

"Shit. Uh, hi, Kyle."

Kyle glanced around the store, then back at Noah. Noah gave him a weak grin. "You caught me. I talk to myself a lot. Sometimes I have conversations with the dog too."

Jake huffed in response.

"Okay. I guess I do that too, but just not out loud."

"Come on in. What can I do for you?"

"Um. I was passing by, and I thought... I wondered. I thought maybe there was something I could do to help out? Miss Sarah said Miss Edna said you were working really hard, and I don't have anything to do today, and I thought maybe you could use some help?"

"I can't afford it, Kyle." Noah smiled at his generosity. "But I appreciate the offer."

But Kyle was shaking his head. "Oh, no, no. I don't mean pay me. I mean helping out. Like a neighbor thing. Miss Sarah says people around here do that. I could help out. And do stuff. Whatever you need. I'm stronger than I look."

"Hell, a green bean is stronger than he looks," Henry observed.

Noah bit his lip. It wasn't that Kyle was skinny. He was slim, though, and Noah wondered how strong he really could be.

IT TURNED out to be a lot stronger than he looked. He hefted boxes in the storeroom like a stevedore, putting them wherever Noah needed them to open and look through. He was tireless, carrying piles of books back and forth and doing grunt work like sweeping floors and dusting without any dawdling or complaints. With his help, they got the store cleaned up and ready to open again in just under a day, where Noah had expected it to take three or four.

He was a cheerful worker too. They didn't talk much, but more than once Noah heard him humming something that sounded like a hymn.

Miss Sarah stopped by late in the afternoon with sandwiches and a thermos of the ubiquitous sweet tea. It was the first time Jake had roused from his bed in the main room all day. They both stopped what they were doing with grateful sighs. Kyle came down the ladder he was using to put books away on the highest shelf of the classics section, and Noah closed the computer program he was using to record new inventory. "My goodness," Miss Sarah said, "you boys have been working hard! The place looks—and smells—wonderful!"

"That lemon wood stuff is nice," Kyle said. "It's the same spray as you use, Miss Sarah."

"Kyle's been working his butt off," Noah said gratefully. "He's such a hard worker."

"Oh, I know it. My garden hasn't been so well tended in ages."

Kyle's face was red. "It wasn't all that much. I just did what Noah told me to do."

"And then some," Noah added.

"Well, it looks like it," Sarah said. "I figured you boys would be hungry, even if you did take time for lunch—which I bet you didn't!"

"I kinda forgot," Noah said, shamefaced. "I'm sorry, Kyle. I get that way sometimes when I'm working on something. Are you starving?"

"I had a granola bar a couple of hours ago." Kyle flushed again. "I ate it in the kitchen and washed my hands so the books wouldn't get sticky."

"Jeez. You should have said something—I didn't mean for you to go without lunch." Noah turned to Sarah. "Thanks for bringing this, Miss Sarah." His stomach growled.

Miss Sarah laughed. "You boys take that back into the kitchen and eat up. Kyle can bring the thermos back when he comes home." She waved at them as she left the store.

Noah picked up the bag of sandwiches and the thermos. "Come on, Kyle."

OVER SANDWICHES, Noah got a little more out of Kyle than he had during the course of the day. He told Noah again he'd grown up "out west" before his stint in Chicago, and that he didn't have much education aside from being homeschooled. He did have his GED, which he'd gotten when he was living with relatives in Chicago, and he liked reading books on different subjects. He mostly didn't read fiction. Noah got the impression that literature hadn't been a big thing in his homeschooling, and, worse, that it had been actively avoided. It was weird. Noah couldn't imagine it. Books—whether physical or virtual—were so much a part of his psyche that the idea of being without their comfort was, well, uncomfortable.

But something about Kyle's expression when he said he didn't read fiction…. Noah got the distinct feeling that Kyle wasn't being quite honest about that. Maybe he thought Noah wouldn't respect him if he did. He couldn't figure out where Kyle had gotten that notion.

"Can I ask a question?"

"Sure." Noah finished the last bite of his sandwich and washed it down with sweet, cold tea. Then he brushed a crumb from Kyle's lips, which turned up into a smile.

"You—when you were talking to yourself—it sounded like you were upset about something. Is there anything I can do to help?"

Noah shook his head. "Not unless you have fifty grand in your pocket. I need to pay off debt my dad had. I think part of it went to all that equipment we got. Maybe he'd planned to expand the store, or maybe had the loans for something else, but if I don't come up with the money, I might lose my father's house and the store—everything I have left of him. It's insane. He never said anything about taking out new mortgages, but the papers are there. I suppose I could sell the store, but I don't know if I want to. Or even if I can, with the debt hanging over it."

"Would you stay here instead of going back to New York?"

"I dunno. I still have a lot of decisions to make, and they aren't getting any easier." Noah put his head down on his arms. From their shelter, he mumbled, "Everything's happening so fast, and I can't seem to keep up."

A gentle, warm hand settled on his shoulder. "I know. I felt like that when I got to Chicago from… where I grew up. Everything was just so different, and I didn't know what to do first."

Noah sighed heavily. "Yeah, I hear you. Henry said I have to figure out what I have before I decide what I need, but I have so much and I don't know what to do with it all. A job, an apartment, a life in New York—and this store, and the house, and the people here…. It's overwhelming."

Kyle squeezed his shoulder gently, then released him. "Who's Henry?"

"He's… a friend of mine. He's… wise."

Noah heard a disembodied snort but ignored it. Henry had disappeared when Kyle had come into the store and hadn't shown up since, but Noah had the feeling he was always around.

"Maybe he could help?"

"He has, a lot. But there's only so much he can do… from where he is."

"Oh, right. I guess he couldn't do much from New York."

"Mm." Noah sat up and busied himself with cleaning up the remnants of their lunch. As he was screwing the lid on the now-empty thermos, Kyle said, "I guess I'd better get going. You look tired—maybe you should too. I can come back for a couple of hours in the morning if you need me to."

Noah hesitated. "I'd really like you to—but I can't afford to pay you, and I'd really rather I did."

"I told you." Kyle smiled at him. "I'm just being neighborly. And, well, I like being with you. It makes me happy."

"It makes me happy too. I promise not to work you so hard tomorrow."

"It's okay. I like it."

Noah followed him to the front door so he could lock up behind him. "Thanks again," he said. "If I could hire you, I would in a flash. You worked really hard today."

Kyle held the door open a moment, looking back at Noah. "Like I said, I liked it. I worked a lot harder on the coffee cart in Chicago."

Then he was gone, Noah staring after him, stunned. "Coffee cart?"

CHAPTER ELEVEN

UNCLE JAMES was waiting when Noah arrived at the restaurant on Thursday morning, one of the newer ones that had popped up around the edges of the historic district. It was what Noah and his dad had called a "tablecloth" restaurant, as opposed to the barbeque and burger places they used to hang out at. The table was right by the window, with a view of the Victorian-era town hall and the town square.

The waiter showed him to the table, then took drink orders and headed off. "You ever been here before?" James asked.

Noah looked up from the menu. "No. A little outside of my price range."

"It's not bad. I'm sure you've eaten at nicer places up north. New York's got a reputation for good food."

"Maybe, but aside from pizza and shawarma, it doesn't have anything more than Aster—or at least Atlanta."

"What the hell is shawarma?"

"It's kind of like gyros, but different."

James snorted. "We have gyros and pizza here, son."

"No, not really." Noah grinned. "Trust me on this, Uncle James."

His uncle laughed. "Charlie used to say that when we were kids—'trust me on this'—and you could. You could trust him to know just about anything. Everyone was so in awe of him 'cause he was so smart. We all thought he'd go off to some fancy college and never come back. It was strange to see him cooped up all his life in that bookstore."

"That bookstore *was* his life," Noah pointed out. "He loved it."

"Oh, I know, I know. The steak here is pretty good. Order whatever you want."

Noah glanced at the menu again. "How's the crab cake Benedict?"

"Eggs are for breakfast, son."

Noah chuckled. "I like breakfast. I think I'll try that."

"Suit yourself." When the waiter came back with their drinks, Noah noted that James ordered the steak, but the waiter nodded approvingly when Noah ordered the crab cake Benedict. "It's really good," the waiter murmured with a wink.

When he'd disappeared again, James was watching Noah with a thoughtful expression. "That boy bothering you?"

"What? No! He just said the Benedict is good."

"I didn't care for the way he looked at you."

"Really?" Noah bit back an irritated snort. "'Cause I think it was nice. Uncle James, you know I'm gay. You've known for years."

"Yeah, well, I'd kind of hoped you'd gotten over it by now."

"*Really?*"

James laughed. "Oh, don't be so sensitive, boy. I love you in spite of it, but I don't pussyfoot around when I'm talking, you know that. I don't mean nothing by it. So. How's it going with the store?"

"It's going." Noah sighed. "I haven't quite decided what to do yet. I need to do an inventory of the stock, there's loans against the house and the store, and I can't sell the house until it goes through probate."

"What about the store?"

"Dad incorporated the business, so that's not included in the probate, though the building and the corporation stock are. It's more complicated than that, but right now I pretty much don't know what I can do with it or what to do about the loans. As it is, I'll need to get it open again, because I can't sell anything if the store's closed, right?"

"Too right, son. Tell me about the loans."

Noah explained about the two different mortgages while they waited for their lunch to arrive. James's questions showed he had been listening closely, and some of the comments he made had made Noah feel like he'd really been interested in helping. Then the meal came, and they were quiet while they ate.

Over dessert—which Noah really hadn't wanted but Uncle James had insisted on—James said, "That's prime real estate, the shop, you know. Right smack-dab in the heart of the historic district. I'd have a half dozen interested parties before I even finished writing up the listing. Even if you can't sell immediately, I could probably work out an advance against a sale, if we can get at least a contract. Since you're kin. That would free up the mortgage on the building at least. You'd have to talk to that lawyer of yours about it, but I think then the proceeds from the sale could go into a trust representing the stockholders until after probate's done. I don't know for sure, but he would."

"Fact is, I don't know if I want to sell," Noah said morosely. "I mean, I do, but I don't. It's like home to me, even more than the house, and it was Dad's. I already have about four thousand from his life insurance and some first editions we sold."

"Noah, son, you got to give up on that sentimentality. Do you *really* want to be stuck in Bumfuck, Georgia, the rest of your life?"

"You have."

James laughed. "Yeah, but I have a really good business here. And with all the new subdivisions goin' up around here, I'm only gonna get richer. In fact, I've got property rights for a new strip mall on the north side of town where the old Barker farm used to be. I just need the damn Merchants Council to get their thumbs out of their asses and approve the zoning." He waved his hand dismissively. "Never mind all that. Look, you're family." He leaned forward across the table, his expression intent. "I will be willing to buy the business—lock, stock, and barrel—for a cool three hundred K. That'll not only take care of the mortgages, it'll pay off those school loans you've had hanging over your head for so long. Yeah, don't look surprised—your dad told me about them. He was worried about those."

Three hundred thousand? Noah could barely breathe. It *would* take care of all his debt, and, carefully marshalled, would be a cushion against catastrophe the rest of his life.

He could even take time off to write his book....

He opened his mouth to say yes, but what came out was "Thanks, Uncle James. I'll think about it."

"You do that. Like I said, I could have a new tenant in there in no time."

Noah frowned. "You wouldn't keep it a bookstore?"

"Good gravy, son! What do we need with a bookstore in Aster?"

Aster wouldn't be Aster without the Stardust. But it shouldn't matter, should it? His life was in New York, not Bumfuck, Georgia. "What would you do with the books?"

James waved a pudgy hand again. "Whatever. You could take what you want. The rest could be recycled. It's the store I want, not the books. Hell, for that amount of money, you could go online and sell there. It's a way cheaper proposition these days."

"True." Noah tried for a smile, and it seemed to placate James, who said, "You go ahead and think about it, Noah. But don't take too long. I didn't get where I was by lollygaggin'."

"Sure, Uncle James."

NOAH WALKED slowly back to the historic district, deep in thought. True, he had been focused on dealing with the store so he could get home to New York, but he'd had a vague idea of the bookstore just continuing to go on, maybe under new management. But James had hit him right in the chops with reality. Yeah, if it weren't for the mortgages, the store would do okay with the current interest in antiques and tchotchkes, but how long would that go on? He could move the business online, keep it going that way. Sure, he'd have to find a way to warehouse the books and to weed out the really valuable ones, but it was doable. Especially with a couple hundred grand to work with....

He needed to talk to someone. Maybe he'd call Yeira when he got home. She'd have a fresh, uninvested perspective.

Someone was lurking around the door of the shop—no, not someone, some*thing*. As Noah came down the sidewalk, he realized it was a large shuck of cornstalk set against the storefront. As he watched, a slender, fussily dressed man came out of the antique store across the street, a huge basket in his arms. He set down the basket and pulled out a couple of pumpkins, setting them at the base of the vegetation, then began wiring Indian corn to the top. "Thad?" Noah said as he approached.

The little antique gallery owner jumped in shock. "Oh! Noah! You scared the bejeebers out of me!" His beringed hand fluttered at his chest. "Give a girl a little warning next time!"

Noah laughed. "What are you doing?"

"Well, decorating for Halloween, of course! Charlie always waited until the last minute, and, well, he didn't get to it before...." Thad's face screwed up in genuine grief a moment; then he visibly collected himself.

"So I reckoned you wouldn't have had any time to get something up, and I had these things left over from my own decorating." He withdrew a length of burlap ribbon crafted into a huge bow, with silk sunflowers. "Isn't it gorgeous?"

"Gorgeous," Noah agreed.

Thad hummed approval and turned to wire the burlap onto the arrangement. Noah watched him a moment, smiling despite himself. The gallery owner had been part of his childhood as much as Ananda at Mystic Crystals, the shop next door, and Miss Edna and Fred the postman. He was the first gay man Noah had ever known. In fact, it had created a lot of confusion—Noah had been pretty sure he was gay his whole life but had never felt the slightest compulsion to behave at all like Thad. His dad had had to take him aside and explain that there were as many types of gay people as there were straight, and that some were a little more demonstrative, like Thad. He'd also warned Noah that there were bad gay men too, and to always be careful when meeting new people.

"This is really nice of you, Thad."

"Oh, sweetheart, it's no problem. We're family."

"We are." Noah put a hand on his shoulder.

"Speaking of being close, that young redhead you've got coming in every other day is adorable." Thad wiggled his eyebrows like a fiend, and Noah laughed.

"Kyle? Yeah, he is. I really like him and he really likes me, I think."

"What are you waiting for, then?"

"There's something about him. He's hiding something." Noah pushed a piece of the straw around the sidewalk with his foot.

"Aren't we all?"

"That's fair. Maybe I'll ask him out after work one night."

"Don't let it pass you by, or you're going to be a lonely old queen like me one day."

"You're not old," Noah said.

"Oh bless your little heart. You go on about your business now, and I'll clean up when I'm done." Thad gave him a half hug and went back to his décor.

"Come on over sometime and we'll have some tea."

"Of course!"

Noah unlocked the door, deactivated the alarm, and went into the store. Family. Yeah. He'd known most of the people on this block his entire life, and those he hadn't—the art gallery woman; Rosalie who owned Pots and Posies, the upscale indoor gardeners' store on the other side of his storefront from Ananda's; the yarn shop lady with the cute dog; Hiram who owned the old-fashioned stationery place—they had become friends with Charlie, and through Charlie, Noah. He wondered who Uncle James would sell the store to, and would they fit in with everyone here.

"Lunch that bad?"

Noah glanced up at Henry, who was sitting atop the sliding ladder that let customers look at the upper shelves. "No, pretty good actually. Uncle James had some ideas about this place. Henry, when did you open the bookstore?"

Henry pursed his lips. "Hm. I think I told you it was *maman*'s dress shop first—she had that as long as I can remember, and I was born in 1904.... I took it over after *maman* retired in thirty-three. Times were pretty hard then, and not too many people were buying nice dresses. We weren't big on banks at the time, so we still had some cash, and Daddy's farm was doing okay, so she decided to give up the shop and let me take over. Of course, I wasn't good about dressmaking." Henry grinned. "All thumbs. Anyway, Renee and Berenice and I moved into the apartment upstairs, and I turned it into a bookstore. People needed books to keep them from thinking how lousy their lives were. Aster was too small a place for a movie palace then, so the only escape was books. So yeah, 1933."

"Wow. That's like almost ninety years."

"Almost. Berenice grew up here, just like you."

"I hope to meet her someday."

"I hope you do too. I'd love to see her one last time."

Noah sank down on the barstool behind the counter. "Uncle James wants me to sell the store." He didn't look at Henry.

After a moment Henry said gently, "That's an option."

"I know. I kind of thought I wanted to too. But I don't know. And there's my job and Karen...."

"Well, child, you don't have to make the decision this moment. Best you sleep on it."

"I have too much to do."

"It'll keep, Noah. Go home, have a nap. See how you feel later. I always felt better after a nap."

A nap. Noah was suddenly tired, down to his soul. "Yeah. Maybe. It's an idea."

"A good one. Go on, then. Git."

Noah got.

CHAPTER TWELVE

NOAH FLIPPED the sign on the bookstore door over to Open and turned on the lights. It was probably stupid to open for just a few hours, and on a Saturday, no less, but the store'd been closed for over a week, and even if he was going to end up selling it, he needed to be doing something. There probably wouldn't be much in the way of business, but Saturdays had always been a good day, especially nice fall Saturdays—there was always a good number of tourists from the Atlanta area stopping to shop the antique stores and gift shops here on Sycamore. It was only nine thirty, and most of the stores opened at ten, but he was here, and he was ready.

More or less. While he'd often manned the store alone when he was in high school and Charlie had auctions or sales to attend, it was definitely weird to be in charge and solely responsible for the place. He was kind of nauseated. How could he manage this alone? He sat on the stool and put his forehead on the cool counter.

"It'll be fine," Henry said.

Well, not really alone.

He picked up the glass of tea from the coaster Charlie had always used and toasted the air. "To Dad, to Henry, and to the Stardust."

"Amen and hallelujah," Henry agreed, toasting back with a ghostly coffee cup. Noah didn't even ask where that had come from.

"Speaking of coffees and teas, I called the company where that stuff"—he nodded toward the crated equipment sitting off the main room—"came from. Seems I can return the supplies, but the actual machines can't go back."

"Are they defective?" Henry took another sip.

"No, they were on clearance. They said my dad got them for a steal." Noah made air quotes around that word and snorted. "The total start-up invoice is a little over ten grand. I'd say that wasn't much of a bargain."

"Do you know anything about coffee machines?"

"Well, no, but Kyle does."

"Then you don't know if it was a bargain or not," Henry reasoned.

"You're right, but how was he going to get this stuff set up and working? My dad didn't know anything about commercial coffee machines. He couldn't even work the Keurig."

Henry was about to reply when the wind chimes over the door jingled and his next-store neighbor wafted in on a wave of sage and patchouli. "Hi, Ananda."

"Hello, darling! I just wanted to stop by and see how you were doing today. Is all well?"

"As can be expected. What can I do for you?"

"For me? Nothing. It's what I can do for you!"

"What the devil is she wearing?" Henry demanded.

Noah looked at her critically. She had on her usual flowing cotton caftan in muted rainbow designs, her artificially scarlet curls done up in a purple silk scarf. Nothing unusual in that—she'd run Mystic Crystals for as long as Noah had been alive, and he couldn't remember her looking any other way. She'd even worn a silk caftan to Charlie's funeral—in white and lavender, to remind him that Charlie had gone on to a better place or nirvana or satori or some such thing.

"I know that it's going to be difficult, and I thought perhaps a cleansing would be a good way for you to start the business back up again." She held up the bronze bowl she carried. A thin stream of smoke wafted from it. "I'm going to smudge the place for you to remove all evil influences."

"Holy mother of pearl," Henry said, then sneezed.

She ran a metal rod around the edge of the bowl, creating a low, musical tone, then lifted the sage stick from the bowl. Chanting something not English in a soft voice, she waved the stick as she swayed around the store.

Henry sneezed again. And again.

"I can feel the impact on the spirits," Ananda chanted. "Flee, evil ones! Bother this place no more!"

"Noah!"

"Um, Ananda? Can you stop?"

She did. She'd made it as far as the children's section. "Yes, sweetie?"

"I think the evil spirits got the message, and your sage is messing with the good ones."

She glanced around the store, smiling complacently. "Yes, I don't sense the evil spirits any longer, and we don't want to chase out Charlie's influence. Just let me know if you need me to come back."

"I sure will."

"And don't forget to stop by later and have your chakras aligned."

"Sure thing."

"Then if you don't have any more need for me, I'd best go get ready to open up." She gave Noah her biggest smile. "It's so nice to have you back, Noah. Charlie would be so happy."

"Thanks, Ananda. See you later."

The door had barely closed behind her when Henry exploded. "Good God in heaven, Noah, what was that old hippie talkin' about?"

"She's not a hippie. She's a...." Noah struggled a moment. "Okay, she's a hippie. But she means well. She's a really kind lady."

"A kind lady with funky incense." Henry waved a hand in front of his face. "Sweet baby Jesus, that stuff stinks."

"I'll tell her next time not to use sage because my resident specter is allergic to it. She'll just bring over a stack of healing crystals instead."

"Say what?"

"Never mind. Hippies weren't into crystals in your day?"

"Child, hippies were into marijuana and free love. Not that we had many around here—hippies were mostly privileged white children—but I met a few in my day."

"Well, Ananda's mostly into holistic stuff, not pot, and if she has any lovers, she keeps it pretty quiet. I dunno. She's got to be in her sixties, at least."

"Being in your sixties doesn't mean you stop being interested in romance, Noah."

Noah shivered. "Ew."

Henry rolled his eyes.

THE STORE got its first customer at 10:01, and a slow, steady stream came through after that. They mostly came to browse, but some people bought, especially the children's books. Noah heard more than one squeal from a browser who'd found a book they'd loved as a child, and once they'd gotten hooked on that, they tended to hunt for other favorites. It didn't take long for him to fall back into the once-familiar rhythm of bookselling.

He definitely needed an updated register. While the antique was attractive, having to write down the book information every time he made a sale slowed things down to a ridiculous pace. Most of the customers were pretty patient, though, accepting it as part of the antiquey feel of the store. He wondered if there was a way to integrate the old brass register with a computer the way that some old typewriters had been. He'd have to ask one of his techy friends.

Before he knew it, it was 6:00 p.m. and his stomach was growling. He'd grabbed a PBJ at lunchtime, but aside from that, he hadn't eaten most of the day. He'd drunk quite a lot of sweet tea, though, and the sugar was already hitting his stomach hard. With a sigh of relief, he flipped the sign over to Closed and locked up.

"A good day," Henry said from the wing chair in the corner.

"Yeah, not too shabby. We brought in about fifteen hundred, so I think we made a profit, anyway. How much it helps, I dunno."

"Every little bit counts. Everything you make can go toward the loan. You don't need to restock just yet. It's more important that you reestablish that Stardust is still here and still functioning."

"Until it isn't." Noah flicked off the lights and wandered to the back.

CHAPTER THIRTEEN

ON SUNDAY Noah drove Miss Edna to church in the rental car. The minister was the same man who'd handled his dad's service, a large but soft-spoken black man with a warm grin and a gentle way with a sermon. Neither Noah nor Charlie had been much of a churchgoer, but Noah liked this guy and didn't mind sitting in the pew with Miss Edna.

Miss Sarah and Kyle were there too, but sat behind them, so Noah didn't see them until they were leaving. As they walked out into the churchyard, the two ladies drifted over to a knot of other women, abandoning their escorts. Noah grinned wryly at Kyle. "Church ladies," he said.

Kyle frowned faintly but didn't seem to get the joke. Instead he said, "Why do they wear those big hats? Is that part of the religion? The younger ladies don't wear hats at all."

"Part of the religion? No—why? Do ladies not wear hats where you come from? I mean, I never went to church in New York, so I don't know if older ladies wear hats there, but here in Aster they always did. I kind of thought it was a small-town thing, maybe a Southern thing. Even though my dad and I hardly ever went, you see them all over town in the hats. It's a thing." Noah shrugged. "Dad said it started with the black ladies getting all dressed up for church, 'cause they always did that, and then the white ladies started doing it, and then there was kind of an informal competition for who could wear the fanciest hat. The pastor who was in charge then put the kibosh on that, though, now they just coordinate their outfits."

"The women in my church don't wear hats. Nobody does. It's considered disrespectful."

"Huh."

Edna and Sarah looked settled in for a while, so Noah wandered over toward the little graveyard attached to the church. The dirt was still mounded over his dad's grave, but they had put several pieces of sod over the top to keep the dirt from getting washed away by rain, which meant it didn't look as raw as Noah's heart felt. Fresh flowers were scattered across it, and he smiled at the kindness of their little town. They did love Charlie.

Beside him, Kyle said, "The other people here have markers. Will your dad have a marker too?"

"Yeah. They have to carve it yet."

"Is your mama buried here too?"

Noah blinked. "My mother's not dead. At least not that I know of. Last I heard she was living in Vegas."

"Oh. I thought—Miss Sarah mentioned it was sad about your mom, and I thought she meant she had passed. She doesn't live with you?"

"Oh, hell no. She dumped us years ago and took off. Dad had to hire a detective to find her to serve the divorce papers."

"Oh," Kyle said again. "I knew there were people in Chicago who were divorced, but I didn't know people from places like this did. I thought it was a city thing."

"Dude, are you saying you don't have divorced people where you came from?"

Kyle flushed. "It was a really small place. Very...."

"Conservative?"

"Yes. Conservative."

They walked out of earshot of the milling crowd saying their Southern goodbyes. They were usually about half an hour from the initial goodbye to actually leaving.

"Sounds like it. Can I ask you something?" Noah touched his arm.

"Sure you can." Kyle stopped next to him.

"You mentioned you worked a coffee cart in Chicago? You were a barista?"

"Yeah, I guess that's what it's called, a barista. I don't really know what that means, but it's what I did. I have a certificate and stuff."

"'Cause Dad was making plans to introduce a coffee bar in the bookstore, and I don't know diddly about coffee, and I thought maybe we could work out a deal. Like I'd help you get set up, and you could run the coffee bar, and we could work out percentages and stuff. On the net profits and all. If there are any. I don't know jack about running a coffee bar."

Kyle's eyes were wide. "I can't. I mean, it would have to be cash—"

Noah blinked, but Kyle didn't look shady to him. Maybe he had some kind of tax problem.

"The stuff is all sitting right there, and it would bring people into the store, maybe. We could talk to Miss Jessie down at the diner and see if we could buy some pastries from her. That might get people interested. I have no idea how much it would cost to keep it going, but if it's within reason, maybe we could do it. Like, fancy coffee, how do we keep it going…?"

"Looks like you've got a multifunction espresso maker with a frother and grinder, according to the box, but it won't handle a huge number of people…."

"There aren't a huge number of people *in* Aster," Noah pointed out.

"Yeah. So if you're only expecting to sell a few cups a day, you can use that one."

"How few?"

Kyle shrugged. "Less than fifty? You'd burn out the machine if you did much more. We handled way more than that from the cart, but then we were in a really busy office building that didn't have a restaurant on site. We probably couldn't charge what he did for coffee."

"I think it could work, maybe?"

"Maybe."

Miss Edna was waving at him, and he waved back. "Duty calls," he said to Kyle. "I imagine Miss Sarah's ready to head home too." He hesitated. "By the way—can you drive a truck?"

"Yes. But—I don't have a valid license."

"I need to return the car to the rental place by the airport, but I need a ride back home. If you haven't gotten your Georgia license yet, your Illinois one would be okay."

"No. I don't have a license at all. Well… I do, but it's not in my name."

"Do I want to know why?"

"Not really."

Noah sighed again. "Okay. Does it *look* legit?"

"Well—yes."

"Okay. Tomorrow morning about nine okay?"

Kyle blinked. "Um, yes?"

"Don't worry, you can just follow me. I've driven to the airport more times than you could imagine."

"Good. Because I've never been there."

Noah grinned. "Piece of cake."

"Cake?"

"I mean it's easy."

"Oh, okay. Piece of cake."

Noah grinned again.

CHAPTER FOURTEEN

NOAH ROLLED his shoulders and grabbed one of the breakfast sandwiches out of the freezer. Miss Edna thought frozen food was a sin, but it was quick and easy and didn't require him to think too much. Wrap it in a paper towel and then nuke for ninety seconds, flip it and fifty-five more seconds—for which he hit a minute anyway because he was lazy.

While the biscuit turned in the microwave, Noah grabbed both of Jake's bowls. He rinsed out and refilled the water, and then dumped both wet and dry food into the other. They'd gotten into a practiced routine in the mornings since he had gotten there almost two weeks before. Just as Noah set the bowl down on the floor, the microwave beeped. He grabbed the sandwich and a Coke (another breakfast sin) and sat down at the table.

He'd stopped stepping around *that spot* on the floor. It seemed like such a childish thing to do. Like that game 'step on a crack and break your mother's back.' What happened if you stepped on the place where your dad died? What did you break, then?

Noah ate in silence with Jake's head on his foot. Jake seemed to need a lot of affection; he wanted to be constantly touching Noah. Either when they sat on the couch, or they were at the bookstore, or even just hanging out in the backyard. Maybe Jake thought he would leave him too.

His phone beeped and he looked down to see Yeira's name. He'd thought maybe Karen had come to her senses. He hadn't heard from her since she set her arbitrary deadline.

Got a lead on a story today.

Guilt crashed over him. He hadn't even thought about how Yeira's life had changed since he'd been gone or how it would change if he never came back. Noah had been so obsessed with his own problems, he forgot other people in the world existed.

That's great. Your boss going to let you run with it?

I have to validate my sources, but yeah—I think I'll get my first solo story. Normally I'm just doing background for other people.

That's awesome!

Yeah, wish my mom thought so.

I'd say she'd come around, but we know she won't.

She wants me to be a dental hygienist or something. Says I should have had enough tragedy and bad news for ten lifetimes. She doesn't understand that I'm trying to help people. He'd met Yeira's mother a few times when she came to the apartment, and she wasn't a woman he'd want to be on the bad side of. But Yeira had grown up in a war zone, which gave her a stronger backbone than anyone he knew. He envied her strength and confidence.

I know. Maybe once you're writing your own stories, you can show her.

Thanks. How are things there?

About what you'd expect. My boss threatened to fire me, my dad was over his head in debt, and I'm trying to run a business that I know nothing about. A lump formed in his throat as he piled up the list of everything wrong in his life right then.

You're smart. You'll figure it out.

He started to tell her about Henry but stopped. Would she think he was crazy? It didn't seem like something a normal person would talk about. And it felt... well... special to him, like he didn't want to share Henry with anyone.

Hey, I've got to get to the station. They lived a few stops from her job, but she always left early because in New York, anything could happen.

Give 'em hell!

A shadow crossed the back door, and Jake looked up as Kyle knocked.

"Come on in, it's open," Noah called. It hadn't taken long for the twang in his voice to return. In fact, as he called it out, he heard shades of Charlie.

"Good morning." Kyle leaned on the doorframe like he wasn't sure he wanted to enter the room.

"Mornin'." Noah took another bite of his biscuit and nodded toward the chair across. Kyle glanced around first but then pulled out the chair and sat.

"Want a sandwich?" Noah asked. "I can make you one."

"Nah, Miss Sarah already fed me biscuits and gravy. I think I've gained ten pounds since I moved here." He patted his stomach and sat back in the chair.

"You look great to me," Noah muttered and Kyle blushed.

"So, uhm…," he stammered. "You want me to drive the truck to the airport right behind you, right? And then you'll bring us home?"

"Yeah, that's it. I need to return this rental car, which is costing me a fortune. You said you don't have a license. Did you ever have one?"

"No. I wasn't old enough when I left Mon—when I left home, and there wasn't any reason to get one in Chicago. You can get just about anywhere on the El."

"The El?"

"That's what they call the trains in Chicago. Because they're elevated above the city."

"Makes sense—in New York it was the subway, below ground."

"You can't get anywhere here without a car," Kyle mused. "You just have to walk around town. Good thing it's not very big."

"Thought about getting your license here? I could help," Noah offered.

"Nope." Kyle closed the door on the subject with one curt word.

Noah finished up his sandwich in two large bites and screwed the cap back on his Coke. He tossed his paper towel into the trash and glanced around the kitchen. Jake still lay under the table with a hopeful expression.

"Okay, you. I'm going to turn on the TV. Don't look at me like that. You don't get human food at every meal." Noah stepped into the living room and turned on a sports channel. The Falcons would be playing in a while, and every good Southern dog loved his football, right?

"Did you do a lot of driving where you were from?" Noah asked as he grabbed the truck keys from the hook by the door.

"Enough. I drove small trucks around picking up and dropping off stuff around the… neighborhood." He paused like he'd been searching for that last word.

"Okay, use your GPS to find the airport in case we get separated. We're going to the car rental area. They're all in one place."

"My GPS?"

81

"Yeah, on your phone. Haven't you ever used GPS to get somewhere? You lived in Chicago."

"I don't have a phone."

Noah stared at him. "You don't have a cell phone?"

"No. I don't have anyone to talk to. Why would I need a phone?"

That one statement—so simple, but profound. Kyle didn't have a cell phone because he didn't have any friends—not back home, not in Chicago, and not here. It felt like the full truth of Kyle's life had just slammed into the side of his head.

High school had been a bitch, but once Noah got to NYU, he made friends easily. After graduation when he started working, he made friends. But Kyle didn't. He didn't even keep a phone to talk to his parents.

"Do you keep up with your aunt and uncle in Chicago?" Noah managed.

"Yes, but we talk on the house phone. Aunt Mary isn't much for technology either." Kyle smiled.

"I'm not sure I've ever met anyone without a cell phone. You're like one of the seven wonders of the world."

"Now you're poking fun at me." Kyle's face darkened, and he turned toward the door.

"Only a little," Noah said and put his arm around Kyle for a quick squeeze and then headed out onto the back porch. Kyle followed, and Noah tossed him the keys.

"Now you have me," Noah said with a grin.

Kyle blushed. "I'd like that."

Noah couldn't think of anything else to say, so he opened the door of the truck and stood next to it.

"Be careful," Noah said, butterflies hitting him at the thought of something happening to his dad's truck. All of a sudden he was sixteen again and driving that thing for the first time.

"I will. Don't worry, Noah. I *can* drive, even if the state of Georgia doesn't know that." Kyle rolled his eyes and got in the truck.

It took them forty-seven minutes to get to the airport, and Kyle stayed on his ass the entire way, even when he nearly missed an exit. That was an impressive maneuver. Together they'd nearly taken out the roadside hotel sign, but they made it. Noah could see the fear and excitement in Kyle's eyes when he pulled up next to him. Kyle grinned back.

"Wow," Noah said, the sting of the final rental bill ringing in his ears as he headed back out to where Kyle sat on the tailgate of the pickup.

"Wow?"

"It was expensive. It's been two weeks, and I should have taken this back days ago, but—"

"But you couldn't face that your father was really dead." Kyle slid down and closed the tailgate with a metallic clang.

"Yeah."

"There have been a lot of things in my life I've had to face. You do it, and you get past it. If you don't, then life just gets harder." He shrugged and walked around to the passenger side.

Noah wanted to press, to ask what kinds of things he'd had to face, but he got the feeling that Kyle didn't want to talk about it, so he changed gears. "When did you come live with Miss Sarah?" he asked, turning the ignition and letting the big truck shudder to life.

"I've been here about a month and a half, maybe? Came down on a bus from Chicago. Uncle Frank wanted to drive me, but he didn't want to leave Aunt Mary by herself. I didn't mind, really. I had a couple of books; they got me through." Kyle pulled one foot up to cross the opposite knee.

"I thought you didn't like to read." Noah checked the mirror and pulled out onto the roundabout that circled the airport.

"I said I didn't like to read fiction. They were both kind of Bible study books. My aunt got them for me."

"And you read them anyway?"

Kyle shrugged. "I colored a bit too."

"You mean, like, with crayons?" Noah asked with surprise.

"Yeah. When I was a kid that's pretty much all we had, pieces of paper and this box of broken crayons someone had left. It's calming." Kyle gazed out the window again.

"So what happened when you got here?"

"Miss Sarah picked me up at the bus station and I came to live with her. We spent a lot of time in those first two weeks watching TV. I think she was happy to have someone to watch with. I didn't really care. I hadn't watched TV much growing up."

"So if you didn't read and you didn't watch TV, what did you do growing up?" Noah changed lanes into the far left to hang out until his exit.

"I dunno. Normal stuff, I guess. We worked in the garden, helped my dad with church stuff, and helped Mama make meals." Kyle watched the miles of green rush past the window.

"So your dad was a preacher?"

"I guess."

They sat in silence for a bit, watching the miles of I-85 whir past under the tires of the old truck. Noah couldn't think of anything else to ask Kyle, who seemed to be getting uncomfortable talking about himself.

"How did they die?" Noah asked quietly.

Kyle ripped his eyes from the scenery to stare at him.

"You got on a bus and came here all alone as a teenager to your aunt's house. I guess I assumed—"

"My father is alive, so far as I know. Aunt Mary tried to find out how my mama was, but she couldn't. I just hope…." What little life had been in Kyle's eyes drained from them.

"I know how that feels," Noah said.

"You can't possibly."

The rest of the ride was quiet as Noah tried to puzzle out what Kyle had meant. He'd lost his own father; surely Kyle could see how they were the same. He wanted to be angry about it, but the pain in Kyle's expression stopped him. Something bad lurked beyond the shadows of Kyle's admission, something dark, and it haunted him.

Noah reached across the console and held Kyle's hand.

"Kyle—" He was interrupted by the shrill ring of his cell phone. It was a Manhattan number, but one he didn't recognize. He touched the button on the steering wheel to answer.

"Hello?"

"Noah, it's Karen." He glanced at his cell phone lying on the console beside him.

"Hi, Karen."

"Are you still in Georgia?" Her voice was flat and heavy, like cream on the verge of spoiling.

"Listen, Karen, about that—I think we should talk to—"

"Are you still in Georgia, Noah?"

"Yes."

The line went quiet for a long moment, and Noah held his breath, afraid to speak and afraid of what would come next. The silence in the car felt absolute. He couldn't hear Kyle breathing either—just the steady flap of the tires hitting the road.

"Noah, this is James Tim from Human Resources," another voice, firm but dispassionate, said through the harsh connection. "I'm sorry, Mr. Hitchens, but we need to terminate your employment as of today. Your desk contents will be shipped to you, and any PTO you had accumulated prior to your bereavement leave will be paid out in your final check. Do you have any questions for me?"

Noah's hands tingled. His arms, even his chest, had this weird disconnected feeling of panic. They were firing him. He had no job. How would he pay his rent on the apartment? What the hell was he going to do? Noah took a deep breath and collected himself.

"Is this your direct line that you've called me from?" he asked.

"It is."

"My attorney may have some questions, so I wanted to make sure I had your number," Noah said, more calmly than he felt. It was a bluff, but all he had.

"Of course."

Noah disconnected the line and sat in stunned silence, his eyes fixed on the road. Kyle held his hand tighter like they were both waiting for a storm.

CHAPTER FIFTEEN

THE BASEMENT light came on without flickering, which Noah was grateful for. If there were going to be spiders—and of course there would be spiders—maybe the lights would keep them away. Hiding in the boxes that he needed to open, probably. Ugh.

"Careful on the steps, they're kind of uneven," he called over his shoulder.

Kyle followed him down into the depths of the cellar. "Wow," he said.

Wow was right. It had been years since Noah had been down there. The walls were lined with boxes—plastic bins on the floor, wooden crates piled on some and cardboard boxes on others. There were piles in the middle of the floor too. "Gah," Noah groaned. "I'm never gonna get through all these. Good thing the basement never flooded—all these would be ruined."

"That's probably why the plastic boxes are on the bottom. Keep them off the floor so the others don't get wet. That's how we stored stuff back... home."

"Makes sense. Okay. We found some nice first editions, so let's see if there's anything valuable down there. Can you read any of these labels?"

Kyle bent over and peered at one. Noah admired his butt in the snug jeans but dragged his perverted mind back to the subject at hand. "Estate Sale, June 2017," Kyle read off. "Leather bound and Book Club." He made a note on the clipboard he carried.

"From the sublime to the ridiculous."

"Why?"

"Well, leather-bound books are sometimes valuable, but book club editions usually aren't. They're printed on cheap paper, and the covers aren't the same as the regular published editions. That's how come the clubs can afford to sell them so cheap. I wonder what the leather-bound ones are. Bet they bought a set from, like, Time Life or something. World's Greatest Literature—and I'll bet none of them have been read."

"Why wouldn't someone read them?"

"They buy them for decoration and read the book club editions. Of course, that makes them more salable." Noah squinted up at another box. "Okay, this one says Auction—that sounds promising."

It happened so fast neither Noah nor Kyle could react. Noah stepped on an uneven bit of flooring and bumped into a stack of boxes, which teetered and fell...

...but they didn't. Instead they hung a moment in midair over Noah's head, and then he felt a hand shove him forward into Kyle's arms.

Which closed tightly around him as the boxes tumbled into a heap, breaking and spilling books everywhere.

Noah drew back, shocked, and stared into Kyle's eyes. "What? What happened?"

"I have no idea," Kyle started to say, but the words went muffled as Noah leaned forward and kissed him.

Noah drew back, startled at himself. "Gosh," he burbled, "I didn't—I mean, I didn't exactly expect to—is it okay? I'm sorry."

Kyle's face was scarlet, stunned. He put his fingers to his lips.

Then Noah whirled back to the pile of books. "Henry!"

"Take it easy, child," his soft voice drawled. "Not likely those books could hurt me."

"Where are you?"

"I'm right here. But doin' so much physical labor after bein' dead for fifty years takes it out of a body—even a disembody."

"Is that even a word?"

"In the ordinary scheme of things, it's a verb, but I think in my case, it functions just as well as a noun."

Kyle was looking around frantically as if trying to spot the speaker. Could he hear Henry? He never had before, but maybe the exertion stopped Henry from being able to hide. "Who's that, Noah? Where is he?"

Guess he could.

"That's Henry, Kyle. I told you about him."

"You said he was a friend from New York!"

"Well, I never said he was from New York. I just said he couldn't help me much."

"That's an unkind thing to say, child. I thought I'd been very helpful."

"Yeah, you have. But it's not like you can haul boxes. At least not without losing your ectoplasm or whatever."

"Noah—is it a *spirit*?"

"Who, Henry? Nah, he's… well, yeah, I guess he is. A ghost, anyway."

"Spirits are evil, Noah! He needs to be cast out!"

"Listen up, boy," Henry said sternly, "I've been here a lot longer than you have, and if there's any casting out to be done, I think that's given me the right to do the casting. As for evil—son, I was deacon at the First Baptist for nigh on forty years." He muttered, "Evil. Bah."

"Henry's not evil, Kyle. He's been a big help to me. I grew up in this store, but I never really did much more than occasionally run the register for Dad. Henry knows all about books." Noah sighed and sat on one of the boxes. "I'm a freaking literature major and a dead guy knows more about books than I ever will. Maybe I should have majored in library science."

"Library's a science now?"

"That's so creepy," Kyle said.

"Library science?"

"No, the fact that I can't see who's talking."

"Well, you can hear me, so that's a start. I'd have bet you never would have if I hadn't exerted myself like that. You haven't exactly got an open mind."

"Henry, be nice. He can't help it if he grew up in the back of beyond. When I moved to New York, it was pretty overwhelming to me too." Noah brightened as Henry began to materialize, sitting on a box across from Noah.

Kyle turned and blinked rapidly. "Oh."

"You can see him?"

"Um—is he a, a brown person with glasses?"

"A *brown* person? I am a black man, you skinny white boy. A proud black man."

"I'm sorry. I don't—I never knew any before I moved to Chicago, and the people back home weren't very nice about brown people. I saw some in Chicago but never really met them."

"Brown people?" Henry looked to Noah.

"What?"

"Is that an acceptable term nowadays?"

"Um—more like people of color?"

"Let me get this straight—'colored people' is a no-no but 'people of color' is okay?" Henry shook his head. "I will never understand this age."

"Well, it's because that's a phrase they chose, where the other they didn't. It's like you might hear a Lithuanian person call another one a Lugan, but it's really rude if you do." He glanced at Kyle. "I dated a Lithuanian guy for a while."

"Hmm. Well, that makes sense. At least we've moved that far. So. Are you boys going to pick up these boxes? It's a little bit beyond my capabilities at this juncture and that one"—he pointed at the auction box—"looks promising."

Kyle was still staring at Henry. After a moment he said, "Oh. Yes. Okay."

Noah chuckled and slipped off the box he was sitting on, moving it over to the side so he could work on the piled ones. A moment later Kyle joined him in picking up the rest.

Henry supervised.

Chapter Sixteen

"But you *have* to—it's tradition!" Thad cried. The giant block rows in his Rubik's Cube costume banged together, cardboard clashing as he tried to follow Noah in through the front door of the bookstore. It took some finagling, and finally he had to turn at an angle, but he made it.

"I've got too much to do, Thad. I just got fired. I have to make this work now. Kyle has some experience with all this coffee stuff, so we're trying to get that off the ground. I don't have time to play dress-up with the kids." Noah made his way back up to the counter and the box of books waiting to be put back in their places. Why did people grab books and leave them all over? Did they think he had nothing better to do than clean up after them?

Thad followed, awkwardly trying not to knock books off their shelves.

"You can't afford not to," Thad said, putting a hand on Noah's arm. "When I first started in business here, no one wanted to buy things from me because I was different. I swear to God, you'd think they never saw a fag before. I was like an alien."

Noah sat the box down and turned. "I didn't know that."

"Yep, gay unicorn alien." Thad raised his arm as much as the costume would allow. "Anyway, the way I got people to accept me, to get that I was an eccentric old antiques-selling queer, was by being part of the community. I joined little committees to improve the town, I volunteered for their food drives, and I pass out candy to their kids on Halloween. Get me?"

"So, you're saying to win over the community, I have to dress in drag and do the hula?" Noah hadn't dressed up in a very long time. He didn't really get into Halloween, though his dad loved it.

"Yep." The *p* popped with enthusiasm. "Got any ideas?"

"Nope, but I'll think of something."

"You'd better hurry. The insanity starts at five," Thad said, turning his bulky cube back toward the front of the store. "If you need help, just holler. I've got all kinds of stuff in my closet."

Noah laughed at his lascivious wink.

"What the good gracious was he wearing?" Henry asked, floating in through the wall. "I start to come in here and he's dressed like a boxy stoplight."

"It was a Rubik's Cube. They were a child's toy popular sometime in the eighties. You have to keep turning it until all the colors match."

"Children don't read anymore?"

"Yeah, not so much," Noah admitted.

"That explains a lot," he said, glancing at the box on the counter. "You want me to put those away so you can go dress like a stoplight?"

"Nah, I don't even know what I'd dress up as." Noah pulled a couple books out of the box and checked the titles.

"It's a bookstore, Noah. You need to go as a literary character," Henry stated as if it were obvious. "What's your favorite book?"

"I have millions. But I guess the fastest and easiest costume to put together is Harry Potter."

"Ah, yes. I saw that in the children's section. The series seems to be very popular, by the way your father decorated around it."

"It is." Noah flipped through the titles and frowned.

"What is it?" Henry asked, looking at the stack.

"Most of these are gay books—romances, YA. Why would someone move all these around? You'd think if they were against it, they'd mutilate them, not just move them around," Noah mused.

Henry considered. "When I ran this establishment, we had a lot of teenage girls who'd come in and read some of the risqué parts of those women's romances. Then they'd leave the book where it lay and run out giggling."

"So maybe we've got a gay kid in town? I found these by the chairs. He must have sat and read them because he was afraid to take them home," Noah said sadly. "I'll keep an eye out for him.

"And do what?"

"Let him know it's okay to read them here, that it's a safe place." Noah placed one of the books back on the shelf.

"I have decided to stick with love. Hate is too great a burden to bear," Henry said.

"Martin Luther King."

"Amen, child."

He piddled around the store for another hour, building himself up for what he expected to find at the party store over in Douglasville. Waiting until the last possible second was never a great idea for Halloween, but he'd figure it out. He'd just locked the front door when Kyle showed up on the sidewalk.

"Closing early?" Kyle asked.

"No, I have a little shopping to do. Want to come?"

"Sure." He followed Noah over to the truck and climbed in the passenger side. "Where are we going?"

"First, to the party store in Douglasville to get costumes. Then we're going to hit up a grocery store and see if anyone in a ten-mile radius still has any decent candy." Noah sighed and turned the ignition.

"Costumes?"

"It's Halloween," Noah said with a glance at Kyle. "Did they not celebrate it where you grew up?"

"Celebrate it? No. It was the devil's holiday. We prayed."

"Okay, no costume for you, then." Noah pulled out onto the main road and did a U-turn. Traffic was light as they drove toward the highway.

"What are you going to pretend to be?" Kyle fiddled with the window control and let his roll down a few inches.

"A boy wizard if I can find the stuff. They're probably down to scraps, but all I really need is a cape and a wand. I have black glasses already, and I can draw on my forehead with a pen."

Kyle gaped at him. "You're going to become a wizard. They do black magic, Noah. You can't do—"

"Kyle, it's just a costume. I'm not actually going to pull a rabbit out of a hat. Thad says that it fosters a community spirit, and we need people on our side right now."

"I don't understand how dressing as a servant of the devil is going to help. God won't want to help you."

"I don't think God has a grudge against Harry Potter. What about you? If we find something that won't send you to Hell, you want to dress up?"

"Like what?"

"Clown? Firefighter? You could be a priest?"

"I think I'll just stick with my coffee machines." Kyle scooted lower in the seat, arms crossed, looking less than amused.

It took the better part of half an hour to pick their way through the carnage they found at the costume store. Severed heads, legs, random pieces of clothing, and even a long white beard lay discarded in the middle of an aisle. It was like Dorothy came to find her ruby slippers and accidently brought the tornado. But as Noah had suspected, he was able to find a generic cape and wand. As a bonus he even found a broom and a totally not Harry Potter scarf in the exact gold and rust colors with a generic "wizard's scarf" tag.

Kyle followed him around, wide-eyed at all the masks still on display. Killer clowns, ghouls, zombies, and a wart-nosed witch. He didn't touch any of them; he simply stared, disbelief warring with horror in his expression.

Noah paid for his haul, already half price in anticipation of the overstock the store was going to carry into the next year. It surprised him that he'd thought of it in such business terms. He'd never thought about things like inventory warehousing. Kyle followed him out of the store and stayed quiet as they left the parking lot and headed back toward Aster.

Noah parked in a spot surprisingly far from the front door of the grocery store, given that it was the middle of a Wednesday. He started to get out but noticed Kyle hadn't moved. He closed the door and turned in his seat.

"You didn't have trick-or-treaters in Chicago?" Noah asked quietly.

"No. Aunt Mary said they drove her nuts, so we always went to the movies. I saw the little kids wandering around in their little costumes."

"But you've never done it?"

"Is it normal?" Kyle asked suddenly.

"Is what normal? Trick-or-treating?"

"Yeah. Is it something that everybody does?"

"Sure, most people. All of my friends did, growing up. It was something we looked forward to every year. We liked getting to pretend to be someone else. Mostly we just liked collecting all the candy we could get. When I was younger, we could go for as long as people had lights on. But now you only get two hours," Noah lamented.

"And no one thinks it's against God?"

"I don't think so. Even the preacher has something at the church for the kids."

"Sometimes I feel like I grew up on an alien planet." Kyle opened the door and swung out of the car. Noah wanted to press, wanted to know why Kyle's life had been so different from his own. Didn't most kids dress up for Halloween?

They picked up fifteen bags of candy, everything from Hershey bars to Jolly Ranchers. Noah didn't think he'd need that many but didn't want to run out. They could always put a candy bowl on the counter. Who didn't like a free piece of candy with their coffee and book?

Jake jumped up to greet him when he and Kyle walked into his father's house.

"Hey, buddy," Noah said, rubbing the dog behind the ears. "I think we'll take you back with us tonight. You'll like seeing all the kids, huh?" Jake nuzzled into his hand and gave a deep, happy bark.

"I'm going to go upstairs and change. I think the white shirt and black pants I wore to the funeral will work under the cape," Noah noted. Kyle wandered into the kitchen and Jake followed, assuming that meant some kind of food for the puppy.

Noah got dressed and even found a little beanie Hedwig hiding among his childhood things. He used Krazy Glue to attach the little bird to his cheap cape and laughed at his reflection in the mirror. It had been a long time since he'd felt this young.

Kyle stared at him when he made his way back down to the kitchen. "You don't look like a wizard."

"Why, how do wizards look?" Noah asked, cocking his head before realizing there was a bird in the way.

"Evil."

"Nope. I'm a good wizard. Come on, Jake!" Noah patted his leg and the big dog followed. He noticed Jake's treats had made it from the top of the fridge to the table.

"Why don't you bring those along?" he asked Kyle, nodding toward the treats. "Just in case he needs a little coaxing later."

Kyle grabbed the bag and they all headed back out to the truck.

MAYHEM ENSUED once the clock hands on his father's mantelpiece pointed to five. Thad hadn't been kidding about the turnout. It seemed that most of the kids started here on the main street before venturing off into the neighborhoods. When Noah was a kid, he and his dad would start at Miss Edna's house and keep working their way through the blocks systematically until either Noah was too tired to carry on or hours ended.

He found a big black bowl in one of the displays, almost large enough to be a small cauldron, and moved it out in front of the store. Thad and Ananda were sitting in front of their stores with similar containers. Ananda's actually *was* a cauldron, and she was rocking that haunted witch costume. He could see the wart from two doors down. Thad had some kind of copper pot to hold his candy, sticking with the antique theme—though he was having a hell of a time trying to sit his cubic self down.

As far as Noah could see, there were lights and kids and an atmosphere of fun excitement. Cooper whooped his siren as he passed, lights flashing as he kept an eye on their town's children. Mr. Barnes from the pet store across the street sat outside with a puppy and a bowl of candy. He wasn't in costume, but he smiled and chatted with people as they came to see him.

"Hi, Noah!"

Fred the mailman stood there at his makeshift cauldron with two small kids, a boy and a girl dressed as superheroes. Noah reached into the bowl and grabbed a couple of pieces each and dropped them into the waiting, open bags. Jake woofed as the little girl petted him. He seemed happy for all the attention. Noah had left him home a lot lately. He'd have to bring him more often so Jake could hang out.

"Hi, Fred. Are these your kids?"

"Yep, Melissa—oh, I'm sorry," he amended when she glared at him with her little girl eyes. "Wonder Woman here is six, and Captain America is ten."

"Dad, I'm not *really* Captain America, it's just a—"

"I can't win," Fred lamented.

Noah laughed and gave them both another piece of candy. He expected them to wander off, but the little boy was looking in through the bookstore window.

"Mr. Noah, you have a ghost," he said matter-of-factly. His sister ran over to the door and peered inside next to her brother. Noah stood up, alarmed, and followed their gaze. Sure enough, Henry was roaming around the classics section in full view of the street.

"Oh, he's… is he scary?" Noah asked.

"No, he looks kind of like a librarian," Captain America said, his voice excited.

"Want to go in and see him?" Noah asked, and both kids nodded rapidly. He opened the door and they took off. Fred looked at him.

"He's a hologram. There's a projector in the ceiling," Noah lied and followed them into the store. The kids were standing beneath Henry, who looked down at them, bemused. Then he did a flip midair and the children gasped with delight. He moved down to the end of the row and then flew past them, then up the next aisle. They laughed and followed.

"Guys, don't you want more candy?" Fred yelled and saw two excited faces peek at him from the end of the aisle.

"We want to play with the ghost!" Wonder Woman called, but Fred walked up and took her hand. Her brother followed, looking sullen.

"Bye, Mr. Ghost!" the little girl called, and Henry waved at them, grinning.

"How imaginative children are," Henry remarked, sinking to where Noah stood at the head of the aisle.

"They thought you were amazing."

"And they were correct," Henry said with a smirk. "What did you tell the father? Adults aren't so easily fooled."

"That there's a projector in the ceiling."

"That was fun," Henry admitted.

"Feel free to float around all you want tonight. I think a haunted bookstore has a little charm," Noah laughed and headed back outside. The cluster of children was still going strong when he sat back down in his seat. He gave treats to a group of young teens dressed in coordinating video game character costumes, and then tiny kids dressed as Mr. and Mrs. Potato Head. He thought maybe he liked their costumes best of all.

They all wandered off toward Ananda's store next.

"Your dad would be real proud seeing you out here carrying on tradition."

Noah looked up to see Miss Norma shuffling up to where he sat with Jake. She wasn't in costume but a simple flowy fall-colored dress. Immediately he vacated his chair and held a hand out for her.

"Ma'am," he said, and she smiled at him.

"You're such a good boy. Your daddy did right by you," she said with a warm smile and perched herself lightly on the edge of the chair. Noah dropped candy into the pillowcases of a few more trick-or-treaters as they passed.

"That he did, Miss Norma."

"You must miss him terribly," she said, and he barely heard her over the din of the milling people grabbing treats up and down the sidewalks.

"I do. He always seemed to know what to do, no matter what bad thing happened. I don't seem to ever know what to do," Noah admitted.

He was surprised when she laughed, a quiet tinkle of sound. "You'd be surprised how much old folks like us wing it. He prolly had no good idea what to do either. He was good at not lettin' people see." She put a hand on his arm. "This was a good idea right here, letting people see that you belong in the community, that you care about what's happenin' round here. And if they offer help, you let 'em. You hear me?" Her voice had taken on that take-charge Southern woman quality he'd heard all his life.

"Yes, ma'am." Noah looked in through the window at Kyle, who manned the empty coffee station like the last sentry of a fallen castle, his expression just as puzzled and sad. He stood with his elbows on the counter and his chin resting on his hands. Noah wanted to hug him.

Miss Norma seemed to notice his distraction. "Good boy. Okay, I'm going to take these old bones down the street and keep visitin'. You have a good night, young Mr. Hitchens."

"You too, Miss Norma."

He gave out candy into the night. It was about an hour past curfew when his bowl ran empty. Then he and Jake sat on the front sidewalk of the store and watched folks checking their haul and heading back home. He'd talked to just about everyone in town tonight. Most remembered him or at least knew who he was because of Charlie. They were friendly and concerned about him, both for the store and for losing his father.

This old town had touched him in ways he didn't even understand.

He could do worse than building a life here in Aster, surrounded by books and kind people.

CHAPTER SEVENTEEN

"FREE PEOPLE of color were pretty common in New Orleans," Henry said Friday evening, after Kyle had gone off home and he'd closed the store. He lit a ghostly pipe he'd pulled out of his pants pocket and puffed to get it started. "New Orleans was always a different kind of place."

"Still is," Noah observed.

"Is it? Good. My *maman* was from there—married my papa right after the Spanish-American War."

"Your mama was a dressmaker?"

"Please. A modiste." Henry laughed. "Despite being colored, Aster was as solidly middle-class as any town up north. We had good schools with teachers from places like Tuskegee Institute and Clark College, and children went on to colleges throughout the country. Ladies like to buy nice clothes when they can afford it, and *maman* made nice, nice clothes. There was a dress she'd made from silk and lace made from real gold thread. She had that in a place of honor in her shop—ladies would come in just to look at it and would walk out a few dollars poorer!

"Things changed a lot after the Great War. There used to be a song that said 'How you gonna keep 'em down on the farm, now that they've seen Paree?' We not only lost the boys who died in that war, but the ones that came back were changed. They'd seen what it was to be someplace where there wasn't the prejudice and the Jim Crow laws, where black people were treated like human beings, and while Aster was a good place, it's still in Georgia. So many of them never did come back here, or came back only to leave again for the North.

"Same thing happened in Dubya Dubya Two. Lost a bunch of young men in the war, and so many decided not to come home. Some did, though. And you heard of war brides? Well, some of the ones that came back brought wives, and some of them later brought their wives' families. Of course, Georgia wouldn't recognize their marriages as legal, but Aster did. So the town became a little more integrated—in the opposite direction."

"Mixed-race marriages are legal now," Noah said. "Heck, same-sex marriages are legal now too."

Henry's eyes grew wide. "You mean two homosexuals can get married?"

"Yep. It's only been a few years, and they're still trying to revoke it, but it's legal. About damn time."

"Well. If you don't mind my sayin' so, that's pretty strange." Henry sighed. "Lots of things seem pretty strange to me, though, nowadays." He sucked his pipestem, then reached into his pocket, pulled out his lighter, and lit the pipe again. "Can never keep one of these things going. Spend most of the time trying to light it again."

"Probably why people get less cancer from pipes than they do from cigarettes," Noah said.

Henry said, "I used to have some good books in my parlor upstairs, but I expect Berenice cleared all that out before she sold the place."

Noah blinked. "No, it looks like everything's just the same. There's a dressmaker's dummy and a big wing chair and...."

Henry's eyes had gone wide. "It's still there? *Maman*'s dress?"

"Yeah, it doesn't look like anything's been touched. Come on, I'll show you." Noah led the way up the stairs and opened the door to the sitting room.

"Oh my." Henry touched the dress gently. "This brings back memories. And my books...." He turned around, looking at the full bookcases Noah had missed in his panic at finding Henry. "I'll bet you can find some that are of some value." He drifted around the room, brushing his fingers over the furniture, the drapes, the knickknacks on the table and shelves. Nothing moved at his touch, but he seemed to feel it, and he smiled.

"I didn't want to come up here. I didn't want to see everything gone, all I'd lost."

Noah could understand.

In one corner he stopped and looked down. "Oh," he said softly.

"What is it?"

"Just a cat bed. My kitty's. Her name was Persephone. I wonder what happened to her."

"I don't know. I didn't know you had a pet."

"Cats aren't pets, Noah. They're companions. She kept me company after Berenice got married and moved away. She used to sleep on the top of the bookcase there... Persephone?"

There was a faint mew, and Henry reached up. A moment later a large tortoiseshell calico—as translucent as Henry—was snuggled in his arms. "Oh, Persephone."

"That's a big cat," Noah observed.

"I think she's part Maine Coon. She's about sixteen pounds, and not an inch of it fat. She's mostly fur—sheds like crazy."

"I somehow don't think that'll be an issue. I didn't know cats had ghosts too. Do dogs?"

"I have no idea. I never had a dog. But I bet they do. Maybe more so than cats—cats don't need people as much." He bent his head and nuzzled the calico. "At least they try to pretend they don't."

The cat reached up and batted at Henry's nose.

"Why do some people, or cats, or dogs become ghosts and others don't? I mean, can you see my dad anywhere?" The hope in his voice hurt coming out, but it was a question he'd wanted to ask for some time.

"I don't see anyone here but Miss Persephone and me, son. I'm sorry. And I don't know why I didn't go to the great beyond. Maybe it's because I hadn't been found. Maybe it's because I was meant to help you. I don't know."

They were quiet for a long while before Noah spoke again. "I wonder...."

"What?"

"Jake is always sitting and staring at the door. I wonder if he sensed she was up here? I didn't see her when I came up before—when I found you."

"You wouldn't, if she didn't want you to see her. Cats are like that. But it wouldn't be a bookstore without a cat."

"Will she come downstairs with you?"

"Only one way to find out." Henry sank through the floor, the cat still in his arms.

Noah rolled his eyes and went downstairs the normal way.

Jake was in the office taking a drink from the dog bowl on the floor when Noah got down the stairs, but he lifted his head, gave Noah a betrayed look, then hightailed it into the main part of the store. Noah could hear him growling.

"Jake!" He ran into the store.

Jake was down on his front legs like he was playing, and his tail was wagging slowly, but he was giving off a low, steady warning sound. Henry stood in front of him, the cat in his arms. "Giving mixed messages, dog," Henry said mildly.

Persephone was watching Jake. If she had had eyebrows, one of them would have been raised, Noah thought. No fear, just skepticism. "I don't think he'll hurt her."

"I don't think he *can* hurt her. I don't know if *she* can hurt *him*."

"She's tiny! I mean, compared to Jake."

"You've not had much experience with cats, have you, son?"

Persephone leaped gracefully out of Henry's arms and onto the floor. Casually, her fluffy tail waving leisurely, she approached Jake. His growling deepened.

Then she reached out, still casually, and swiped her claws across his nose. He yelped and ran for the kitchen.

Persephone sat down and began washing the paw.

When Noah went into the kitchen, Jake was seated by the back door. He looked even more betrayed than before. "Okay, let's see what damage she did," Noah said and sat down beside his dog.

But when he looked, there wasn't so much as a scratch on the dog's nose. Nothing.

"I think you'll live," he said dryly. "Scared you, did she?"

Jake crawled into his lap and laid his head on Noah's thigh, giving a huge sigh.

Henry came in a moment later, sans cat. "He okay?"

"Yeah, she didn't hurt him. Scared him, I think. Where's she?"

"Curled up in the window seat, basking in the sunlight." Henry sat on one of the dinette chairs. "Cats are like that. Never any guilt. Leave that to the dogs. She was just trying to establish that she won't be pushed around. I've known some women like that. Good strong women."

"Yeah, me too."

"I imagine you have. Finest kind. My *maman* was like that, and my Renee, and my Berenice after her."

"And your Persephone."

Henry grinned. "And my Persephone. I'm glad I found her—she'll be company when you go home at night. Can't sleep the way I used to, and the night gets long. Although now that I know everything's still up there, I can go through it and find the more valuable stuff—that should help. And I have lots of LPs too, even some old 78s. Do people still use hi-fis?"

"Hi-fis?"

"Record players."

"Oh. Yeah, some do. Collectors mostly. If they're in good shape."

"Should be, if they didn't get warped from the heat. I'll see if I can check that too. Don't know if I can move anything that heavy."

"We can check them together."

Henry nodded. "But for now, you should go home and get some rest. You worked yourself hard today."

"I did. We made almost two thousand dollars, and another three with the rare books we sold on the internet."

"You're getting there."

"Not fast enough. And look, I know you're not crazy about Kyle…."

"The boy said I was evil!"

"He didn't know that you weren't. I don't know where he came from, but it must have been the back of beyond. And he didn't get much of an education, so I think he's from one of those really conservative religions. He's a good guy, Henry. And he works hard. I wish I could afford to pay him."

Henry humphed but said nothing.

"I'm just saying, cut him some slack, okay? He's good people. And you're good people."

"Okay, but the minute he comes around with a sage pot like your crazy hippie woman, I'm done."

CHAPTER EIGHTEEN

"I KNOW, I'm sorry." Noah sat at the counter with his head in one hand and his phone in the other. "I don't know what else to do right now except move back here. I can't look for another job in New York if I'm not in New York."

"It's Manhattan, honey. I'll have another roommate by the end of the week. I hate that I won't be able to see you every day. And it just sucks that you got fired for staying to clear things up after your dad died. It's the twenty-first century, for goodness' sake, they should have worked with you."

"I already paid for November. I know it's only the third, but are you sure you're going to be okay? Let me know if you don't find someone right away and I'll find some way to pay for December too."

"It'll be fine, Noah. What do you want me to do with your stuff?"

That was the harder question. He could see Yeira in his mind's eye, looking around the apartment at the bits of his life he'd collected over the past three years since moving out of the dorms at NYU.

"Sell the furniture if you can. If not, give it to someone who needs it. Dump the blankets and stuff. If you could, box up my clothes and pictures and stuff. Ship it here?"

"Thank you for being a minimalist. It should be fine. We did a piece on the shelter down the street. I know they'll take anything I can't sell. Desperation is funny like that."

"Thank you, Yeira, and I'm sorry."

"You didn't ask for any of this to happen, Noah. It is what it is. Text me the address, and take care of yourself, okay?"

"That's getting harder and harder lately."

They said their goodbyes, and Noah hit the button to disconnect the call. He dropped the cell phone on the counter next to a pile of unpaid bills and sighed. A meow caught his attention, and he looked up to see Henry and Kyle watching him. He hadn't even known they were there.

Noah sighed. "If there is no struggle, there is no progress."

"Frederick Douglass," Henry mused, surprised. "I'm impressed. So it looks like the decision has been made?"

"I didn't appreciate it being made for me, but yes. I'm all in."

"I'm glad you're staying, Noah," Kyle said, his voice quiet, almost reverent.

"Thanks. I'm going to head over to the diner and pick up some pastries for breakfast. Could you get this stuff unstacked and open the boxes? We have that counter over there where we can set it, and they can pay up here at the register. Or maybe we can set up a till."

"I think that sounds like a grand plan," Henry agreed. "Well, except for breakfast. I'd kill for a few beignets."

"I don't think ghosts can kill for donuts." Noah rolled his eyes.

"But you don't *know* it, do you?" Henry countered.

"I'm going now," Noah said, heading for the door as he heard Kyle's laugh behind him. He waved at Ananda as he passed the crystal shop, and she waved a hand back. Yes, there were definitely worse places he could have ended up unemployed.

The door opened with a whoosh, and he stepped into the diner. The place hadn't changed since Noah lived here. He wasn't sure the place had changed since it opened. The owner, Miz Parker, had taken over the business when Noah was a boy, back when his own father used to talk about him taking over the bookstore. Most businesses in Aster were family owned and run; it was life in small-town America.

Miz Parker wasn't behind the counter, but her daughter Jessie was taking Cooper's order as he half stood and half sat on one of the stools. She'd been a few years older than him in school, and all the boys crushed on her.

"Hey, if it isn't little Noah Hitchens," Jessie called, pushing a lock of tight black curls off her pretty face. Noah sat at the counter and smiled.

"Hi, Miss Jessie, how are you?"

"I'm doin' just fine. I was sorry to hear about your daddy. He was a good man," she said quietly, patting his arm.

"Thank you."

Country gossip flowed like water in small towns, so she might have been expecting some news from his life, but he didn't really have any. In the awkwardness, he ordered a half dozen pastries, her choice.

"Take care of that little errand you had to do?" Cooper asked him, sidling up as he waited for his own breakfast.

"Yeah. Not a happy task, but I found out what I needed to know."

"Know what you're going to do yet?"

"I'm staying."

"That's a good kid. Your dad would have been happy to see you take over."

"You say you're taking over at the bookstore?" Jessie asked.

"Yeah. We've already started reopening."

"I'll let people know to come over and see you."

"And I'll tell them to stop by here for lunch after," Noah said back.

"That's a deal."

He came back to the store with half a dozen filled croissants and danishes in a large paper bag. Henry huffed and floated off in search of Persephone, but Kyle dug right in with a ham and cheese croissant in one hand and an apple danish in the other.

"What?" he asked when Noah just looked at him.

"You must be hungry."

"Yeah, it takes a lot of energy to get this stuff set up." He waved toward the coffee room, and Noah's gaze followed. On the counter were two large coffee machines, large and shiny and intimidating.

"If you plan to keep it there, you're going to need a small fridge to keep milk and whipped cream," Kyle observed and Noah wondered if he'd gotten himself into more than he could handle—both with the coffee and the store in general.

"So what's back here?" Noah grabbed a danish and led the way into the room, stepping carefully around the shrapnel of packing materials on the floor.

"Well, you have a drip machine for regular coffee, an espresso machine, an industrial grinder, and six flavor bottles with pumps. Your dad had already run a water line in here." He indicated the line going into the espresso machine.

"That accounts for more of the money he borrowed," Noah observed.

"It looks like the electric has also been rewired to accommodate the machines," Henry said from behind them, sending Noah lurching sideways toward the counter.

"What about supplies?" he asked and glowered at Henry.

"You have coffee here, about a dozen different kinds of teas, cups, lids, stirrers, napkins—pretty much everything you need to get started." Kyle pulled box after box out of the larger shipping crate.

"Let's get to work," Noah said, mesmerized by all of the boxes.

It took them the better part of the day to get everything unpacked, organized, and set in a way that everything would be easily accessible near the counter. Noah took the last of his father's life insurance money and picked up a large dorm fridge for them to store the cold stuff; then he stopped by Publix and grabbed a couple gallons of milk.

"Think we should have hot chocolate?" he asked Kyle after they'd carried in his haul.

"Well, it was popular in Chicago, but it's freezing there. So I'm not sure how well it would do in Georgia. Maybe as a seasonal thing."

"Thank you so much for helping me set all this stuff up. I feel better about staying and putting a real effort into the store now that I know we're going to have this revenue stream."

"Yeah, because it's Saturday and you haven't had very many customers," Kyle observed.

"I noticed that too. We need a sign that lets people know we have this coffee bar. We should also move a couple of the low tables and chairs into this room so people can sit and drink."

"Maybe put out a newspaper or two," Henry offered.

"I don't know that people really read newspapers anymore. We get most of our news online."

"Is everybody online?"

"No, I guess not. Especially older folks who have the time to hang out in coffee bars," Noah noted.

"Okay, I'll get to work on the sign."

Noah grabbed his laptop and pulled up Publisher to see if the internet had any coffee-appropriate templates while Kyle fired up the machines for the first time. They were loud in the small space, but in the main part of the bookstore, the noise was tolerable. Maybe he'd get a small sound system and play soundtracks or classical music. The future seemed like a string of endless possibilities now, both good and bad.

He printed a few signs on his dad's old inkjet printer and put them into wooden frames they'd found in the basement. Noah grinned to himself as he thought about the kiss. He wanted to take Kyle out, do something nice to say thank you for setting up the coffee bar, and really for just being supportive. He didn't have any friends here; all of his childhood friends had moved away. Kyle made it less lonely.

The signs fit in random places throughout the store and in the front window. He liked the way they seemed to belong there with the frames. Lots of stores simply taped printed signs to the window or wall, and it looked tacky.

"Hey, do you have plans tonight?" Noah asked, and Kyle looked up from his counter.

"No. I never have plans," he said with a smile.

"Let's go get some food after the store closes." Noah fiddled with the stack of cups on Kyle's counter, straightening them equidistant from the lids and napkins.

"You mean like a date?"

"Would that be okay if it were?" Noah's heart hammered. He didn't know when it had become so important to hear Kyle say yes.

"I've never been on a date before."

Noah looked at him, stunned.

"What? I didn't get out much," Kyle murmured. "Plus, I couldn't let people know I was… gay. My family doesn't approve of homosexuality. They say it's a sin."

"What do you say?"

"I say I don't know and that they don't either. If God doesn't like gay people, why would he make us this way? If he does, then my family is wrong."

"I don't disagree with any of that. So, a date, then?"

"A date," Kyle agreed.

THEY DIDN'T sell a single cup of coffee, but they drank more than a few while they tried different flavor combinations and played with different configurations on the machines. By the time the store closed, they were both wired, and Henry threw them out of the store, calling them unruly and recalcitrant. Kyle asked Noah what recalcitrant meant, though he admitted he figured it was an insult.

"There are some chain restaurants over by the highway," Noah suggested as he hit the alarm and then locked the door.

"I'll eat just about anything, so it doesn't matter to me."

"You're a pretty easygoing guy."

"I was raised pretty much to take life as it comes," Kyle said and climbed into the passenger side of the truck.

"Where did you grow up?" Noah slid in behind the wheel and fired up the engine.

Kyle hesitated for a long moment and then said, simply, "Montana."

"Wow, I bet that's different from here. All the wide-open spaces. Horses. Lots of green?" Noah pulled out of the lot and onto the main stretch of road in Aster.

"It was different," Kyle admitted.

"I'll admit, I'm only guessing. I've never been to Montana, but it *sounds* open and green."

"It is. When we were younger, my sister, Hope, and me, we used to climb to the top of this hill after all the chores were done. It felt like you could see forever."

"You have a sister? Any other siblings?"

"No, just a sister."

"I don't have any brothers or sisters. Made growing up a little lonely."

"We never got lonely. There was always someone around, and they brought their kids. I don't think my parents knew anyone who didn't have kids."

"Small communities tend to produce lots of kids—there's not much else to do besides procreate," Noah laughed.

"And color," Kyle added.

"And color. There isn't much more to do here. You can go out to eat, bowl, or drive over to the mall and see a movie." Noah turned on the next street, headed toward the highway.

"What did you like to do as a kid?"

"Me? I don't know, the normal stuff. We played baseball a lot. It was the only sport I didn't suck at. I loved to read. More often than not you'd find me hanging out under a tree somewhere, reading a paperback I'd read a hundred times before," Noah reminisced.

"Your dad owned a bookstore. You didn't get new books?"

"Yeah, I could have any book I wanted. Well, I had to ask Dad to make sure it was okay—like age-appropriate. But there were some books I loved, like *Harry Potter* or the Terry Pratchett books. I could read them over and over."

"We didn't read growing up except when we did school." Kyle sat up higher as they pulled into the parking lot of an Olive Garden.

"Did school?" Noah slid into a space near the end of the row.

"Yeah, we all sat down for lessons."

"You and your sister?"

"I guess." Kyle shrugged.

They walked up to the restaurant in silence and were immediately seated. For that, Noah was thankful. He hated milling around in the front like bugs on a burger, waiting for the coaster to buzz and tell him their table was ready.

Kyle studied the menu.

They didn't go to Olive Garden much in Manhattan, with the millions of other restaurant choices, but growing up, this had been one of his favorites. It was the special-occasion place where he and Dad would go for birthdays and such. He hadn't even thought about it that way as he'd driven there. Kyle had agreed to a date—maybe this was something special to celebrate.

Their server, a petite brunette with an impeccable updo, came by with a bottle of white and asked if they'd like to sample.

"I don't drink alcohol," Kyle said.

"No, thank you," Noah said and waved her off.

"Never?" he asked after she'd gone.

Kyle had gone back to looking at the menu. "It's a sin," he said simply.

Noah didn't respond. He'd decided on the build-your-own pasta with cavatappi, his favorite. Maybe they could share a piece of cake after.

"Do you know what this means?" Kyle asked suddenly, turning the menu around. He pointed to an item, and Noah looked down at it.

"Manicotti? Sure, it's a tube of pasta with cheese in the middle."

"Oh."

"Not sure what to get?" Noah nudged.

"I…. My family didn't go out to eat, and in Chicago, we didn't go out often. Some of this stuff. I just… I don't know." Kyle started to get frustrated—Noah could see it in the stiffness of his body, the embarrassment in his expression.

"It's okay. Do you like pasta?"

"Like spaghetti, you mean?"

"Yes."

"Yes." Kyle nodded as he said it.

"Do you like red sauce?"

"Isn't it all red?" Kyle cocked his head.

"No, some of them have white sauces," Noah explained quietly.

"Yes, I like red sauce."

"Do you like cheese?"

"Sure." Kyle sat back in his chair like the questions were too much for him.

"Then why don't you try the manicotti or maybe a ravioli, which is like that but in pieces?" Noah suggested.

When their server returned, they ordered sodas and then cavatappi for Noah and ravioli for Kyle. She smiled at them benignly and went off to find them salad and breadsticks.

"Next time we'll try a Mexican place. In New York you could find any style food you wanted right around the corner—Indian, Thai, Cuban, whatever." Noah unfolded the napkin and dropped it in his lap.

"That seems like a lot of choices I wouldn't want to deal with," Kyle admitted. He mimicked Noah and put his own napkin on his leg.

"Then it's good you live here—you have limited options." Noah smiled and Kyle smiled back, seeming to relax.

It didn't take long for the food to arrive. The entrees appeared almost simultaneously with the breadsticks and salad, so they had a table full of food in front of them when Matt Handley passed. He stopped and looked back, overbalancing, but caught himself. Apparently the wine had already been flowing at his table.

"Hitchens. Having a farewell toast? Or maybe a date?" he asked, smirking at his own joke. His girlfriend, a petite blonde barely out of her college cheerleading days, grabbed his arm.

"Matt." She tried to pull him away. "Come on."

Noah said nothing. Handley, ever the bully, had the ability to call in his loan. He wasn't about to sink to trading insults with him at Olive Garden. Kyle had tensed, and Noah wasn't sure if it was Handley's presence or the word *date*.

"Nah, I'm just seeing my old friend here. Seems he shouldn't be out spending money he doesn't have." Handley's voice got louder.

"Matt," his girlfriend said again. "You're making an ass of yourself. Let's go."

"But I want—"

"My sister said let's go," a linebacker-sized man said from behind the girlfriend. He took a step forward, and Handley stepped back. It was good to see him cower before someone bigger and stronger.

"Fine," he huffed and bumped a server as he passed. She dropped her tray and they hustled off. Noah noticed a man in a long-sleeved shirt and tie with an earpiece follow them.

Noah tried to smile at Kyle, but the mood had been lost.

They ate their food quietly and declined dessert, but fought over the check.

"I asked you out. It's only right that I pay," Noah insisted, but Kyle shook his head.

"You need the money for the store."

"Just like Handley, telling me how and when to spend my money," Noah huffed and sat back in his chair, arms folded. He felt like a pouty kid, but Handley had embarrassed him, reminded him how powerless he was. It hurt, and it made him angry.

"Noah, I want to pay because I care." Kyle's voice had softened, and he glanced around, then reached across the table to cover Noah's hand. "Not because I think you can't."

Noah nodded and pushed the check toward him, shame clogging his chest.

Kyle paid in cash, leaving a modest tip, and they headed back out to the truck. Kyle followed him to the driver's side, which was away from the restaurant. He caught Noah's hand and turned him back.

"Thank you for the date," Kyle said.

"You paid."

"You asked."

With a gentleness that made Noah ache, Kyle leaned forward and kissed him. One soft, sweet kiss, and then another. Noah put a hand on his side, and Kyle stroked Noah's cheek. It seemed to last forever yet be over in a heartbeat. It was rural Georgia, and they weren't about to make out in the parking lot.

"We're going to get you the money for the store," Kyle whispered. "Because I don't want you to go."

"Me either."

They sealed their confessions with another quiet kiss.

CHAPTER NINETEEN

"SO HOW'S the coffee thing going?"

Noah held the door for Thad. "Not well, but today was the first full day we had the station up. We had a couple people try it out. Kyle can do the thing where you make pictures in the foam, which is kinda cool." He followed the antiques dealer into the large conference room where the Merchants Council was having their monthly meeting. He'd been told he needed to be there the first Monday of every month. They were early, but a handful of people were there already. Most of them Noah knew by sight, at least, and Thad made quick work of introducing him.

A couple of them reacted kind of strangely, with either a raised eyebrow or a "huh" expression, but most of them just said they were glad to meet him and that they were sorry to lose Charlie. From what they said, his dad had been very active in the council.

"We were hoping he'd take over as president when the next election came up," Martha, the woman who ran the pharmacy a couple of blocks from Noah's store, told him. "He was dedicated to the welfare of the town, which is more than I can say for our current president. Ed's a nice guy but apparently had his spine surgically removed at a young age. He doesn't have the oomph to stand up to... certain people, if you know what I mean."

Noah hadn't a clue, but he smiled faintly.

"Come on, Martha," Thad said. "It's not Noah's fault he's got James for an uncle."

"What's wrong with Uncle James?"

Martha's lips thinned to an almost invisible line. "Let's just say he doesn't represent the majority opinion around here."

"He wants to bring in a private prison," another man said. He held out his hand. "Spencer Graff. Healthy Eats Health Food."

"You're kidding!"

"Nope. Says that it'll bring all kinds of jobs into the community. Which is baloney, pure and simple. I did some research, and in general, do you know how many hires the average private prison makes from the community it's based in? Twelve. *Twelve.* They'll be hiring from Atlanta and Marietta, and then they'll go home and spend their money on stores in Atlanta and Marietta, and we won't see a dime of it."

"But that's not the worst of it," Thad told Noah. "The worst of it is that he wants to 'rejuvenate' the downtown area." He used his fingers to make quotes.

"I thought they did that already." The streets had been repaved and the new streetlights put in, and Noah was sure his dad had talked about some of the improvements the shop owners had had to make to bring their stores up to snuff.

"They did. What Montgomery wants is to tear down the whole city center and rebuild it to 'modern' standards." Again with the finger-quotes.

"What?" Noah's jaw dropped. "He what?"

"Has he offered to buy you out yet?"

Noah blinked at Martha. "I… well, we talked about it, but I haven't given him an answer yet."

"Well, you decide what you want to do, but just know that your daddy was completely against the idea." Martha patted Noah's arm. "Once James Montgomery gets his hands on even one of those storefronts, he'll make it his life's work to drive out everyone else and pick up the remaining stores. That'll give him a majority on this council, with his toadies. He'll push demolition through, and then we're all out."

"Yeah. He's even graciously offered to let us rent space in the antiques mall he's planning for out on the highway. At a significant increase from our current rents."

"Do any of you own your own buildings?"

"Some of us do. Some of us rent from Omar Lindley, who owns a big chunk of property down there. He hates James Montgomery worse than the rest of us."

Spencer Graff snorted. "I don't know about that."

Thad asked curiously, "What did your uncle offer you for the store?"

"Three hundred thousand. It's tempting, but—"

He was treated to three gasps. "What?"

"Son, those storefronts are assessed at six hundred thousand. Three is an insult."

Noah felt his stomach drop. Had Uncle James tried to rip him off? Was he betting on Noah being so naïve where business was concerned that he'd just jump at the chance to get out from under the responsibility?

Noah was family. How could he do that to family?

Numbly, he followed the rest of them to the table and sat down. They took roll, and as they finished, the door blew open and two men walked in, Uncle James and Mr. Handley, Matt's father. They were laughing as though they had shared a joke. When James saw Noah, something dark flickered across his face; then he gave Noah his usual grin. "Hey, boy. Takin' up your daddy's reins?"

"Looks like," Noah said. To his surprise, his voice was level and didn't give away how shaken he felt.

The president banged the gavel and called the meeting to order.

JAKE WAS waiting anxiously when Noah got home. Noah let him out into the backyard, then poured himself a glass of tea and followed him outside. He sat on the porch steps and took a deep breath. Then he set the glass on the porch, folded himself over his arms, and lost it.

It was like James's betrayal was the proverbial straw. Everything Noah had been trying to suppress—his grief over his dad, his anger and guilt over losing his job, the stress of trying to run a business he had no business trying to run—it all spilled over into great, heaving sobs. Vaguely he felt Jake come and sit beside him, his cold wet nose nudging at Noah's cheek until Noah put his arms around him and turned to cry into the thick black fur. He was shaking so hard he thought he might die of a heart attack, and wished he would, wished this were all just a horrible dream and he'd wake up back in New York, in Yeira's dinky rent-controlled apartment, and that it would turn out that Dad wasn't dead and Uncle James wasn't a jerk, and there wasn't a huge pile of debt Noah had to pay and that there wasn't a ghost haunting his bookstore and that Kyle....

Oh, Kyle. The only good, sweet thing to come out of this whole clusterfuck.

As if summoned, a body settled on the step next to him and put his arms around Noah, a warm cheek against his and the sweet piney scent of Kyle enveloping him. He didn't say anything, just held Noah while he wept and shook and hated everything and grieved. Mostly grieved.

It was nice that Kyle was there, but Dad wasn't and wouldn't ever be again. In the end it didn't matter that he had Miss Edna and Henry and Fred the mailman and Thad and all the people in town who'd loved his dad, or even Kyle and Jake—Noah was alone.

A wracking moan shook him, and he cried harder, grief and loneliness ganging up on him and pounding him into the ground until he wanted to yell "Enough!" and have all this end.

And then warm lips brushed his ear and Kyle's sweet voice said, "I've got you. Let go," and he did, letting everything go until he lay limp and exhausted in Kyle's arms.

He opened his eyes to see Jake watching him, fear and love in his dark eyes, and glanced up to see the same expression in Kyle's. "Sorry," he started to say, but his tears had clogged his throat and nothing came out but a croak.

"Shh," Kyle said and ran his hand gently over Noah's hair. "It's okay."

He cleared his throat and managed, "Thanks."

"Of course."

"What are you doing here? Did you hear me?"

Kyle shook his head. "No, but I wanted to see you. I knew you had that counselor meeting—"

"Merchants Council."

"—and that you'd be home late, so when I saw Jake in the yard, I came over to see you." He smiled gently and rubbed his cheek on Noah's hair. "No reason. I just wanted to see you."

"Well, you've seen me—basically at my worst," Noah said ruefully.

"Did something happen at the meeting?"

Noah hesitated, then went ahead and told Kyle about it. When he got to the part about Uncle James offering him half of what the store was worth, his friend's eyes darkened with anger. "What a, a jerk."

"Yeah, you could say that." Noah had straightened up from his hunched-over posture while he talked, and now gave in to the urge to lean against Kyle's shoulder. For a thin guy, Kyle was strong and solid, and Noah needed solid right then.

"What are you going to do?"

"Not sell the store, anyway." Noah bit his lip, then looked at Kyle. "I want to fight him, I really do. I don't think it's right to try to trick me, and it's rotten what he wants to do to Aster. He's got more money than God and all he can think about is making more of it. Mr. Handley's no better, but I expect it of him—he's a banker, for fuck's sake. What?"

"More money than God?"

Oh, crap. Religion again. Noah started to apologize but was shocked when Kyle burst out laughing. "That's the funniest thing I've ever heard!"

Whew. "That's me, a laugh a minute. Except when things are going wrong, which they seem to always be."

"Murphy's Law," Kyle said wisely.

"Huh. You know about Murphy's Law?"

"Yes. One of my customers at the coffee cart in Chicago explained about it. He also explained about Cole's Law."

"What's Cole's Law?"

"Shredded cabbage in a vinegar dressing." This time Kyle's smile was huge and contagious. Noah lost it again, but this time in a good way.

It was a silly joke, but the fact that it was Kyle who told it and that he was already emotionally raw from his meltdown seemed to make it funnier than it should have been. He was crying again by the time he finished laughing, but this time they were good tears, washing away the last of his stress. He was exhausted, but sitting here on the steps with Jake's head on his lap and Kyle's arm around him, he felt calm for the first time in… weeks.

He turned to tell Kyle that, but his hazel eyes were dark in the shadows and his lips looked soft and inviting, and he had to kiss him, so he did. It was the first time he'd had the opportunity since the night at the Olive Garden when Matt Handley had been a dick, and he wasn't going to think about Matt Handley right now, not when he had an armful of soft, strong Kyle instead.

Kyle who was kissing him back, moving his hands up to cup Noah's head and hold him still. He started when Noah's tongue touched his lips, taking their former sweet kisses into a whole other realm, but he opened his mouth and let Noah in. Noah moaned softly and ran a hand down Kyle's spine, then drew back. "Is this okay?" he murmured.

"Oh, yes. Can we do that again?"

Noah kissed the tip of Kyle's nose, then said, "Oh hell yeah," and dove in for another kiss.

They didn't do much more than that, but the tongue-tangling was really nice, and Kyle's hands found their way under Noah's T-shirt and hoodie, their slightly rough, callused surfaces giving Noah erotic chills. In return, Noah cupped Kyle's rear, pulling him against Noah.

Kyle drew back, his eyes wide and dark. "You—you're hard."

"So are you," Noah pointed out and leaned in to kiss Kyle's throat. He licked Kyle's Adam's apple and Kyle shuddered, closing his eyes. "Oh, like that, do you?"

"I like everything you do." Kyle's voice was soft and shy. "But...."

Noah eased up. "But?"

"I told Miss Sarah I'd be home soon, and she worries...." He bit his lip anxiously, then cried, "I don't want to go home yet!"

Reaching up to cup Kyle's cheek, Noah said, "It's okay, sweetheart. I'm not going anywhere. Besides, I'm wiped." He kissed him again. "Go on and git—it's gotta be ten at least, and we both worked a full day."

"Okay." Kyle kissed him again and reluctantly stood up on the step and held a hand down for Noah. Then he put his arms around him, hugging him tightly.

Noah hugged him back. "Tomorrow after work. We're going on a date, and this time it's on me."

"No place expensive," Kyle warned.

"Nope. Cheap date. I promise."

Kyle kissed him again and then patted Jake and trotted around the side of the house toward the street. Noah watched him go.

Jake nudged his hand with his cold nose, and Noah petted him as requested. Maybe he wasn't completely alone after all.

CHAPTER TWENTY

As SOON as he'd closed the store Tuesday evening, Noah headed home with Jake. While the dog was eating his dinner, Noah showered and put on his nicest pair of jeans and the cashmere sweater Yeira had given him last Christmas. He'd always thought it made him look a little thinner, and it was a pleasant enough night that he didn't need to wear a jacket. Then he got the truck out of the garage and parked it in front of Miss Sarah's.

His phone dinged and he checked the screen.

I got a little over sixteen hundred for your furniture and stuff I knew you wouldn't want.

Are you kidding? I didn't have that much stuff.

No, but my new roommate didn't have anything, so now she has a bed, dresser, and all kinds of other crap that Mommy and Daddy don't have to go out and buy for her. He could almost hear the sarcasm in her voice.

Trust-fund kid?

Yup.

He laughed. Well, at least she'd be able to pay the rent.

What are you up to?

I'm going on a date.

Really? With who, the goat from up the block?

Hush, we're not THAT far out. No, I'm going out with Kyle. He lives across the street.

So you found the only other gay man in a twenty-five-mile radius. I wonder what Grindr looks like out there.

He snorted. He couldn't help it because he'd been wondering the same thing himself.

Hush, I have to go.

Don't bring home anything you don't want to share. Yeira had always been able to make him laugh. Noah shoved the phone in his pocket and jogged up to the door.

Sarah opened the door at his knock. "My, don't you look nice, Noah! Are you and Kyle going anyplace special?"

"We're going to a bunch of special places," Noah said mysteriously. She laughed.

Kyle came down the stairs. Noah looked up at him, smiling, and the answering smile on Kyle's face took Noah's breath away. He barely heard Kyle's goodbyes to Sarah, murmured, "See you, ma'am," and took Kyle's hand to lead him down the steps. Once in the truck and belted up, he let out a sigh of relief.

"What's wrong?"

"Nothing. That's what's so great. I had visions of something happening to stop us from doing this, and I wouldn't believe it until just now."

"Well, if you could tell me what 'this' is, maybe I could help."

Noah grinned. "Well, I'm going to take you on a tour. The life and times of Noah Hitchens. Miss Sarah said you haven't gotten out much to see the splendor that is Aster, so I thought I'd show you the sights."

"Are there any?"

"Oh, child," Noah said in a gravelly voice, "prepare to be amazed. Or at least amused." He put the truck in gear and drove down into town.

"Now, you've seen the wonders of Sycamore Street," Noah said as they passed the bookshop and then the grocery store where Kyle worked. "Did you ever wonder why some people still call Leroy's the feed store?"

"No. I just figured it was because it used to be a feed store."

"Ding ding ding! Excellent response. Ten points to Gryffindor."

"What's Gryffindor?"

"What? You haven't read *Harry Potter*?"

"Um… no?"

"Oh, honey," he said again. "We will need to remedy that. Add it to the list."

"What list?"

Noah ignored him. "Now, coming up on the right is the First National Bank of Aster. This is the bank owned by Fucking Matt Handley's family. We hates him, yes, my precious."

Kyle was giggling now. "I didn't know you were so silly."

"Oh, not silly, precious. We hates orcses like Fucking Matt Handley." In a normal voice, Noah said, "And up on the left is Aster

Elementary, where I went to grammar school. There were fourteen kids in my graduating class. That's because there's another school on the far side of town where most of the farm kids went. We all went to Aster High because there was only one of those. Here we are passing Aster High. Note the fine crenellations on the roof—excellent for grappling hooks in the case of siege warfare. Though why anyone would want to break in there, I don't know."

He turned down Maple. "Here is Tyler's Tailors—yes, that's its real name—where all the haut ton of Aster acquire their tuxedoes for special events at the country club."

"What's hot tone?"

"*Haut ton* means upper class. The snooty rich. Also on Maple we find a couple of boutiques and a computer store. This is where those same snooty rich shop when they're not slumming it down on Sycamore. And"—he turned left onto a tree-lined residential street—"this is Mulberry Street."

"Is that important?"

"Very. Rumor has it that Dr. Seuss references this very street in his classic novel, *And To Think That I Saw It on Mulberry Street*. First editions are going for upwards of seven hundred dollars."

"Is that true?"

"What, the seven hundred dollars?"

"No, that this doctor wrote a book about this street?"

"Not a bit of it. I made it up. The seven hundred dollars is true, though."

They drove on through the town, Noah making stuff up the whole way, until Kyle was bent over clutching his belly from laughing. Eventually they made it to Noah's destination, the high point over the town called Mitchell's Hill by adults and Make-out Hill by teenagers. The peak was bare of parked cars, since it was a Tuesday and a school night, but the view of the town below was as lovely as Noah remembered. He backed up so that the bed of the truck faced the town, then got out and dropped the tailgate, pulling the cushions and quilt he'd put in there earlier onto the gate.

Kyle got out and wandered over, jumping up onto the tailgate when Noah did. "This is nice," he said. "I didn't know this was up here. You can see the whole town."

"Yep. I used to ride my bike up here and sit and look. See, there's the high school, and there's the Methodist church and cemetery, and there's First Baptist and the cemetery, and the bank. And under those trees is Sycamore Street and the store and Leroy's, and under those trees is Oak Street where we live."

"It looks like a picture."

"You can see more during the day. Mostly at night it's just lights, but they light up enough that you can figure out where things are."

"You really love this place," Kyle said softly.

"Yeah, I guess. I really loved New York too. They were different enough that they didn't compete or something." He pulled the cooler from behind himself. "You ate dinner, right?"

"Yeah, you told me to."

"Good. I brought dessert."

It was Miss Edna's orange cake with peach frosting, and two bottles of sweet tea. They shared the cake, eating with their fingers as they sat on the edge of the tailgate, their feet swinging. When they'd finished, Noah said, "Okay, interrogation time."

Kyle went very quiet. Noah glanced at him and said reassuringly, "Nothing bad, Kyle. Just—I want to get to know you better."

"Okay." His voice was uncertain.

"Favorite color?"

"Purple?"

"Good choice. Favorite movie."

"Um… I don't know a lot of movies."

"Doesn't matter. Which one do you like best of the ones you've seen?"

"Do cartoons count?"

"Yep."

"Um… *Moana*."

"Oh, good choice. That movie rocks."

"My aunt Mary said it was heretical and that I was going to go to hell, but I thought it was beautiful."

"You're right. Okay. Favorite book?"

"You know I don't read a lot. The Bible, I guess."

"Pfft. Okay, the Bible can be a good book—lots of adventure and romance and sex in there—"

"In the Bible?"

"You haven't read a lot of it, have you?"

"No, not really. Just the parts that were authorized."

"By your religion, right?"

Kyle was quiet a moment, then said, "I don't want to talk about that."

"Okay, we won't, then. Do you like living in Aster?"

Another moment of quiet, then: "Yes. It's not what I expected. I thought all the South was, I don't know, kind of like how it was where I lived before. Miss Sarah uses the word *conservative*, and I guess that's how I imagined everywhere in Georgia."

"There are a lot of conservative places in Georgia. But Aster's different. It was founded by former slaves and had a hard time getting started. You should talk to Henry about that—he knows all about it."

"He's...." Kyle sighed. "I'm a little scared of him. He's so... stern."

"Henry? Nah. He doesn't know you. He's a good guy. Get him talking about something he's interested in—and believe me, he's interested in everything—and he'll like you just fine."

"Is he okay with you being gay?"

"He doesn't talk much about it. That's okay, though. Most people don't. But most of them know." Noah cocked his head. "They don't know about you back where you come from, do they?"

Kyle shivered. "God, no. I think maybe that's why—why I ended up here."

"I'm glad you did." Noah put his arm around Kyle. "I'm really glad you did."

CHAPTER TWENTY-ONE

"YEAH, BEEN sittin' there all night." Fred picked up his toast and took a huge bite. Peach preserves oozed onto the side of his lip, and he wiped it away with a rueful grin to Miss Jessie. She rolled her eyes and turned to Noah.

"Hey there, what can I get for you?" She smiled and it felt genuine to him. He'd been afraid that after the bookstore started serving coffee, folks at the Aster Café might take exception.

"Could I get two country breakfasts to go?" he asked, flipping a sugar packet between his fingers.

"No coffee?" she asked, and the smirk in her expression made his face go hot.

"Uhm… no, thank you."

"You wanna get Mama on your side?" she asked, leaning low. "You should start sellin' her pies and such. That's where our coffee business is. People might like a slice of blackberry cobbler with their fancy coffee and books."

Noah stared at her.

"What?"

"I was going to talk to you about that," he whispered a little too loudly. "Let me talk to—" He was about to say Henry, but then he caught himself. "Let me think about how that would work with the space, and I'll be back to talk to y'all."

"Good man," she said and patted his arm. Then, more loudly, she asked, "Fred, what were you talkin' about with that truck?"

She turned and handed his order to the line cook.

"Out on 92, there's a truck just sittin' in that old parking lot where Jack's used to be."

"I know where you mean." She started wiping down the already clean counter. "You didn't see nobody?"

125

"No, but the back was open and you could see the ends of sleeping bags. Someone's livin' in it. Or they're camping in early November."

"You tell Cooper?" she asked, referring to the town's sheriff, who had been the only police Aster'd had in years.

"Yeah, but they ain't doin nothin' wrong. People camp around here all the time." He shoveled another bite of eggs into his mouth.

"Not in parking lots," she said.

"We're about to find out," he said, his eyes wide as he glanced to his left. "It just pulled up outside."

Out of sheer curiosity, Noah turned full in his seat and watched a man and a very young woman climb out of a beat-up Chevy pickup. The camper on the bed looked even older than the truck and appeared crusted with mud and muck.

The bell above the door rang, and Noah avoided eye contact by playing with the sugar packet. They didn't get strangers much in Aster. Kyle was probably the first one in forever.

The young man had a flannel shirt on, keeping him warm against the chill of a fifty-degree morning, and clean but unkempt brown hair and a scraggly beard across his thin face. He was tall and just this side of gaunt. The woman had auburn hair pulled back from her face with a rubber band. She was half a head shorter than the man and was wearing a calico print dress. She held the man's hand tightly. They scanned the room like they wanted to escape. Instead they sat at the very end of the counter closest to the door.

Miss Jessie raised her eyebrows at Fred, who sat up a little higher on his stool.

"Hello. Is there something I can get for you folks today?" she asked, shuffling toward that end of the counter but staying close to Fred, who sat in the middle.

"Yes, ma'am. Do you have oatmeal?" the man asked quietly. His voice was quiet, almost strained.

"Sure, honey. Do you want anything in it? Brown sugar or—"

"No, ma'am, just oatmeal and some water, please." He pushed the unused menu aside.

"And you?" she asked the young woman, who glanced at the man beside her.

"She'll have the same." His eyes didn't leave Jessie's. Though they didn't say anything menacing, Noah's gut churned as he waited for his order to come up.

They spoke to each other in low, quiet tones, and the redhead pulled out a map. They studied it together, pointing and dragging a finger down one road or another. Maybe they were lost. They'd stopped for the night to get their bearings and some breakfast. It wasn't like Aster was a booming metropolis. They were prolly just a couple of 'Bama folks headed east.

"Noah, here's your order," Miss Jessie said, handing him a bag and his check. He paid with a twenty and left her the change.

The couple watched him leave.

The bell jingled as he exited, and instead of turning immediately left for the two-block walk back to the bookstore, he crossed the main street, but as he did, he turned to study the truck. Rust held it together in places, especially over the wheel wells. He couldn't tell what color it had originally been because of the thick overlaying splatters of mud and something darker, tar maybe. The license plate, which Cooper would no doubt run when he saw it, came from Montana. These folks were a long way from home.

He hurried past the feed store and crossed back over toward Stardust. Some things, like small-town skepticism, must not go away completely. He'd met hundreds of strangers when he'd lived in New York. None had unsettled him like those two.

The wind chimes announced his arrival, and Kyle glanced up from his equipment with a shy smile. It turned to a full grin when he saw the food.

"That for me?" Kyle pulled down two mugs from the shelf behind him.

"Well, it ain't for Henry."

"I'd love a big ol' steak and eggs with grits," Henry lamented as he glided in through the wall. "Summa Miss Betsy's fluffy biscuits and gravy."

"You seemed to be a pretty thin guy in life. Where did you put all that food?" Noah set the Styrofoam containers on one of the tables and pulled up a couple of chairs. Henry lounged on a couch nearby.

Kyle brought over the mugs of coffee, cream, and a little sugar.

"I had a hollow leg." Henry pulled Persephone onto his legs and stroked her translucent fur.

"Well, now you have two," Kyle murmured, and Noah laughed.

"Damn, I forgot to get silverware." Noah searched through the bag and found nothing but napkins.

"I'm surprised she didn't put it in. Miss Jessie's always real good about that." Kyle opened his container and grabbed a piece of bacon.

"These two folks came into the diner—a man and a woman. Plates on the truck said they were from Montana, which is weird. I think they made her nervous. Made me nervous." Noah shrugged and turned, headed for the kitchenette in the back. "I got some stuff in the back."

"Wait—" Kyle started but stopped himself.

"I'll be right back." Noah jogged out of the coffee bar, through the main shelves, and back to the small kitchenette his dad had always used as an office. The plastic utensils were in a baggie in the desk drawer. He pulled out two forks and searched fruitlessly for knives.

"Bleh," he said, closing the drawer and retracing his steps back to Kyle and Henry.

Only Kyle wasn't there.

"Kyle?" Noah called and set the silverware between the two Styrofoam containers.

"He just ran out. I told you he was a strange boy," Henry said, propping his insubstantial feet on the table in front of him.

"I should…," Noah said with a general wave at the door as he walked.

"Boy, aren't you gonna take this food?" Henry called after him as he made his way to the front door. "Why do you torture me with food I can't eat?"

Noah checked around, but Kyle had already left the main street. He hadn't mentioned having to be anywhere, so Noah closed up the store again and headed home. He'd check with Miss Sarah first and then look in on Jake. The big guy hadn't been feeling well that morning, so Noah had given him a little pumpkin in his food and set him up with a nice cooking show.

The drive home seemed longer than normal. He saw Fred's kids playing baseball with the Mallory boys as he crossed Forest Road. They paid him no mind because the older Mallory boy had just knocked a small dent into a little Ford Escort that seemed to have more rust than paint. They were scampering as one block turned into the next. They ticked away, one by one, until he reached the street he'd lived on his entire childhood. It seemed different now, quieter than in his youth. He could remember playing that same game of ball right there under the tall oaks.

About halfway up the block, he noticed the truck sitting in front of Miss Sarah's house, parked neatly against the curb on the far side of the street. The couple he'd seen at the diner were talking to her on the porch. They didn't appear to be menacing her, just having a conversation. Noah kept walking to his father's yard and then around the drive to the back.

He opened the gate and went into the yard. Kyle sat on the padded bench inside the screened porch. Jake lay sprawled across the bench with his head in Kyle's lap. As he approached, Noah watched Kyle stroking the big dog absently behind the ears.

"Hey." Noah opened the screen door and stepped up into the porch. Jake's tail started to wag, but he didn't get up. He'd found his happy place.

"Sorry."

"Those folks are here looking for you, aren't they?" Noah asked, dropping into the wicker chair next to the bench. Jake's head popped up, but he didn't make the effort to get up. At first Kyle's only response was a sigh. Noah sat back in the chair and waited.

Soft pillowy clouds raced across the sky on the back of an autumn breeze, chased by the storm close on their heels. The sun played peekaboo across the morning, but not enough to be warm. Noah pushed his sunglasses to the top of his head and waited. The tension in Kyle's shoulders made his tight as the man's gaze focused hundreds of miles away. The sorrow in his face twisted Noah's chest, and he took a deep breath to try to loosen it.

"I saw them talking to Miss Sarah. It's my sister. I think the guy is her husband. I'm not sure."

"What do they want?"

"It's a long story," Kyle hedged, but Noah simply put his feet up on the flimsy plastic table and his hands behind his head like he had all the time in the world.

"Fine. I guess it started when Mama took Joseph and me and little Abigail out to find donations. Papa and my sister Hope went to sell some of the stuff the womenfolk had made, blankets and stuff. It was summer, so they weren't hopeful, but the camp was almost out of food." His eyes stayed on the horizon. Noah wanted to interrupt and ask a thousand questions, but he bit the inside of his cheek. He didn't want Kyle to stop talking, stop showing him something real.

"We went up to this big house. It had these flowers out front like nothing I'd ever seen—every color you could think of. There were these stones going up to the porch rather than a walk. I remember little Abigail hopping from stone to stone. She was about four, I think. We didn't celebrate birthdays or anything. I didn't even know when mine was until Aunt Mary told me." Kyle paused then. He glanced over at Noah with a question, like he was waiting for a rebuke or to be mocked. Noah simply put a hand on his where it rested on the swing between them.

"Mama knocked on the door and this lady answered. We was all wearin' our fancy clothes, the ones we only wore when we went to town for donations. Abigail had little ribbons in her hair, which Mama had curled. She wasn't my sister. I don't have any other sisters, just Hope, but we were raised that everyone was a brother or sister, aunt or uncle. We were a family, they said. Anyway, Joseph was younger than me, maybe ten. He had fair skin like me, and we was all red from the sun, so the lady asked us in for some sweet tea. That half hour we spent in her kitchen was life-altering." He squeezed Noah's hand.

"What do you mean?" Noah asked and squeezed back, mostly to stop Kyle's hand from shaking.

"It was the first time I really saw how outsiders lived. They had plenty of food. They had air-conditioning. No one hit them. We were different. We were so different." He closed his eyes and took a long breath. "When Mama said it was time to leave, the woman gave her some money. Abigail and Joseph were playing with the woman's little pup. Lot like Jake in temperament, very sweet, and she just loved the attention. Anyway, they were crying when Mama made us go. I could tell she was angry—no, more than angry—but I didn't know why. Not then." He fell silent. Noah didn't say anything. He knew Kyle'd had a difficult life before he moved to Aster, and he needed to hear the details. Noah didn't know how, but one day they'd make a life together. There was no other option for him.

"What did you do then?"

"We went back to the camp, but Mama, she wasn't the same. About three months later, when we went out for donations again, it was just me and her and little Abigail. She gave me a bag with my clothes, a bus ticket, and a little bit of food and told me to run. She said that there was a better life out there for me. The bus ended up in Chicago, where her sister Mary lived, and I stayed there for five years, trying to figure out the outside world." Kyle looked him long and hard in the eyes.

"How did you end up here?" Noah rubbed little circles on the backs of Kyle's knuckles, trying to soothe him.

"They showed up at Aunt Mary's, and I ran. Mary's husband, Tommy, sent me here to his sister."

"What do they want?"

Kyle shook his head violently. Noah knew there would be a line, and he didn't want to cross it.

Kyle turned his gaze back to the clouds.

"Your family is in some kind of religious… group?" Noah sat up a little higher in the chair.

"Cult. You can say it. I finally can. And yes."

"Your family is still with them?"

Kyle nodded. "My mom said she couldn't get Papa to let Hope come to get donations with us, so I had to go by myself. I didn't want to leave, but she said she wanted a different life for me. So I got on that bus. I was fifteen. When I got off the bus, my aunt Mary and uncle Tommy were waiting there. I'd never even met them before. But they just opened their arms up. Aunt Mary cried. I think she was hoping that my mom and sister would be with me."

"How did you like Chicago?" Noah said, changing the subject, giving Kyle time to breathe.

"It was so different. Noisy and bright and everything felt so close. I had panic attacks for a while. Aunt Mary took me to the doctor for them. It was the first time I'd ever been to a doctor before. They gave me some medicine that helped. They also took me to a different doctor to talk to about the camp. I don't know if it made me feel any better or not. Everything happened at once." Kyle put a hand down to scratch Jake behind the ears.

"Is that why you left and came here? Because it's quieter?"

Kyle didn't say anything; he just kept rubbing behind Jake's ears.

"Why are you telling me now? Did something happen?" Noah asked. Kyle hadn't been exactly forthcoming in the month since they'd met, even though Noah could feel that they were getting closer. It was difficult to be with someone who you knew so little about. Trying to get Kyle to start talking was kind of like trying to get Henry to stop talking.

"Aunt Mary called Sarah this morning. The police came and told her Mama was dead. Been dead since about the time I left, but they just found her… her…. And now my sister is here looking for me. She must be after the box Mama gave me. Papa sent her." Kyle's face suddenly turned imploring.

"Box?"

"Yeah, it's got some papers and pictures in it. Mama said it was to protect me. I'm not sure how it's supposed to do that. But I guess the camp could get into real trouble if the systemites… government people… got ahold of it. That's what they want. That, and to bring me back with them." He looked out over the yard, and the storm clouds reflected in his bright green eyes. "I'll never go back."

"You don't have to. They don't need to know you're here. You can stay above the store until they leave. You don't have to go back to Sarah's." Noah squeezed his hand again. "It'll be okay. You have friends here."

"Henry won't like me staying up there. He don't like me much."

"It's my store. He'll live with it. But you need to get that box from Sarah's so we can see what's inside it. We need a plan."

"You have so much to do already with the store. You don't need to take this on."

"At the very least, you're my friend and I'm going to help you. I'd like for us to be much more than that," Noah finished shyly.

Kyle squeezed his hand back. "I'd like that too."

"Let's take a peek out front and see if the truck is still there. Where is the box?"

"It's a wooden box inside a shoebox on the floor of the closet."

"If they're gone, I'll go over and get it. I'll grab some clothes too. Do you need anything else if you're going to stay at the store awhile?"

"No, I think anything else I can pick up at a store."

"They're going to look for you at the bookstore. They'll look for you anywhere." Noah stood up and straightened the wicker chair.

"They won't draw attention to themselves. That's not their way." Kyle rubbed Jake's head again and then stood up. Jake got to his feet as well, as if he knew his new friend needed backup. "And if they do threaten me, I can always run again."

"No, we're not going to let that happen. You've built a life here." Noah wanted to say that they were going to build one together, but it felt wrong to bring up that sentiment then.

Kyle nodded and they went into the main part of the house, Jake right on their heels. The curtains were pulled back from the big living room picture window. Kyle hung back while Noah scanned the street. The truck had gone.

"I'm going to see Miss Sarah. Does she know about all this?" Noah opened the front door and then turned back to Kyle.

"Yes, she knows." The pain and fear in Kyle's expression broke Noah's heart.

"Okay. Lock up behind me and stay here with Jake. He sucks as a guard dog because he loves people, but maybe he can look menacing if the situation calls for it." He chuckled and then stepped out onto the front porch. Noah saw no signs of life on their sleepy street, so he jogged across the road to Miss Sarah's house.

She asked about Kyle and then let him in.

"They know he's here, and they've been talking to folks. They know he works at your daddy's store." She looked shaken from her encounter with the couple.

"Did they hurt you or threaten you, Miss Sarah?" Noah asked, and she wrapped her arms around herself.

"Not in so many words, but I've heard stories about those camps and how women are treated as slaves for... you know." She looked away, her face slightly flushed. "Seeing the blackness in that girl's eyes, just—"

"You can stay at Daddy's if you want, if you're afraid they'll come back." Noah caught her gaze.

"I'm going to go talk to Coop first, see if he thinks it's warranted. I don't want to be a nervous biddy."

Noah nodded as he slid past her in the tight hallway and headed for the stairs. He'd been in this house years ago when the Murphys lived in it. He'd come over and play ball in the backyard. He remembered pushing the brother, whose name he'd forgotten, to let the little sister play. As a boy with no siblings, he remembered being jealous of their relationship, of the boy having a built-in playmate.

He turned at the top of the stairs into a small room that could have passed any Army inspection. The bed had been neatly made, no clothes lay on the floor, and even the dresser contents were laid out in perfect little rows. Noah looked around and saw a small duffel bag hanging from the closet door handle. He tossed it on the bed and went to the closet first. It took some digging, but he found the shoebox that contained a small wooden chest. It just fit, nestled inside the cardboard. Noah set it on the bed next to the bag. Then he went through the drawers.

Crawling through Kyle's underwear made him flush, feeling a little pervy, but he got enough clothes packed for a week. He grabbed the bag and the box and was nearly out the door before he saw Kyle's jacket hung neatly over the back of a desk chair. When he grabbed it, he noticed an envelope lying there with the name *Samuel* slashed across the front in quick, jarring letters. He slid it between the wood and cardboard in the box.

He left Miss Sarah with assurances that he would care for Kyle. As he crossed back to his father's house, he caught a glimpse of the beat-up truck backed behind the Walters' hedges at the end of the block.

CHAPTER TWENTY-TWO

KYLE SAT in the back of the truck behind the tinted windows. Jake sat beside him with one paw on his leg. He'd tucked the box and bag neatly beneath Noah's seat in the big Ford, and they drove back to the bookstore. Noah parked behind the building and let them both in through the back. Usually Noah only used this door to take garbage to the dumpster, but he didn't want to parade Kyle in front of the store as a show for the neighbors.

Henry waited for them in the kitchenette.

"I think those people you were talking about before you left me with your congealing breakfast stopped by the street a few minutes ago. They didn't come here, but they went in across the street. The owner didn't seem very pleased with them. In fact, he seemed rather put out when he tossed them into the street," Henry mused.

Still, Kyle said nothing. He hadn't uttered a word since his confession.

"They're here for Kyle." Noah gave Henry an abbreviated version of the story Kyle had told him. Henry's eyes widened with each word.

"They're here for this." Kyle pulled the wooden chest out of the Nike box and let the cardboard shell fall onto the table.

"My goodness." Henry tried to take the chest from Kyle's hands, but his grip was insubstantial compared to Kyle's, and his hands went right through it.

"Kyle," Noah said gently, "why don't we see what we've got in here?" He took the chest from Kyle's less resistant fingers and sat down at the kitchenette table. Henry took the seat beside him, but Kyle stood, leaning against the counter.

Noah flipped open the lid. Inside were papers, pictures, certificates, and video cassettes that he remembered seeing people rent when he was a kid. He glanced up at Henry, then began to remove them from the box. Henry shuffled around a few papers to get a better look, but Noah went for the pictures. The first showed two adults and two children in rags, bundled tightly together. The adults were smiling, but the kids' expressions held twin grimaces. He held the picture up to Kyle.

"That's me and Hope, Mama, and Daddy," he said, his voice quiet and toneless. Noah turned over the picture and read "Jonah, Moonglow, Samuel, and Hope."

Kyle confirmed with a nod.

"Your name is Samuel?" Noah whispered. Kyle nodded again.

The next picture depicted the same man from the picture surrounded by six women. It looked like maybe three of them were pregnant. They were all smiling, and the women were dressed in similar simple but low-cut dresses.

"That's my father and his wives. The higher up you got in the cult, the more wives you were able to take. That's how it worked. My father was the leader of our camp," he said to the floor. "I was fifteen when I left the camp, but already they wanted me to pick out a wife. Because I was Jonah's son, I could have anyone but Daisy."

"Daisy?" Henry asked.

"She was Luna's little girl. When she got her womanhood, she was to become another sister-wife for my mother. My father's wife," he explained.

"Womanhood?" Noah had an idea what that meant, but he couldn't fathom it meant—

"When she gets her flow and becomes a woman. That's when all the girls in the camp got married."

"That's what, like, twelve? Thirteen?" Noah asked Henry, who appeared to pale just a little further than normal.

"'Bout that, yeah. My sister was getting close when Mama sent me away. The man she's with may be her husband, I don't know."

"I don't want to look at any more," Noah said and pushed the pictures away.

"Take the receipts," Henry suggested, pushing the pile toward him.

"If there's any weird stuff in here…."

"Just look. Don't be a child."

Noah flipped through the pile of receipts. Most were from a farm supply store in a place called Lakewood, Montana. They were handwritten and always paid in cash.

"Your camp must have done a lot of farming," Noah observed.

"We had little gardens that we used to grow vegetables."

"Wait. Henry, do you know anything about farming?"

"Some. Why?" He looked up from the certificates he was studying.

"Because these receipts are for tons of fertilizer. I think probably more than you'd need for a small garden? But I've never gardened. This just looks like a lot." He handed the papers to Henry.

"This one is for a bunch of batteries and a dozen kitchen timers."

"That's a lot of—" Noah stopped and grabbed his phone. He googled a few things and then looked back at the papers, sick.

"You use all of those things in bombs."

The room went silent. Noah stared at the pages for a long time while an enormous number of *tick tock* sounds echoed from the old alarm clock on the counter.

Tick.

Tock.

Kyle—Samuel—Kyle left the group five years ago. How many places had they blown up since his mother had been brave enough to collect this information and put her oldest son on a bus? Had it been a government building? A school? His stomach churned as he looked at receipt after receipt.

"I didn't know," Kyle breathed. "I didn't know anything about that."

"These papers are interesting," Henry said, organizing them into rows. "They're life events—births, deaths, marriages, and the like. No divorces. But if my math is right, and it always is, he's right about the average marrying age of girls in this camp. There's enough right here in this box to bury these people."

"My father is still there. He's one of the leaders," Kyle implored, conflict written plainly across his face. "My sister wouldn't hurt me."

"Religious fanatics will do just about anything to anyone," Henry said. "When I died, they were still burning crosses in black folks' yards, stringin' us up from trees, all in the name of their version of Jesus." Even in his translucence, Henry's eyes blazed.

"Okay, if Kyle is right about his sister, that's fine. But what about the guy? What about the explosives? What if they brought this kind of stuff with them? If they couldn't convince Kyle to come back with them, what would they do to protect the group?" Noah implored. "And what about these little girls? Don't you think someone should help them? What if your sister is one of them?"

"What are you suggesting?" Henry asked.

"We need to tell someone. Cooper or the staties. Maybe take it to a journalist who can blow it open so that someone has to investigate." Noah stood up and dropped the papers to the table. "Whatever happens, we can't simply do nothing." He put a hand on Kyle's shoulder.

"Do what you want with it," Kyle said and pushed Noah away.

"We do have to do something about this, right?" he asked Henry.

"Yeah, son. We do."

"Should we go to the police?" Noah wondered aloud.

"Police have been out to the camp before. They won't do nothin'," Kyle said as he picked up the picture of his family and studied it.

"Do you still have newspapers?" Henry asked.

"Yeira."

"Bless you?" Henry said, half in question.

"Yeira is… was… my roommate in New York. She's a television journalist. We met in English courses at NYU—that's how we got to be friends. What if she did a story on the cult? The press of public opinion might get the police more engaged." Noah stood up and grabbed his phone from the table. He'd dialed before anyone else had a chance to move or speak.

"Hey, I shipped your stuff out this morning. You should have it—"

"Yeira, I need your help," Noah cut her off, anxiety pushing the words out as they tumbled over one another.

"What's up, Noah?" Her voice took on a seriousness he rarely heard, and he explained Kyle's situation in a rush, finishing up with the receipts and their suspicions. The other end of the line was silent for a long moment. Noah could almost hear her brain working.

"Where is this?" she asked, and he could hear her moving around, probably looking for a pen. Yeira rarely went anywhere without her notebook.

"Montana."

"Do you know exactly where?"

"There are addresses on the receipts," Noah said, flipping through them. "Kyle, do you know where this place is?"

"No. I mean, I'd know it if I saw it. It's outside Missoula. That's where Mama put me on the bus, anyway," Kyle said to the picture.

"Missoula," Noah told Yeira.

"Okay, can you scan me copies of everything you have? I need to talk to my boss, but I think homegrown terrorists warrant a plane ride. What are you going to do?" He heard her typing, probably already messaging someone at the station.

"We're going to try to keep Kyle hidden until someone can help him. His sister and some guy are here looking for this box. They know it exposes the camp. They'll try to take it and him." Noah looked at Kyle, who kept staring at the picture.

"You should get out of there," Yeira warned. "Some of these people are militia and not to be messed with."

"I can't. I don't have much time left."

"I know you care about him, Noah. Is the store worth his life?" Her question punched him in the gut.

"We'll be careful." Noah disconnected the call and started to gather up all of the stuff from the box. His father had a multifunction scanner printer in the office. He could use that to send everything to her. Hopefully she'd be able to convince her boss to let her do something.

Henry drifted up through the ceiling to the apartment he'd once shared with Persephone. Noah knew the old man was going up there to think. He scraped the papers back together and put them neatly into the box. Then he took the box over to the scanner and powered it up.

When he came back out, Kyle was sitting in the window seat, watching the street. The old pickup rolled past, and Kyle rested his head back against the wall with a sigh. They wouldn't see him there, not with the lettering across the window, but the guy was taking an awful risk by putting himself out there like that.

"You really shouldn't be in the window." Noah put a hand on Kyle's shoulder.

Kyle sat up a little higher in the window box. "Someone's coming."

Whoever it was wouldn't be able to see Kyle because of the window front lettering, but he got up and stepped back behind a shelf anyway. Noah pulled the I Heart New York keychain from his pocket and headed for the door.

Noah unlocked the door and pulled it open with a jingle for two elderly black women. The first must have been close to ninety, walking with a cane and a spine of steel. Her gaze caught Noah's and held it while the other woman, who appeared to be just a few decades younger, followed the woman in. Noah stood back while they passed and then closed the door behind them.

"Good morning, ladies. I'm Noah. Is there something I can help you find?" he offered when they stood unmoving in the doorway.

"I haven't been in this place for so long," the older woman said, her voice a reverent whisper.

"I don't even remember it," the other woman said, glancing around with wide eyes like she hoped to conjure something from deep in her mind.

"Chile, the police came and told me they found my daddy up in the dusty rafters here. Do you know who owns this store now? I'd just… I'd like to hear about it." She trailed off, still gazing around the store. He wondered if she saw it as it was now or as it had been when her father owned it.

"I found your father," Noah said quietly. "Why don't we come over here and sit down." He nodded toward a small cluster of chairs in the general fiction section and relocked the door. Not that they had a lot of traffic on a weekday morning, but she deserved to hear it undisturbed.

"I'm sorry, I don't know where my manners went. Seein' this place…." She glanced around like she wanted to commit every book to memory. "I'm Berenice Johnson, and this is my daughter, Ellie."

"It so nice to meet you both. I've h—seen pictures. The owner had them in his apartment upstairs." He'd almost said he'd heard so much about her, but that would lead to a lot of questions he didn't want to answer.

"My father was Henry McDaniel. A better man you couldn't find. The police said that he'd been in the attic?" she prompted.

"Yes, ma'am. My father died just a couple weeks ago, and I was up there trying to get a feel for the place again. I found an old trapdoor up to the attic, so I went to check it out. Hen— Your father was there, surrounded by some old Christmas decorations."

"Daddy went missin' round about January, so he was probably up there putting stuff away. Maybe he had himself a heart attack. I didn't even know this place had an attic." She shifted to her left, and it looked like she was trying to take a little pressure off her right hip. Noah couldn't bring himself to tell her about the robbery. Better she thought he died peacefully.

"Did you sell this place to my granddad, Robert Hitchens?"

"Whoo, chile, that was a lifetime ago. I sold the store after Daddy went missin', musta been in the seventies?" She removed a handkerchief from a tiny handbag and dabbed at her face with it.

"I am so sorry, ma'am. Would you like something to drink? I have some bottles of sweet tea in the back."

"That's be nice," she said, shifting again and glancing down the aisle.

"You're more than welcome to take a look around. I'll be back in just a minute." Noah started toward the back and heard the chimes again. He glanced toward the door to see Kyle's back. He hoped Kyle had more sense than to go to work or to Sarah's. He grabbed three bottles of tea and took three cups from the coffee bar. When he came back to the main room, the women weren't in their seats. He found them in the classic book section.

"I like all the detail your daddy put around these books. The décor in the cases. It gives the place a homey feel," Berenice said as she ran a finger over a standing globe that had been there as long as Noah could remember.

"He loved this store, put everything he had into it," Noah told her.

"It shows." She followed him back to their seats. Noah poured out tea and handed them both cups, then set the empty bottles on a nearby table.

"It may not matter," Noah said with a sigh big enough to fill the room.

"What does that mean?" Ellie said, speaking for the first time. Her voice was quiet, shy compared to her mother's.

"He left it in debt. With the e-readers and big chains, even large bookstores are going out of business. My dad saw that he needed another line of money coming in, so he started to build a coffee bar." Noah nodded toward the small room with the machines. "Took out a loan for the renovations and equipment. We set it up, but so far it's been a bust."

"So if you can't make it work, you'll sell the store."

"I already have an offer. They want to tear down the block and build something else. If I sell, they have leverage to get other people to sell too."

"Tear down Stardust," Berenice said, her hand coming up to her throat. "I can't imagine."

"We're trying to stop that from happening," Noah said, a little defensive.

"This is a good old town," Berenice said. "You should hold some events here. Maybe get some authors to come and sign. Get some people in through those doors."

"That would take time to coordinate, and I only have a few weeks left. To be honest, right now I'm hoping for a miracle."

"Miracles are for suckers," Berenice spat.

Noah stared at her, wide-eyed.

"You need to get up off yo' ass and make something happen. Young people feel so entitled these days, like everything should be handed to them. You gotta work for what you want, son. There's folks in this town who would help. You need to let them." Berenice sat back in the chair and looked thoughtful.

Noah didn't dare speak.

"Ellie, honey, hand me my cellular phone," she said suddenly, sitting up straighter in the chair.

"Yes, ma'am." Ellie dug through an old handbag that she'd sat on the floor next to her chair. It was about the size of a rolled-up sleeping bag. It took her a minute, but she came out unscathed and handed her mother the phone.

Miss Berenice flipped it open. Noah hadn't seen a flip phone in years. She clicked through a couple of buttons and then hit one in the upper corner. The phone shook just a bit as she brought it to her ear.

"Norma, it's Berenice. Want to have some fun?"

CHAPTER TWENTY-THREE

EVERYONE IN a small Southern town rallied around the church, and in Aster, the church meant Norma Jackson. She might not have been the preacher or the preacher's wife, but she ran the extra social activities with military precision and care. In a matter of hours, Miss Norma and Berenice, put together an event to help raise money for the bookstore. They got all the ladies in town to bake something, because in the South, that's what people do. They bake—pies, cakes, and a ton of casseroles.

She put out the word that after church on Sunday, people should stop by the bookstore, where she'd be selling her world-famous apple pie. Miss Edna would be baking cobblers, lots of them. And Miss Ellie had taken it on herself to make some fall pastries, making use of the pumpkins and sweet potatoes of the season. Other ladies would be pitching in as well.

Henry gave Noah a fierce smile of pride.

"That's my Berenice," he said in a choked voice, "always helping others." Henry had floated down from the upstairs apartment a few minutes after his daughter and granddaughter had left the store a few days before. A stunned, harsh pain swept his translucent features. It took a moment before he'd been able to speak, which surprised Noah, since Henry never really shut up.

"I didn't want to frighten her," he'd said. "But goodness, I wanted to come down and talk with her again. I missed my little girl."

"Maybe we could ease her into it." Noah smiled at Henry.

Kyle and Noah had been busy making sure the coffee bar was ready—folks did like coffee with their pies. They set up some extra tables and chairs that Miss Norma had sent over from the church. Cooper said they could bring them out onto the sidewalk. Miss Ananda let him put a few in front of her store in exchange for a piece of Miss Norma's apple pie.

Sunday dawned a clear, crisp morning. The day started out in the fifties, but by lunchtime, it would be seventy and clear, a beautiful Georgia afternoon. Kyle and Noah sat side by side in church with Miss Edna and Miss Sarah. Noah didn't pay much attention to the sermon—he couldn't. Kyle's sister and her companion were there. Miss Sarah had noticed them when she came back from the ladies'. They sat in the very last row, usually reserved for women and their babies. Side by side, they sat rigid, dressed in what passed for their Sunday best. He wore a button-down shirt that had started to yellow with age. She had her hair up off her face in a bow that matched her fraying sundress, out of place on a fall morning. Noah was surprised at just how much she looked like Kyle: same red hair, same freckles, same pale complexion.

Kyle was watching the preacher. Noah didn't know if he'd seen his sister or not. The sermon rose and fell, holding the congregation's rapt attention, except for Noah, who glanced at his phone screen every few minutes through the story of Abraham's sacrifice. By the time they reached the moral, Noah's leg was bouncing. The preacher called up anyone who wanted to be saved. There was a teenage boy with his parents watching proudly. The preacher prayed with him, encouraging and kind.

Then it was over, and the congregation murmured quietly as they got ready to leave.

"I'll take you boys through the office and out," Miss Sarah whispered, and Miss Edna looked around.

"I don't see them," Miss Edna told her.

"Yes, but that doesn't mean they're not still here."

"My sister?" Kyle asked, looking around, his voice almost hopeful.

"Come with me," Miss Sarah whispered. It was the start of a cloak-and-dagger mission to get back to the bookstore without being seen and before everyone arrived for food. They snuck back through the baptismal area, where a large pool sat empty, then through a door and across a lush hidden courtyard. They came out the back door, quiet as mice, to find Miss Edna there with Noah's dad's truck.

She rode in the back as they headed for the bookstore. He didn't see Kyle's sister or the man as he headed for the Stardust with half the town on his heels. The Southern goodbye would give them about half an hour to get things ready before the hordes descended.

Noah parked behind the store in the alley and unlocked the back door. Miss Norma and her church ladies had his spare key because they'd been by before service to set everything up. Kyle and Miss Edna slid out of the truck and waited for him. Then he held the door open as they passed. He followed, then locked the door behind. Henry's feet disappeared through the ceiling as they came into the main room.

Table after table of baked goods lined the coffee bar, while smaller ones sat randomly throughout the rows of shelves. Noah didn't relish the thought of sticky books when people started eating and browsing, but it was better than going out of business.

His phone buzzed in his pocket, and he pulled it out to see a text from Yeira.

Flight to Montana in an hour. I'll keep you posted.

Be safe, he sent back.

Noah pulled the bins of discounted books outside to the sidewalk while Kyle brought tables and chairs. Then he went back in and got the coffee machines ready. By the time people started to arrive, things were already in motion.

They figured Kyle would be safe enough surrounded by half the town.

Miss Norma, Berenice, and Ellie arrived first, flitting around straightening the food, making it as presentable as possible. They set out dainty paper plates and napkins from the dollar store up the road. Children darted in soon after, dollar bills clutched in small hands. They went for the cookies and cupcakes first, their eyes hungrily determining which were the best. Then they brought their treasures to Noah at the register.

They'd made it very simple. Each item was three dollars, or you could have two items for five dollars. Miss Edna had taken some cash to the bank and changed it out for fives and singles so they'd have enough change.

Fred's daughter, Melissa, brought him a chocolate cupcake with rainbow frosting and paid him all in change. He wondered if she'd raided her piggy bank. The concentration she'd shown counting out all the change to make three dollars disappeared in an instant when Noah scooped it into the register, and she headed back to mailman Fred to enjoy her bakery delight.

Parents wandered in soon after. Noah hoped no one on the street got angry for them taking up all the parking. But maybe after they filled up on sugar, they could stroll down the sidewalk and pick up a crystal, or maybe a knickknack from one of his neighbors in another shop.

Miss Berenice wandered up the classics aisle with a Langston Hughes book in one hand and her cane in the other. Miss Ellie followed up from behind with two plates of peach cobbler, one in each hand. As she got closer, an idea struck Noah, and he glanced around.

"Miss Berenice," he said, coming closer, "may I ask you something?"

"Sure you can, young Noah." She stopped and closed her book, balancing it on her slender hip.

"All these classics back here with those things from the beyond like *Hamlet* or *The Legend of Sleepy Hollow*." He waved his hand at the shelves surrounding them. "Do you believe in ghosts?"

"Well, I'll tell you. As a good Christian woman, I'd have to say no. When we die, God takes our souls. But as a human being who has lived a long lifetime, I think there are things that happen we can't explain. One day we'll learn the truth, but for now, we have to take things on faith. Why?"

"I was just curious."

She scrutinized his face. "That's an odd question to come up out of the blue."

"I'm writing a book. Trying to come up with ideas." It wasn't a complete lie, but he felt bad saying it anyway.

They'd left the door open to the cool morning to keep the chimes from constantly sounding, so he didn't hear when Hope arrived, but simply glanced up to see her staring at him from the door. She was a ragdoll come to life. A young, red-haired girl with a button nose in a hand-sewn dress. A foot shorter than her companion, who stood with a protective hand on her shoulder, she held his gaze for a long time.

Then a teenager came up to the counter and handed him a piece of chocolate cake, and when Noah looked up again, she was gone.

"Miss Edna, could you take the register, please?" Noah asked, his eyes darting across the room, frantically searching for the girl. He needed to warn Kyle. "You just hit the total amount of each sale and put the money in the drawer."

"Noah, I know how to run a register, even this old thing." She gave him a sardonic look and he headed straight for the coffee bar, which seemed to be doing a brisk business. Miss Sarah was making change out of a cigar box as Kyle served cup after cup to waiting patrons.

"My God, have you tried these hand pies?" Thad asked, spinning to face Noah in the coffee bar doorway. "They are heaven in fried dough!" He took another bite, daintily wiping the sticky glaze from the corners of his mouth.

"I haven't," Noah said, searching over Thad's shoulder.

"Oh, this is my last one, don't tell my trainer." He put a hand on Noah's arm.

"Found her," Noah said.

"Found who—" Thad started to ask when Noah darted into the coffee bar. He couldn't get very far because of the milling crowed, but she shifted from foot to foot near the window. Kyle was preoccupied filling orders and hadn't seen her. Her companion took a step forward, but Hope put a delicate hand on his arm. She looked up at him, and there was no challenge in her expression. He stepped back and let her get in line for the counter. Noah couldn't stop himself from watching as she moved to third in line, then second. Kyle looked up, ready to take the next order, and froze. Miss Sarah froze too. Time itself came to a halt.

Noah sidestepped a few people and then stood near the end of the counter, his eyes on the newly reunited siblings.

"Hello, brother," Hope said. "May I have some tea?"

It took a long moment for Kyle to move. The length of the line behind her must have spurred him on. He grabbed a cup, filled it with hot water, and turned to the packets.

"What kind would you like?" He showed her the choices, and she selected one with a bright orange hue.

She stood at the counter a little too long, making a show of opening the tea bag and dropping it into the water. With a flick of annoyance at Kyle and Miss Sarah, she turned and walked back to her companion, leaving the wrapper on the counter and no money in the till. Kyle watched her walk away with a look that broke Noah's heart.

Then he swiped the garbage and dropped it into his little can under the counter. The pair watched him for five, maybe ten minutes as he stood in public, surrounded by people. Noah couldn't stand the pain in Kyle's face, so he skirted the room to where they were standing.

Hope sipped her tea, and her companion stood in stony silence with an expression of unquelled rage.

"Is there anything I can help you find?" Noah asked with a false cheeriness that fooled no one.

"Did you know my brother is a thief? I'm not sure why you would employ him," Hope said by way of reply.

"I'm sorry?" he asked, stunned at the quiet venom in her voice.

"He stole a box from our late mother, one that the family would like to get back. Have him bring it to me and we'll leave quietly," Hope told him, even as her companion's head jerked toward her. It seemed they weren't on the same page about leaving quietly. Maybe they had instructions, and after seeing her brother, Hope wasn't going to stay with the program.

Then she looked up at him, and the man relaxed.

Or she was lying.

"I don't know anything about a box, but if you're going to threaten my barista, you can leave. Now." He didn't break her cold gaze, nor did she move.

She simply watched him, and Noah saw her spine of steel. This was not the broken little girl he had pictured.

"Officer Thompson is standing right there next to the magazines. Shall I call him over and have him ask you?" Noah charged, and then said a little prayer of thanks when they left with angry looks but no more trouble. He didn't think for a moment that was the end of it, but it was another obstacle they had overcome.

Noah popped behind the counter and grabbed a packet of hot chocolate. He put a hand on Kyle's arm, a quiet show of support, and then filled his cup with hot water. He grabbed a second cup of water and a tea bag and headed back to the register.

"Thank you, Noah," Miss Edna said as he handed her the tea. "You've got quite a turnout here." Her gaze swept the room from the kids playing around with the toys in the children's section to Miss Norma surreptitiously checking out the romance novels. A few older folks were looking at the Christian section with Preacher Dan. His motions were animated as he pulled one book after another off the shelf and showed them to his congregation of three in the aisle.

Ananda was dazzling children in the back with her crystals. Noah swore he saw her make a book disappear. Kids were raiding the shelves looking for magic books. Bless her.

"This isn't going to save you."

Noah set his cocoa down and turned to see Matt Handley standing next to the register, sober this time, in a baseball jersey and a wry smile. The jersey had started to get tight in the arms and around the chest, but Noah was sure Handley showed it off with pride. Vanity seemed to mean everything to the man.

"We have a great selection of self-help books down that aisle," Noah said loudly, wafting his hand vaguely to his right. "Lots on moral superiority—you should check them out." He was done taking shit from Handley. If he was going to go down, it wasn't going to be with Matt Handley's boot on his neck. Fuck him.

"You're fifty grand in the hole and you think pie is going to help? You should be packing this place up to be sold," Handley growled in response.

"What, you want pie? I think Miss Norma has some excellent choices in that self-help section," Noah said, pointing again. Miss Norma looked up at the movement and waved at him. He waved back.

"I'm not the one with the dough-boy physique," Handley countered and stormed out the front door.

"I don't know who is more unpleasant, him or your uncle James," Miss Edna commented as she took another sip of her tea. "But I'd like some of that pie, so I think I'm going to go see Miss Norma." Her quiet laugh galvanized his soul.

"Bring me a slice of pumpkin?" Noah asked.

"Now that's the spirit."

CHAPTER TWENTY-FOUR

"YOU'RE SURE Henry won't mind if I stay up here?"

Noah glanced around the empty room. "I can't figure out why he would. It's not like you're taking over or kicking him out or anything."

"He doesn't like me."

"That's because you said he was evil." Noah shrugged. "You both know better now." He plugged in the pump for the queen-sized double-height air mattress and turned it on. "I wish we could get you a better bed, but right now we can't afford for your sister and that guy to see us moving furniture in here."

"They'll probably figure it out anyway." Kyle sat on the floor, cross-legged. "They've seen me here, and once they find out I'm not staying with Miss Sarah anymore...."

"That's why you need to make sure the doors are locked and the alarm is set before you go to bed. The blinds in the parlor are closed, but the ones in the hall are broken. I never thought to have them fixed before now since no one was up here." Noah chewed his lip anxiously.

"I'll be careful not to show much light. Just enough to read by."

"The kitchen's pretty safe—there's no windows in there and you can close the door. Plus you have the table and chairs, so you have someplace to sit. Don't go out into the main part of the bookstore— you'll set off the alarm."

"He can sit in the parlor, if he likes." Henry's voice was doubtful. "As long as he doesn't preach at me. Or try to exorcise me or anything. No bell, book, or candle around here."

"Well, we need candles in case of a power outage, and you really can't escape books around here, but why would you want to? And what's the bell for?"

Henry rolled his eyes. "Do you know?" he demanded of Kyle.

"No...."

"Those are the traditional accoutrements of an exorcism."

"What's an 'oh-coot-tray-mont'?"

Henry winked out of existence. Kyle said, "See? He doesn't like me."

"You just frustrate him. Besides, it doesn't matter if he doesn't like you—he won't hurt you. And I like you... a lot."

Kyle smiled shyly. "I like you a lot too."

Noah reached over and drew him up into his arms. He fit so perfectly, his head resting on Noah's shoulder and the clean soap smell of him in Noah's nose. They stood there a long moment; then Noah drew back and kissed Kyle before bending to turn off the pump. They made up the bed with the sheets Noah had snuck over from the house and threw a thick comforter Sarah had contributed over the top. It was starting to get cold at night.

"Okay. The fridge doesn't seem to be working, but the hot water is on the same line as the bookstore, so your bathroom should work. I guess depending on how long you're gonna stay here, we can start moving over some other stuff like a teapot and a pot to make soup in or something. At least it's not too dusty."

"Of course not," Henry said, rematerializing in the room. "I keep a clean house, even if it's not mine anymore. What kind of music do you like, boy?"

"Um... I don't know. We didn't have much except hymns, and they weren't ones I've ever heard anywhere else." Kyle shrugged. "Ours had much more death and destruction in them. Not so much glory of God, more 'God will smite our enemies, hallelujah.'"

"Merciful heavens. And when there are so many beautiful spiritual songs. I'll have to play some of the records I have. We can go through them and see what ones are salable for Noah, at any rate." He faded out again, leaving the hummed strains of "Shall We Gather at the River" echoing behind him.

"I don't think I'll ever get used to that."

"You will. I've only known him a few weeks longer than you, and I hardly even notice anymore."

They went downstairs again and Noah flipped over the Open sign. "Fire up the kettle, Maw, and git that coffee boilin'."

"You should never boil coffee," Kyle said soberly. "It makes for bitterness."

151

"Well, there's enough bitterness in this building right now." Noah went behind the counter and started organizing the stuff there. "There's some stuff left from yesterday's bake sale—why don't you add it to the cart?"

"Any more of those lemon bars? That would make an awesome breakfast."

"Look at you!" Noah said, mock admiringly. "Using words like *awesome*."

"Oh, hush." Kyle stalked back into the office and came out a few minutes later with a laden tray of pastries. "Just for that, no lemon bars for you."

"Seriously?"

"No. There are a few left. Since they're a day old, should I sell these or give them away?"

"Sell 'em, but only charge a dollar instead of the three they were going for yesterday. Worst-case scenario, we'll eat 'em for dinner tonight." Noah poked at his soft middle. "Though to be honest, I need to lay off the sweets. I always have a problem with my weight, and I haven't had time or enough energy to go running lately. Plus people are always making me eat—you'd think I was wasting away instead of getting fat!"

"You're not fat!" Kyle was horrified.

Noah poked his middle again. "Fat," he confirmed.

"Give it up, son." Henry appeared and spoke to Kyle. "He's got anorexia or something."

"I so do not! Okay, I weigh what I should for my height, but it's all mushy."

Kyle and Henry rolled their eyes at the same time, the expressions on their faces identical. Noah had to laugh despite himself.

"Haul a few more boxes of books," Henry advised. "That'll toughen you up."

The door chimes rang and Henry vanished.

YESTERDAY'S BAKE sale had apparently whetted local interest in the coffee stand, so despite it being a Monday, there was a steady stream of shoppers. Some lingered to talk to Kyle and Noah, some left with packages of pastry, and some actually bought books. There was only one accident involving coffee, and it was a spill onto a rug Noah had always disliked. They moved a little table over the spot and kept on working.

When they closed up that evening, Kyle was damp with sweat from the heat of the coffee and the activity, but he was beaming. "Twenty-two dollars in tips! That's almost as good as in Chicago!"

"I wish it would last." Noah made a face. "How did the pastries go?"

"They're gone. They were a big hit despite being a day old. Maybe we should offer those on a regular basis." Kyle dug in his cashbox. "I set that money aside. We made another thirty-six dollars on the pastries. And we got enough from the coffee sales to cover another shipment of those organic beans."

"Well, we made about twenty-five hundred yesterday and another thousand today, so we're about a third of the way there. I don't think we're going to make it in time," Noah observed, finishing up the books.

"We will, but right now, boy, am I tired!"

"Yeah, me too. I gotta get home and let Jake out. He's probably crossing his legs."

"Poor Jake."

"Yeah. I should probably start bringing him to the store, but then he's just cooped up here. And he's not fond of the cat. Speaking of being cooped up—did you want me to run over to the diner and get you something for dinner?"

"Oh, would you mind? I'm kind of starving."

"If I brought Jake to work, I could have dinner with you in the evenings. We might even be able to cook if we got some supplies in upstairs."

"I would love it if you would cook with me. I do know how. It wasn't considered 'men's work,' but I used to watch Mama and the other wives when they were doing it, and when the men weren't around, they would teach me. I couldn't do it where the men could see."

"Wow. Toxic masculinity in action."

"Yeah. Miss Sarah lets me cook sometimes, but she's so good it's kind of intimidating. I'd never be able to bake as well as she does. But I'm learning a few Georgia recipes, like barbeque and grits and biscuits and gravy. Mm. I love biscuits and gravy."

Noah closed out the register. It had slowed down later in the afternoon, so he'd been able to balance the books already. "Funny thing about biscuits and gravy. I dated a guy in New York once that was from England. We got to talking about our favorite foods, and when I mentioned biscuits and gravy, he almost puked."

"Why?"

"Because in England, they call cookies 'biscuits,' and he thought I was talking about cookies and gravy."

"Ew! That's disgusting!"

Noah laughed. "I thought it was hilarious. Especially when they have food they call things like 'toad in the hole' and 'bubble and squeak' and 'spotted dick.'"

"What?"

"Yeah. It's not really a toad or a dick—thank God! It's like sausages and stuff. But they have weird shit over there. I take it you want biscuits and gravy for dinner?"

"If they have any. I know it's more a breakfast food."

"If Jessie is there, she'll make it for you. They might be frozen biscuits, but you won't know the difference. Her mama is another awesome cook."

NOAH CHECKED carefully around the diner before he went up to order from Jessie, just to make sure Hope and the guy weren't around. He did the same as he left the diner a few minutes later, feeling like a spy as he slipped into the store via the back door.

Kyle was waiting. "Thanks. Did you get anything?"

"Yeah, a club sandwich. I gotta go let Jake out." He leaned over and kissed Kyle. "Enjoy your dinner. I gave you the Wi-Fi password for the tablet, right?" He had lent Kyle the tablet so he could watch some movies in the evening when Noah wasn't there.

"You did. And I thought Henry might not mind if I looked at some of the stuff in the parlor. It looks interesting."

"And maybe if you were interested, he might be a little nicer to you?"

Kyle gave Noah his sweet smile. "Couldn't hurt."

Noah had to kiss him again. "I'll see you in the morning. I'll bring breakfast."

CHAPTER TWENTY-FIVE

"YOU WANT to get some dinner before you go up?" Noah asked as he finished counting twenties from the register the next night. He added the total to the spreadsheet on the laptop and grabbed the tens. It took a long time each night to match the till against what they sold because of the manual process. Once he got everything straightened out with the bank, he really needed to figure out some updated equipment, or at least software for the laptop. He had one of those little card readers, but it was so slow with their Wi-Fi. Ah well, one battle at a time.

He added another couple thousand to the total in his special spreadsheet, the one that would tell him if he'd still have a home in just over a month.

"No, I'm tired. I think I'm going to read for a while and go to bed."

Noah didn't look up from where he grabbed a few supplies from the storage area for the next morning. They were starting to get a few coffee addicts trickling in for some of Kyle's "fancy coffee."

"What are you reading?" Noah moved on to the singles.

"*Harry Potter.*"

Noah's head jerked up. "I thought you didn't read fiction."

"I never had any. Now I'm surrounded by shelves and shelves of it." He set aside a sleeve of cups.

"And you started with a story about witchcraft?" He didn't want to appear too excited, because Kyle should make his own literary decisions, but it would be great to sit and talk to him about all the amazing worldbuilding and subplots as he got through each book. They hadn't talked much since Hope showed up, and he didn't know how to help.

"A friend recommended it."

Noah smiled at Kyle before hefting his box and heading toward the coffee bar. "He must be a smart friend."

"She. Miss Sarah loves it," Kyle called over his shoulder. Noah's sound of protest just made him laugh, and it was a delight to hear.

Noah finished with the change and smiled when both totals came down to within a dime of each other. That was close enough for him. Plus or minus a dollar was good with him, though a year of that would be a much larger disparity. He'd work it out, assuming he didn't have to sell.

"I'm gonna head up," Kyle said, giving Noah a small peck as he went by. They'd been doing that a lot lately, just small tokens of affection.

"Do you need anything from the kitchen? I'm going to hit the alarm as I go out."

"No, Henry talked me through getting the refrigerator upstairs to work. Nothing else does, but that's okay. It's clean and safe—better than some places I've lived." Kyle shrugged and headed toward the stairs.

Noah wanted to ask about those places, but deep down, he didn't think he'd want to know. "Okay, I'll see you tomorrow." Noah locked the till in the safe and headed for the door. He had to decide what he'd be having for dinner. Maybe he'd stop by the diner and talk to Miss Jessie a bit about buying their pastries for the coffee bar.

Headlights caught his vision, and Noah looked up to see the truck drive past again. It looked like they were waiting for Kyle to come out.

They'd have a long wait.

Miss Jessie wasn't working, so he picked up a burger for himself and grabbed a grilled chicken sandwich for Jake, who greeted him at the door with paws up and mouth open.

"Dude, I get it," Noah said with a laugh and pushed the big dog back. Jake sniffed the bag all the way into the kitchen and then dropped his furry butt to the floor in a perfect sit.

"Show-off." Noah pulled the sandwiches out and opened up the wrapper for the chicken. He ripped each bun into chunks and then the chicken before tossing a piece of meat for Jake to catch. Then he leaned over and dropped the whole mess into Jake's steel food bowl. He grinned around his burger at the appreciative noises coming from under the table.

Yeah, there were worse things than being here with that big lug at his feet. He'd been back in Georgia for almost a month to the day, and he'd already started to forget the sharper, shiny points of New York. Seeing and being seen every Saturday night didn't seem important anymore. Hanging out on the couch with a pup in his lap and a book in his hand felt right. Kyle felt right. The bookstore felt right. These things felt more right and more comfortable than he'd been in New York.

He finished the book he'd been reading about small business and wandered upstairs to brush his teeth and crawl into bed. The big bedroom at the end of the hall still loomed like a shadow over him, empty and overwhelming, so Noah turned left before he reached it and grabbed his toothbrush from the cup. He'd just put the paste on his brush when his phone started to ring, and he pulled it from his pocket and checked the display.

It was a number he didn't recognize, but he slid the bar across the screen to answer anyway. Maybe he'd won the lottery.

"This message is for... Charlie Hitchens from... Prism Security Detection. An alarm has been triggered at... Stardust Books. We are sending emergency assistance. If this is a false alarm, please press zero to speak to an operator," an automated voice read to him.

Noah dropped the toothbrush into the sink and ran for the stairs. He all but leaped over Jake to get to the door and barely closed it behind him as he raced to the truck. The key was in the ignition and he was turning it with one hand and summoning Siri with the other.

"Siri, call the bookstore," Noah said, his voice frantic as he rammed the truck into Reverse and pulled slowly back to the street. It wouldn't help Kyle if he got into an accident. Tires squealed when he dropped the truck into Drive on the road and sped toward the store.

On a good day, it took six minutes to get to the store on the low-limit small-town roads. He made it there in three, the phone ringing over and over through the car speakers.

Cooper hadn't arrived when he reached the store to find a jagged hole in the glass door, which was slightly ajar. He couldn't think about whether Hope or her companion had guns. He couldn't think about whether they'd already taken Kyle. He couldn't think about losing his life if he walked through that door. All he could think about was getting to Kyle.

Noah flung the door open with a crashing of glass and ran in through the main part of the store. When he reached the end of the aisle, a book went whizzing by him, and he heard an unearthly shriek. Hope's companion had Kyle by the arm, dragging him toward the door, but had stopped. Noah watched his face drain of color when more books flew at him, seemingly from nowhere.

"Who's there?" he demanded as he and Hope looked around wildly. They were both dressed in dark clothes, making their pallor more pronounced.

The man jerked to the side like someone had jabbed him in the ribs, and he struck out with the hand not holding Kyle. Noah froze, hidden behind one of the displays.

"What devilry is this?"

"Elijah, maybe we should—"

"Don't presume, woman," he said, clearly trying to maintain his composure.

Henry batted him right between the eyes.

He dropped Kyle's arms, waved his hands frenetically around his head, and screamed. Hope careened sideways from the force of his blow.

In a voice lower than Noah had ever heard, Henry boomed, "Be gone from this place and never return."

The man screamed and pushed past Hope as he ran. Hope glanced at her brother, who still looked shaken, and ran after Elijah. The remaining glass from the door's pane crashed to the ground as they fled.

Kyle slid to the floor, and Noah scrambled the last few feet between them to kneel beside him. "Are you okay?"

"They didn't even ask about the box," Kyle whispered.

"What?"

"They came for me."

"Did they say anything?"

"No, he just dragged me downstairs. I don't remember him from the camp at all. I don't know who he was." Kyle looked up above the counter and said, "Thank you, Henry."

Henry flicked into existence about six inches from Kyle, also somewhat kneeling on the floor. Kyle jumped and listed sideways.

"Sorry," Henry said, his voice sheepish and rather pleased with himself. "I didn't know what else to do, but this young man had been so disturbed by my presence, calling me evil and such. I took a chance that they would be as unnerved."

Blue light swam off and on around the books, and Noah looked up to see a police car pulling up in front of the store. He was about to get up and greet Cooper, but then he saw the man coming through the door, gun drawn.

"They ran out," Noah called. "It's just me and Kyle here. You can put the gun away."

Cooper's stance relaxed and he came up through the aisle. He looked disheveled, his hair at odd angles without the hat and his uniform askew. His skin and clothes were tinged with black, and he looked more harried than someone who'd shown up for a simple nighttime robbery.

"I'm sorry I wasn't here sooner. There was a fire out by Jonas's place. Someone lit up the barn where he keeps his horses. We lost one but got the rest out, and the volunteer fire department has it contained. Gas cans were still layin' out front." Cooper leaned heavily against the counter.

"Think they set that as a diversion?" Noah asked. He kept a hand on Kyle's arm, not caring if their contact bothered the old cop or not.

"Probably. I can't imagine we'd suddenly have a crime wave in the middle of November. If kids were going to do something stupid, they'd have done it on Halloween. And this wasn't a bunch of kids," Cooper spat out. "Do you know who they were?"

Kyle looked at Noah, who nodded to him, a silent reassurance that they could trust Cooper.

"Almost six years ago, my mother put me on a bus to her sister's in Chicago. Before that, I'd lived my entire life in a Montana compound with what you would call a cult," Kyle began.

"Okay." Cooper cocked his head, his body leaning forward.

"The girl is my sister, but I don't know who the man is."

"So you were here when they broke in?" Cooper ran a hand down over his tired face.

"Yes, we moved him into the room upstairs so he would be safe," Noah chimed in. "They'd already been to Miss Sarah's, looking for him."

"We thought they were here for the box, but they didn't even ask about it when they dragged me down here."

"They must know that Yeira already has it and that's why she's there investigating," Noah said. "I need to text—"

"What's in the box?" Cooper's hands and jaw were clenched. Noah had seen that reaction plenty of times when he'd come home after curfew.

"Pictures, videos, some birth and death certificates, and... receipts for bomb-making materials," Noah finished in a whisper.

"And you didn't call me, why?" Cooper asked, his voice rising from annoyance to anger.

"Policemen came to the camp a few times. They never did anything. And we were raised to believe that the government wanted to hurt us. That they would take us and throw us into prisons. We weren't to trust systemites, ever," Kyle explained. "Noah called a friend of his who is a journalist. He said she could help."

Cooper sighed, a tired and soggy sound. "Do you still have the box?"

"Yes." Kyle sagged back against the wall.

"Go get it."

Noah glanced at Kyle, who heaved himself off the floor. They shared a long look before Kyle headed for the stairs.

"Why didn't you call me? Why? This is serious. These people could be getting ready to blow up half the Northwest."

"Kyle's been gone for five years. Those receipts are at least that old, some more. And just because you bring injustice to someone's attention doesn't mean it stops. Cracking it open in the court of public opinion may pressure someone to do something." Noah started picking up the books Henry had used as projectiles toward their intruders.

"What does that mean, exactly?"

"That means when I needed help because I was being tortured every day at school, no one did anything because of who Handley's family was. Today we would call the shit he did to me assault. He should have been arrested. Instead, he just came back to school day after day," Noah spat. He hadn't realized how deep the hurt and anger went until it pooled like acid at his feet.

Cooper closed his eyes, fatigue dulling his features. "You're right. We gave him too much leeway, and things were different then. Back then it was 'kids will be kids,' but that wasn't right. Today I'd haul the kid off, ask the parents if they wanted to press charges."

Kyle returned with the box and handed it to Cooper.

"Is everything in here?"

"Yes. We scanned it all to send it to my friend," Noah assured him.

"I'm going to start going through this tomorrow. I may have more questions," he said, looking at Kyle, who nodded. "In the meantime I'm going to call in a few volunteer deputies to keep an eye on this place and to look for your sister. I'm guessing they're the ones creeping around in the old truck people have mentioned?"

"Yes."

"Fantastic. Noah, head over to Home Depot in Douglasville tomorrow to get plywood for that door. It will take them at least a week to get out here and fix it. And Kyle, you don't want to stay here," he advised.

"He's going to come stay with me. I've got Jake and my dad's guns."

"Can you shoot one?" Cooper raised an eyebrow.

"I was going to YouTube it," Noah admitted.

"For God's sake, ask Edna Mackey, then. She's won awards for marksmanship. I'm sure she can teach you."

"Wait, what? Miss Edna?"

"Yep, she's a hell of a shot."

CHAPTER TWENTY-SIX

"YOU'RE ABOUT as intimidating as Big Bird—how the hell did you scare off two would-be kidnappers in the middle of the night?" Yeira demanded from hundreds of miles away as she sat in some rinky-dink Montana no-tell motel.

"Well, I pretended to be a ghost. I threw some books at them from where they couldn't see me and made some ghoulish noises," Noah replied lamely, and Henry snorted at the table next to him.

"And that worked?" The skepticism in her voice rang clearly through the cellular airwaves. He glanced at Henry, who nodded.

"Yeah, but the cops showed up like sixty seconds after they ran out anyway. Do you have any news?" Noah asked, changing the subject.

"Well, I've found out several important things about Montana. One, they really don't like the government out here. Two, they really don't like foreigners out here. And three, two government offices and a school have had minor explosions here over the last five years. I got close to Kyle's camp using the geographic indicators he gave me. Our local affiliate station said that this place is relatively quiet but doesn't respond well to outsiders. They go into the bigger towns and try to collect donations. They sell some of the produce they grow. They're pretty self-sustaining. It's like a militia camp." He could hear her moving around papers in front of her. Yeira had never been a fan of digital note-taking. He'd teased her about it a few times, but she said a pen in her hand made her think.

She went on. "I verified the receipts and the certificates—they're authentic. The guy at the store also agrees that it's too much fertilizer for a small garden, and they compost anyway. I have most of what I need for a story, I want to round out some more details so that it's bulletproof before going on air. Tomorrow I'm checking around with local healers to see if they've been out to the camp. People like this wouldn't go to hospitals because they're part of the system."

"You need to be careful. Like I said in the text, I think they know about you. They weren't looking for the box when they came in, just Kyle. Oh, and when the police got here last night, Cooper asked about the people who broke in. We admitted to who they were and gave him the box," Noah said.

"Good, maybe they'll start doing something about these people. I've been watching them bring little girls in and out of the camp as they go out and beg for money and food. They're malnourished and cowed. I still have nightmares about being a little girl like that in Syria. Someone needs to help them—whether it's the cops or us." Pain laced her voice, and he hated it. He remembered how she'd wake up yelling in the middle of the night from her nightmares. She'd get up each morning after and call her little brother. Noah would eat breakfast while they talked, and she never mentioned the nightmares, just listened as he talked. Maybe it grounded her. Maybe the dreams were about him.

"Okay, let us know. Hopefully Cooper can do something too. Setting a fire and breaking into the store were bold. I don't want to know what else they're capable of," Noah admitted.

"Will do. You guys keep your heads down," she said with a gravity that made him shiver.

"You too."

"And I'll be through on my way back to New York to interview Kyle for the piece. Is he up for that?"

Noah looked up at Kyle, who seemed to be concentrating very hard on his bowl of instant oatmeal. The tension in his shoulders betrayed his unease. Noah hated adding to it. He reached a hand across the table, and Kyle took it with his left, spoon still in his right.

"Yeira is going to wrap up there in the next day or two and then head here when she's finished to talk to you in person, maybe on camera. Would that be okay?" Noah squeezed his hand.

"I guess I don't have much of a choice if I want them to leave me alone," he said miserably.

"Yes, he'll speak with you. You can stay with me if you want. The house has another bedroom," Noah said, his eyes on Kyle.

"It will probably just be an in-and-out trip. My boss is excited about this piece, especially the progress we've made on it. He wants to run with it as soon as everything is vetted." She sounded distracted now, like she'd already started to plan her next move.

"You think it will be that soon?"

"They're sending out a white guy from the affiliate station to see if he can get into the camp or talk to a few of the members as they're leaving. We're also trying to track down any ex-members to see if they'll talk to us. Kyle didn't remember anyone leaving, but he was a kid then. We're talking to people who live nearby. I've also spoken to family members like Kyle's aunt Mary in Chicago. If I had to guess, I'd say two weeks, maybe a little less. Reinterviewing Kyle with more informed questions from our investigation will be my last bit, unless he can get his sister to talk to us?" She ended the phrase on a question.

Noah thought about Hope and the fierceness in her eyes when she looked at her brother. "I don't see that happening, plus the police are looking for them. They may be in jail by the time you get here," he said, letting a little bit of the fear creep into his voice for the first time.

"Good point. Okay, I'll keep you up-to-date if I have more, and when I'm going to be there." Her papers were shuffling again.

"Okay. I can pick you up if you need me to."

"No need. I'll schedule a car service. The network will take care of it," she said lightly.

"Thank you, Yeira," Noah told her earnestly. "We didn't know what else to do."

"Don't thank me. You guys may have gotten me a promotion, which makes me feel both guilty and elated."

They hung up the phone, and Noah glanced at Kyle, whose face had drained of color. It stood out stark and white against his flaming hair and vibrant blue shirt. Noah took a step forward and opened his mouth to tell Kyle that it would be okay, but he spun on his heel and fled into the coffee bar.

Noah looked up at Henry, who floated just above him.

"Tell you what, why don't you go and talk to them diner folks about buying pastries for the store to go with his coffee? I'll go talk to him," Henry said. "I know a little bit about being different."

"Because you're a ghost? I'm not sure that relates here," Noah said, cocking his head to the side.

"Because I'm black, child. In the South, during my time, that made you different. To most folks, it made you scary too," Henry said and started to float off toward the coffee bar. Then, abruptly, he turned. "That's really the first place your mind went? To the ghost, not the black?"

"Henry, I don't think about you being black. It's not something that makes me look at you differently than I would look at Thad or Miss Edna. The ghost part, on the other hand...."

"Touché."

Noah hollered after them both that he was headed out for the diner and that he'd bring back lunch. Henry grumped about not being able to eat, and Noah set out down the street. Ananda waved from the front of her store as he passed. Her rings glittered in the morning sun when she shielded her eyes. Thad wasn't outside, but Noah could see him through the window, talking with a customer. Smiling and animated, he was explaining something in his hand. Noah relaxed. Walking along this street made him feel good. It gave him a sense of belonging, and he could keep it for a bit since the bank was behind him and the diner lay ahead.

He didn't see the truck in the lot when he headed for the door. At least he wouldn't have that constant knot in his stomach while he talked to Miss Jessie about a partnership that would be in both their interests.

His stomach twisted anyway when he opened the door to see Matt Handley sitting at the counter. He'd taken hold of Miss Jessie's hand, and she looked at him like he was something on her shoe.

"Come on, Jessie. I'd give it all up for you if you just give it up for me," he said with one hand over his heart while the other held hers tightly. She wasn't struggling to get away, but it did look like she was struggling not to punch him in his smug, laughing face.

"Hey—" Noah started, but Jessie beat him to the punch. She pulled a long butcher's knife from under the counter.

"Normally I use this to cut through them pies in the case when someone asks for a slice." She pulled the knife in a long slicing motion as she said it. Handley's eyes got as big as the saucer his coffee cup sat on. "I reckon if it works on them pies, it'll gut a pig. Don't you?"

She stared right into his face as it drained of color. The only coloring in it were the red tinges around his eyes and a faint bruising beneath them. He released her hand and glanced around.

"Well, if it isn't the wannabe librarian. Where's your boyfriend? Is he—"

This time it was Handley who didn't get to finish his sentence, because Miss Jessie slammed the knife hilt down on the counter so hard he nearly fell out of his seat. Handley spun to face her, and she smiled an angel's smile.

"I'm sorry, I thought I saw a rat," she said, emphasizing the last word.

Handley looked from Noah to Miss Jessie and back.

"Now, Mr. Noah, why don't you take a seat at the other end of the counter. Let me finish him off and then you and I can talk business. That's why you're here, right? To talk about my offer?" she asked, and Noah loved that she'd been deliberately vague because it would drive Handley crazy. First, he would hate that Miss Jessie liked Noah more than him. Second, he'd be dying to know what business they could have together.

"Matt, here's your check," she said, slapping a bill down in front of his plate.

"But I wasn't done—" he started, but she cut him off with a curt explanation that he was, indeed, done here. Then she came down to the other end of the counter where Noah sat.

"He's disgusting," Miss Jessie said, and Noah felt that was the perfect way to start the conversation.

"Ever since high school," Noah agreed. "Is he bothering you? I could—"

"Nah, he's too afraid of me to give me any grief outside here. Plus he's scared it will get back to that pretty little fiancée in Atlanta."

"You did just threaten to gut him like a pig."

"Yep, 'bout once a week or so."

"Why don't you tell Cooper?"

"So he can issue him a citation?" she asked, drawing out the *ci*. "Nah, it's more fun to put the fear of God into him every once in a while. He knows if he ever really messes with me, Uncle Fred will put him under his mail truck."

"Good to know."

"You want something to eat? Maybe sample some of the pastries you'll be buyin' for the bookstore?" She laughed. They both turned as Handley slammed cash down on the table and walked out.

"I think that's a fine idea," Noah said. "Sample with me?"

"Absolutely."

CHAPTER TWENTY-SEVEN

"I'VE FIGURED out what the boxes in the basement are for," Kyle announced the following Saturday.

Noah looked up from his laptop, where he'd been writing up his notes on Henry's last ramble. "Spill."

Kyle tossed a battered file folder into the counter. "Well, not figured out so much as discovered. Your dad was great about organizing stuff, but he had a tendency to put the folders in pretty random places. I found this one in with the warranties for the office equipment."

Noah thought a moment. "Yeah, that would be 'miscellaneous stuff in the building.' You just have to know how Dad thought."

"Okay. So I found this, and it turns out that a bunch of people have been trying to get a library and historical center going, and your dad was collecting books for the library. But I'm confused, Noah. Wouldn't a library cut into your dad's business?"

"Some. But Dad always felt that so many people couldn't afford to buy books that would like to, and some of them would later become readers, so he wanted to help them as much as he could. He was big on literacy and all that. What's the matter?"

"He sounds like such a great guy. I wish I knew him. I only ever saw him to wave at sometimes from the porch." Kyle wiped his eyes.

Noah hugged him. "I wish you could have too."

They held each other a bit longer, then mopped up damp faces with the tissues Noah kept behind the counter. Kyle fetched them each a coffee.

"Historical center, huh?" Noah flipped through the contents of the folder.

"Yeah. I was thinking that maybe you could put all your notes on what Henry told you together for like a Henry's-eye-view of the town. I mean, he goes way back—over a hundred years. And you said he's really interesting in a historical way." Kyle sounded a bit doubtful. Noah didn't blame him; Kyle knew less than nothing about history, and a lot of what Henry talked about went right over his head. Particularly the civil rights movement; apparently according to the cult it never happened.

"Yeah, I bet they'd like that. Whoever was in charge. I'll have to talk to Thad about it. He knows everything that goes on in town."

"You need to have him over more often," Henry said, appearing at Kyle's shoulder. Kyle jumped but said nothing. Noah suspected Henry kept trying to get a rise out of Kyle, but so far he'd failed. Probably more of the cult's upbringing. "He's an interesting fella once you get past the um...."

"The 'um'?"

"The flamboyant gay stuff," Noah explained.

"Okay." Kyle glanced over his shoulder at Henry. "Are you ready to get back to work?"

"If I must. Miles Davis will keep."

Noah fished his phone out of his back pocket and queued up the classic jazz station on Pandora. "Here. This will keep you entertained." He handed the phone to Kyle. The two of them had been working on inputting the older paper catalog into Charlie's computer, Henry reading the information from the ledgers and Kyle typing it into the program.

AROUND LUNCHTIME he had Kyle take over the counter while he ran to the diner for carryout. His timing was good—the only person there was Thad, who greeted him effusively as usual. While they waited for Jessie to put together their orders, Noah mentioned Kyle's discovery.

"Oh, yes! We've been working on that for a while. The old Methodist church next to the village hall is for sale, and the Merchants Council has put a motion before the town to buy it for the library. It just blows my mind that there isn't one since the old one closed back in the seventies. That building had dry rot and black mold, and they ended up tearing it down. The BP station took that corner. But the Methodist church will be perfect—it even has a parking lot, and the church itself is lovely. But"— he lowered his voice to a dramatic whisper—"some people have alternate plans for the site. In one word: Costco."

"No way."

"Yes way. Three guesses who's behind that one."

"Uncle James."

"Got it in one. Only thing holding him up is zoning issues."

"That would suck. That building is beautiful. Historic."

"Yes. Perfect for an historical society." Thad cocked his head. "You're interested in history, aren't you?"

"I never was, but Aster is different. I, I actually am sort of working on a little book on the history of the town. Just from some of the people who've lived here forever."

"Between fighting off murderous cult members and single-handedly saving your dad's business?" Jessie interjected as she brought over Thad's lunch and rang him up.

"Yeah, well, the last ain't going so well."

Thad patted him on the back as he left. "It'll happen, darling. It'll happen."

"Better be careful or that one will have you running the place," Jessie advised. "But it's nice to know some other young people are takin' an interest in the town. Especially since safe places like Aster were so rare in the history of the South."

"I know," Noah said. "I've been reading about Jim Crow laws and sunset laws and everything black travelers used to have to do to be safe not so very long ago. I want to put that up front in the thing I'm writing."

"Still a lot of places you have to be careful. Can't take anything for granted. You know, gays have some of the same issues." Jessie patted his hand. "Should put an interesting perspective on things."

"I hope." Noah handed her the cash and took the bag. "Thanks, Miss Jessie."

HE DIDN'T think much more of the conversation through the rest of the afternoon, but a little after three, the front door chimed. Noah came around the counter to help Miss Berenice and Miss Ellie with the shopping bags they carried. "Wow, these are heavy! You should have come in to get me or Kyle to help you."

"Mama's too impatient," Ellie said.

Berenice waved her hand, it must be said, impatiently. "Jessie over at the diner said you were working on a history of Aster."

"I, well, yes, I sorta am—"

"Did you hear that?" Berenice stopped and asked, turning to look over her shoulder toward the back of the store.

"I didn't hear anything," Noah said, when in fact he'd heard Henry talking to Kyle, who whispered something back.

"That's odd. Well, you remember I told you my daddy could talk the hind leg off a donkey? Well, he kept journals too. I guess for when there was no one around to listen to him. So I figured if you're going to write about Aster, you should have the words of someone who lived it." She took a battered notebook out of one of the bags. "Daddy started keeping one when he was about ten years old, so some of these are about a hundred years old. You use them, write the realities in them, and then they go to the town historical society when you're done."

"Um, technically the town doesn't have—"

"It will. You'll make one." She took out another book. "This was the last one before he disappeared." She stroked it lovingly and pressed a kiss to the cover.

"Noah, did you call me?" Henry wafted into the front of the store, Kyle on his heels.

Miss Berenice's eyes went wide and her face went ashy. Noah glanced quickly at Ellie, whose eyes were just as wide. Henry stopped stock-still.

"Daddy?" Berenice's voice was plaintive, almost like a little girl's.

Wordlessly, Henry opened his arms. Berenice stepped forward, but of course she couldn't touch him.

But as Noah watched, a pale, silvery fog settled around Berenice, morphing into a ghost-image of a tall young woman, her lovely face framed in an old-style Afro held back by a beaded headband. She wore a print dashiki tunic over bell-bottom jeans.

This image reached out and wrapped her arms around Henry. With a sob, Henry pulled her into the tightest of hugs.

Berenice stood motionless beneath the superimposed image, but her face was that of the young woman, joyful, though wet with tears.

Persephone appeared out of nowhere and leaped up onto the counter, purring loudly. She rubbed past Noah to jump up on Henry's shoulder. Henry opened eyes that glittered with happiness and tears. "Thank you," he said soundlessly.

Noah could only nod and watch as Henry, the young Berenice, and Persephone all faded. Then it was just the four of them.

Finally, Ellie broke the silence. "Mama, was that Grandpa?"

"You saw him too?" Berenice turned and clutched Ellie's arms. "He was here? He was real?"

"He was real, Mama!" The two women fell into each other's arms.

Kyle said softly to Noah, "He's gone, isn't he?"

Noah nodded and dropped his head to Kyle's shoulder. "I think so."

"You boys knew he was here?" Miss Berenice asked in hoarse whisper. "How long—"

"Since I found him," Noah admitted.

Her hand flew up to her mouth, and she glanced around at the books. She didn't appear to see any of them. "Why? Why didn't you tell me? I helped you boys raise money for this place and you kept that from me?" She looked furiously between them, and Ellie put a hand on her arm.

"Mama," she said quietly, but Berenice brushed her off.

"He didn't want to scare you. Your father was a ghost, ma'am. He thought it…." Noah looked rueful for a moment and then continued. "He thought it might not be good for your heart."

"My aunt Fanny!" she said. "He didn't want to admit he'd been stuffed in the attic for fifty years."

"No, ma'am. He really didn't want to frighten you. Some God-fearin' folks don't take well to the idea of ghosts. It flies in the face of God," Kyle said. "I had a hard time with Mr. Henry for a while."

"Well, okay, I can see that. Seeing a ghost does make me wonder about what happens… you know, after. But Daddy, he was right here."

"Yes he was."

"Thank you, God," she whispered.

CHAPTER TWENTY-EIGHT

"BLACK FRIDAY. Sounds a little like All Hallows' Eve or Samhain—a devil's celebration," Kyle said as he sat on the counter watching Noah go through their inventory.

"All Hallows' Eve and Samhain are the same thing, and you lived through it—it's also called Halloween," Noah said and swiped the highlighter across the page twice in rapid succession. "But I guess Black Friday is rather evil, if you find consumerism a work of the devil."

"Wait, they are? But it was just a bunch of little kids dressed up like superheroes and stuff, asking for candy."

"I'm sure different people celebrate it in different ways, but here in Aster, that's what it means. Black Friday isn't a holiday, per se, and while people do it religiously every year, it's not exactly sacred." Noah snorted and flipped the page.

"So what is it?" He took the paper Noah offered with six highlighted books on the inventory list.

"Black Friday is the day after Thanksgiving where people lose their minds and have a marathon shopping day. This frenzy is exacerbated by stores like us, who drop prices drastically on things to get people in the door. Since we're so tiny, it'll be like standing in the back of a crowd jumping up and down yelling 'Pick me! Pick me,' but it's tradition, and it may help the store." Noah swiped the highlighter across another page.

"So you're picking books out to put on sale?"

"Yes, and then I need to put together some signs and flyers we're going to put in the local businesses here. Thad and Ananda are putting a couple up in ours. Thad is having some great sales, so maybe we'll get a bit of his overflow," Noah said.

"Why so many?" Kyle watched him flip another page.

"I just wanted to do one or two deep discounts and three moderate discounts in each section. We have lots of sections."

"Did your dad do this?" Kyle took another sheet.

"No, he figured folks would go into Douglasville to the retail stores, that they wouldn't have time to mess with us. We'll see. We're running out of time, and I'll do anything," Noah admitted.

"What can I do?"

"I'm going to print some sale tags. Could you put them on these books while I work on the flyers?"

"Sure," Kyle said and hopped down from the counter.

"Do you have any ideas on discounting coffee?" Noah asked as he finished highlighting the last page.

"We just got in a pumpkin spiced syrup. It's nasty, but people had been asking for it. I've been experimenting with different kinds of coffees. We could discount that, especially since it's something you only do in fall. We could also do hot cocoa, because we have a ton and we get it really cheap," Kyle offered, and Noah smiled at how knowledgeable Kyle had become since taking over the coffee bar. He really had a sense of what people liked.

"Okay. I'll add that we now have pastries from the diner. People love Miz Parker's pies and strudel." Noah headed back into the office and used a template his dad had designed to make sale tags. Kyle stood by quietly and then took them as they came off the printer onto mailing label stickers.

A deep sense of loss hit Noah then. It should have been his dad putting this stuff together. Or Henry should have been there lamenting that businesses were not only open on Thanksgiving, but making people work. Noah should be at his desk in New York, waiting for them to light up the Christmas tree at Rockefeller Center. He'd lost so much in the past month, it felt like he was on a boat listing from side to side. Sometimes he even had the nausea that accompanied it.

But then, he'd gained too. He had Kyle. He had Miss Edna. He had the goodwill of a small town that wanted him to succeed. The bookstore made him happy, like he was accomplishing something rather than churning out another manual. Being here made him want to write when the store was quiet. Just sit down by that big fireplace with a notebook and pen, not even a laptop, but simply listen to the quiet and put words to the page.

"I have the tags out," Kyle said from the doorway. "Are you okay?"

"It hit me for a minute. Maybe it's the holidays, but I miss my dad and I miss Henry."

"Sometimes I miss my family too. It wasn't all bad. On Christmas morning Mama would call us in to the living room. It was the one day of the year we ate until we were full and we didn't have to sit in church. Christmas was for celebrating Jesus in our own ways. Anyway, Mama would call us in and we'd each get one present. It was usually something we could use. Hope got a pretty dress one year that she loved. I usually got crayons or a coloring book. Another year I got a box as big as my head. That one lasted a while, though some of the colors were really strange." Kyle looked uncomfortable when Noah stared at him. "What?"

"Christmases growing up for me were just different, that's all."

"Different how?"

"I'd feel ashamed to tell you now, to be honest. But in a month, I'll show you," he said, breaking into a grin for the first time that day.

"Okay, I can wait. Did you finish the signs?"

"Yeah, the ones for the store anyway." He handed a stack of papers to Kyle, who grabbed a roll of packing tape on his way out to load the store with signs. It was nice not to have to do this alone.

Once he printed out the signs for the other stores, Noah had a sudden inspiration. He went back to the computer and searched for a coupon template. He made a hundred of them and used the paper cutter on the desk to slice them apart. Then he left Kyle putting together his coffee bar for the day and headed out along the street.

"Hello, dahling!" Thad drawled as Noah entered the store. Upon first inspection, it looked like a junk shop with eclectic pieces in seemingly random clusters all over the showroom floor. There were scenes in more clusters along the wall. An antique bed sat on an oriental-style rug, covered with an ancient quilt. There was a side table arranged next to it with an oil lamp and reading glasses. A bookshelf sat on the other side of the bed, covered in leather-bound books and knickknacks he was sure were older than he was. It felt like a colonial museum, except maybe for the pattern on the rug. Thad had an eye for design. He could have done well in any fancy New York gallery.

175

"Hi, Thad! I have the flyer. Where would you like me to hang it?" Noah asked, holding up the sheaf of papers.

"Right here, lovely." Thad gingerly handed him a gilded frame. "Hold this. No, turn it around, like that, yes."

Noah held the frame so the front faced him and saw a small white tag dangling from the frame on a string. Thad was putting his cheap paper flyer into a three-hundred-dollar frame. He slid the back into place and set the frame on a table at the front of the nearest display.

"That frame is the one object in this store that people pick up and look at most often before returning it to the table and moving on," he said with a laugh. "You should see some traffic from that." He read through the sign with a smile. "Pumpkin spice lattes? I'm so there."

Noah laughed and then asked, "Did I do okay with the sign?"

"Well, it's a little pedestrian for my tastes, but then they are a little gaudy by human standards. It looks bookish and offers practically free coffee. I think it's fine," he said. "Besides, you'll get better at the business part each year. Lord knows I did, honey. It was a wonder I stayed in business those first few years."

"If I'm still open next year," Noah sighed.

"You will be. Ananda has been saging herself silly over there on your behalf," Thad said, nodding to indicate a couple of box fans pointed out a window. "Never thought I'd have to use a box fan in self-defense."

"I appreciate all the help I can get. Speaking of, I have something else for you. I made some five-dollar-off coupons. I figured you could tell people if they spent a certain dollar amount or bought a certain thing, they could get some money off with us. Does that sound like a good idea?" Noah asked, desperate hope clear in his voice, counting out twenty-five of them.

"I think that's a great idea, maybe for the diner or Ananda's. Unless you have any books on antiquing or furniture history, I doubt they'll do much good here. I'll just hand them out. They don't need to buy anything," Thad said with a smile and a shrug.

"Thank you. I have some for Ananda and Miss Jessie too. Did you have anything you wanted me to put up for you?" Noah asked, anxious to keep going. For the past week, there'd been a tingling under his skin, an anxiety he couldn't shake. Maybe it was an allergic reaction to sage.

"Indeed I do." Thad turned and skipped back to his counter. He came back with a sign printed on what looked like parchment paper. There was a hole punched in the top, and Noah was going ask about it, but then Thad handed him a suction-cup-tipped arrow. "Hang it on this."

"You do have a flair," Noah said, amazed.

"It's a gift," he said, bridging his fingers under his chin with an angelic smile.

"It surely is," Noah laughed and headed on to the next store. His eyes had already started to sting before he ever opened Ananda's front door.

CHAPTER TWENTY-NINE

"NOAH HITCHENS, you're the one who invited all these people to my house. You boys move that table and chairs into the living room so they have a place to eat!" Miss Edna called from the kitchen, even over a disturbing clatter of pots against the stove. Noah grabbed one end of a large folding banquet table and motioned with his head for Kyle to grab the other. She must have gotten them from the church, along with the dozen or so metal folding chairs holding up the wall to his left. They set the table in an open space, and Kyle turned it on its side to fold down the legs while Noah popped into the kitchen.

"You don't mind, do you, Miss Edna? If you do, I'll take them to my place and we can—"

"Nuke some turkey pot pies?" she asked, one gray brow raised behind her big bifocals.

"I was thinking more along the lines of frozen pizza, but...." His grin was sheepish, and she put a hand on his cheek.

"Of course I don't mind, sweet boy. My Tommy and his wife couldn't get away anyway, and I like cookin' for folks. My dinette table just isn't big enough. You bringin' Jake over?" She turned to the oven and put her hands on the handles of a huge roasting pan.

"Miss Edna, please let me get that." Noah slapped her hands away gently and hefted the turkey from the fridge. Jesus, it must have weighed thirty pounds. "Holy... sh—moly, where did you even find a turkey that big?"

"At the grocery store, Noah. It's only a twenty-five-pound bird. You need to start working out," she told him as he set it on the counter with a bang.

"So people keep telling me," he mumbled and then glanced around at the counters littered with Corningware. "You know it's only six people, right?"

"And leftovers—that's what Thanksgiving is all about. Leftovers."

"Funny, I thought it was about community."

"Psssht. Community is for the young. When you're old, it's all about the leftovers." She smacked him on the arm and laughed.

"All of this isn't going to fit in your oven," he observed.

"Nope, but it will fit in yours and mine. Yours is already heatin' up." She pushed two pie plates and a tin of rolls into his arms. "Go put these on your counter until it's time for them to go in. Push 'em back so Jake doesn't get any fancy doggie ideas."

"Kyle!" Noah called, and pushed the rolls into his hands when he entered. "We need to drop this at my house and pick up Jake. I can't get the door with all this stuff in my hands."

"Amateur," Miss Edna said under her breath, and Noah laughed. They headed out the back door and across the big driveway to Noah's yard. Kyle pulled the gate open, and they carried their haul to the porch. Jake met them at the back door, nose already in the air. *Is that for me?*

"Back up, buddy," Noah said sternly, and Jake begrudged them a step into the kitchen, and then another. They put the pies and rolls on the back of the stove, which was already warm. Kyle turned back toward the door, but Noah caught his hand.

"Just a sec."

Kyle looked at him, and Noah stepped closer. "I wanted to steal a kiss before we went back. Is that okay?"

Noah gasped as Kyle bridged the distance in a step and brought his lips to Noah's in a fierce kiss. He loved the way Kyle touched his hair and his face, like Noah was something precious to him. Noah had never felt cherished. It was addictive.

They broke apart, breathless and hard. Noah was about to ask Kyle if he wanted to go upstairs, but Kyle patted his leg, and Jake followed him to the back door. Noah took a breath and grabbed a Coke from the fridge before following. It almost went to the front of his pants to kill his erection, but instead he took a cold drink, which helped as they made their way back across the yard.

Miss Edna had told folks to start showing up around two, but they made it there in varying degrees. Miss Sarah arrived about one thirty to help pull everything together. She went over to check the pies while Miss Edna put together the green bean casserole. Another casserole. Noah was pretty sure that's all Southerners did. Maybe they had casserole clubs. Or subscribed to the casserole of the month.

Ananda came by about a quarter till two with a Jell-O ring that matched her blazingly purple caftan. There were bits of red in the gelatin that coordinated with her red accessories. After a moment Noah remembered his manners and stopped staring. He tried to take the mold from her to set it in the kitchen, but she grabbed his arm.

"Oh, Noah, thank you for inviting me. Can I do something for you?"

"As long as it doesn't involve saging my store," he said, trying not to giggle as he recalled the look on Henry's face as he sneezed his way through her last visit. Then he sobered, remembering Henry was gone.

"No, child. I'd like to come and do a ritual at your house. Your father, he passed there."

"I know," he said warily. "But he's not still there. I would know."

"Oh, I don't want to upset you on such a glorious day. Let's talk about it later," she said and flittered off to the kitchen with her coordinated dessert. He rolled his eyes, and Kyle glanced at the door to the kitchen.

"What does she want to do to your house?"

"God knows," he said with a sigh. "Looks like we have enough chairs. Let's put the tablecloth on and see if Miss Edna wants us to set the table."

"God does what he does for a reason. He may not like Miss Ananda meddling with it."

"She's harmless, honestly. Just well-meaning and a little... odd." Noah grabbed the tablecloth and began to unfold it. He held the opposite end to Kyle, and they spread it over the long table. The cloth was the normal institutional white of any church linen, but Miss Edna had colorful dishes and placemats to warm up the table.

"Noah!" Miss Edna called from the kitchen. "Could you boys put the cloth on and set the table?"

Noah smiled at Kyle. "We're on it, Miss Edna!" he laughed and felt warmer than he had in ages.

THAD WANDERED in at five after two, fashionably late, he said. The platter he brought had stuffed mushrooms, bacon-wrapped scallops, and tiny striped cucumber crudités. He must have spent all morning putting it together, and Noah suspected that was why he was a little late. Well, and that he had to find a bow tie that coordinated with his sweater.

"Thad, that plate is beautiful," Miss Sarah crooned. "They're so delicate." He pulled back the plastic and she took one of the mushrooms. They could have been on any menu in New York.

"You boys are supposed to—" Miss Edna said, bustling into the room. "Oh, Thad! Hello, son, how are you?"

Thad's face clouded over for the smallest of moments, and then he handed the plate to Noah—shoved it at him, actually—and wrapped Miss Edna in a warm hug. He didn't say anything, he just hugged her.

Noah took the plate into the kitchen, and Kyle followed right behind.

"Is he okay?" Kyle asked as Noah piled placemats into his arms.

"Yeah. I get the impression Thad's family doesn't like that he's gay, and Miss Edna accepting him freely may have made him feel really good." Noah explained the best he could, but he guessed Kyle understood about families and their issues. Kyle's family didn't have issues, they had entire volumes.

Noah took plates out of the china cabinet, and together he and Kyle set the table while the others mingled around talking. Then everyone sat down at the table out of the way while Miss Edna and Noah brought in dish after dish of food. It covered the entire center of the eight-foot table. A magazine-perfect turkey, golden brown and succulent, sat at the head of the table, stuffing tumbling out of its… innards. Mashed potatoes and gravy sat in their place of honor next to it, then the green bean casserole, deviled eggs, rolls, cranberry sauce, and a bevy of other accoutrements.

No one seemed to want to be the first to break the plane of the perfect meal. Miss Edna took Noah's hand on her right and Miss Sarah's across the table. Each person followed suit until their little ring sat unbroken.

"Lord, we thank you for your blessings and your kindness in bringing us all together for this beautiful meal. We thank you for keeping our family here safe, and for our bounties and gifts. Please watch over us—Noah and Kyle as they start their new relationship together, Miss

Sarah and her new job, Thad and Ananda as they continue to bring beauty to our community. In Jesus's name we pray. Amen," she finished, surrounded by a chorus of "Amens" around the table. Kyle squeezed Noah's hand tight before letting go.

"Miss Edna," Thad said quietly from next to Ananda on the opposite side of the table.

"Yes, son?" she asked, handing the carving knife to Noah.

"Thank you," he whispered, like the sound was all he could manage.

"Honey, you are welcome at my table anytime," she said with a smile, taking the carving knife back from Noah when he just looked at her blankly. She stood up at the head of the table and sank the huge knife into the bird, cutting remorselessly down its back. Noah remembered what Cooper had said about Miss Edna being really good with guns. This was not a woman you wanted to mess with.

"You scare me a little, Miss Edna," Noah admitted.

"Fear is a healthy thing," she said with a smile.

CHAPTER THIRTY

MORNING CAME long before he wanted it to, but the shoppers would be out in full force well before the sun rose on this glorious day of consumer frenzy. He lay in bed for a long time, trying to prepare himself for what was coming. They were a week away from his deadline with the bank and nowhere near where they needed to be in terms of savings. As much hope as he held in his heart, very soon he'd have to come to accept that he would lose his father's store. No huge sales or gimmicks were going to get them to the total they needed. For now, he had to simply keep on pushing.

Noah threw the covers back and immediately wished he hadn't. Georgia had finally found the AC switch, and a chill swept the small room. Damn, he might actually have to break out a sweatshirt at this rate.

The hot shower did wonders for the tension in his back and shoulders. The stress of the last few weeks drained away with the sluice of water. It would come back, but for right then, he felt good. Out of the shower, he wrapped a towel around his waist and opened the door to head back to his room, nearly bumping into Kyle coming up the hall.

"Hi," Noah said, a little self-conscious when Kyle simply stared. The look started at his tousled hair and might have been a caress down his face, over his shoulder, along his hip. It gave Noah a shiver even without Kyle's hands on him. The hallway warmed, sending a blast of heat through him. And all of it without a word spoken.

Noah felt the blush hit his cheeks when his cock started to tent the towel, and he excused himself back into his bedroom. When the door closed, he leaned against it, letting the cold wood work to staunch his hot wood. He really didn't want to sit in here and jack off while Kyle showered across the... oh hell.

Thirty minutes later, after a quick cleanup and thorough hand-washing, Noah stood at the stove, putting together french toast for them both. It was one of the few things he could make really well. They were starting to spend a lot of money with Miss Jessie at the diner simply because he didn't know how to make anything more than grilled cheese. Miss Edna had promised to teach him, but she'd been busy with Thanksgiving preparations. Besides, she'd said, they had all the time in the world.

"Morning again," Kyle said as he came into the kitchen. "Can I help with anything?" He gave Noah a shy kiss.

"You're getting to be a good Southerner," Noah said with a laugh. "You can pour a couple glasses of milk. Maybe feed Jake? This'll be done in a minute."

Kyle started with Jake's food, and it felt so domestic, Noah's breath caught. He didn't know if Kyle would stay at the house with him after Cooper and Yeira had resolved the situation with his sister, but right then, he felt a contentment that had never been there before.

"Do you think it will be busy today?" Kyle asked when Noah sat a plate in front of him.

Noah sat down in his father's seat since Kyle had taken his. The kitchen looked different from this perspective. The world seemed to look different. Now he was the man of the house and everything fell to him. He wasn't sure he liked that seat.

"I don't know. My dad was always closed today. He took a four-day weekend at the store, and we always took a mini vacation somewhere." Noah had forgotten that somewhere in the chaos of life. It was information that sat in his permanent memory banks, like math or how to tie his shoes, but it bubbled to the surface then.

"What's a mini vacation?" Kyle poured syrup on his food and cut out large slices. He always cut every bit of his food before he started to eat. One of those eccentricities Noah was starting to learn.

"My dad and I would get in the car and go somewhere for a few days. Sometimes we went camping. Sometimes we went into Savannah to the shore. Sometimes we went to the gulf. I think we went to Birmingham once. Just some time away together. Looking back, I think he wanted to make sure I knew I was a priority." Noah watched as Kyle chewed thoughtfully for a moment.

"My family never did stuff like that. The only time we traveled at all was to go to another camp."

"I thought you stayed at that one," Noah said.

"No, they liked to move the elders around some. Keep them from getting too much power in one place. I heard my father telling Mama about it. We lived in a couple different places in Montana. All over, really." Kyle wolfed down a bite so large, he looked like a squirrel in a nut race.

"There are other camps?" Noah took a smaller bite.

"Sure. Light of God has little communes all over the world."

"What does that mean for you? For telling your story? I thought it was just that one little camp in Montana."

"I guess we're going to find out. She's going to be here in a little while, right?" Kyle said, his gaze fixed on Noah's. They looked at each other for a long moment; then Noah leaned forward and they shared a soft, syrupy-sweet kiss.

"Yeah, she's on her way from the airport now. She's going to get a hotel room and then meet us later."

WHEN NOAH unlocked the door to Stardust Books about half an hour later, they had a small gathering of about ten people outside waiting for the store to open. Kyle glanced at Noah, who walked through the door and turned off the alarm. Jake followed, accepting pets from a few folks like a king mingling with the common folk. Noah rolled his eyes and whistled for Jake to follow.

Kyle headed into the coffee bar, with most of the people coming in to follow him. The remaining few strolled up and down the aisles, looking at the books on sale. One guy asked about additional books in a series Noah had put on sale. Another asked if he'd ever read the set he was considering. One woman asked about *Harry Potter* for her daughter and got a resounding yes.

Kyle did a steady business of coffee and pastries. They'd had to roll one of the glass bookcases into the coffee bar to put the pastries on display, but it worked. They sold. Fancy coffee coupled with Miz Parker's hazelnut-filled turnovers in Aster—who'd have thought it?

His dad.

By about six that evening, the steady trickle of people had dried up. Kyle counted down most of his drawer, and Noah did the same. They left some change out in case they had a few last-minute shoppers, but Noah grabbed his Kindle and a leather chair. Kyle pulled out his coloring book and crayons and sat at a table near Noah. They hung out in the coffee bar, quiet and together, waiting for Hope to upend their lives.

CHAPTER THIRTY-ONE

A FARMER'S moon shone down on them as they lay side by side beneath the stars. Jake wallowed in the grass nearby, seemingly unimpressed by the celestial stage. The night had stilled around them as they held hands in the darkness. Noah mused that they'd never be able to do that in New York. First, you couldn't see the stars for the glow of the city; second, they'd get stepped on... or mugged. But here in Aster, they could lie in the grass and their biggest worry would be mosquitos, though as it neared the end of November, they weren't much of a problem. Kyle had been quiet the last few days since the interview, and Noah thought maybe lying out here alone would get him to open up.

"Do you think God is up there?" Kyle asked, breaking the silence. He turned his head to look at Noah, who saw the conflict in his face.

"I don't think anyone can know that for sure, but I like to think so. My dad wasn't real religious, though Miss Edna pushed us to church on Sundays. But I hope my dad is up there like the Bible says." Noah stroked Kyle's hand with his thumb.

"The Bible also says we're an abomination." He'd gone still, his hand limp in Noah's.

"The Bible is an interpretation written by men and retranslated a million times. People make it out to be the rule of law for Christianity, but really it's a book of fables. It's what you believe in your heart that matters. If God is perfect and we're created in his image, then we're exactly who he made us to be." Noah went up on one elbow, looking down at Kyle. He used his free hand to stroke Kyle's cheek.

"I'm scared," he whispered back. "Scared of how I feel. Scared of what I want."

"I'm not scared," Noah murmured against the still of the night. "I love you. I want to spend a long time showing you how much."

"Can you show me now?" The words were out, and Kyle's eyes widened like he hadn't meant to say them.

Noah leaned in closer, his eyes never leaving Kyle's. He saw fear there, but also a kind of quiet resolve. Something had clicked into place. As their lips met, he wondered what it was.

The kiss started slow, and Noah reined in the need to take it deeper. Kyle was still new to all of the emotions and conflicts of being in a gay relationship, and Noah didn't want to push him too far. But Kyle's fingers tugging at his hair made that self-control so fucking hard.

Kyle deepened the kiss, pulling Noah's body against his. He wrapped those strong stock-boy arms tighter as their bodies came together. Noah rubbed against Kyle, their hard cocks separated by nothing but denim.

A tiny whimper issued from Kyle, and Noah barely heard it over the rustling of trees, but it broke his resolve. He needed Kyle. Needed him like sunshine or air or water. He rolled, trying to take Kyle beneath him, hands tightening, hips moving. God, he wanted to make love right there in the grass, he wanted—

Jake nuzzled his nose against Noah's cheek. The cold and wetness shocked him, and he jerked back, but not far enough away that the old dog couldn't lick his face. Kyle started to laugh, moving from giggles to guffaws as Jake's weight threw Noah off balance and he landed on his back with the big dog on top of him.

"Jake, what the—" he sputtered through a face full of tongue and fur.

"We were getting some lovin', and he wanted some too," Kyle managed and sat up. He patted his chest, and Jake went to get some pets from him too.

"I know," he told Jake, "no one loves the poor puppy."

Noah snorted, which brought Jake's attention back to him. The big guy flopped down on his back, legs sprawled in the air, and commanded them to rub his belly. When their fingers touched on his soft fur, they kissed above him. The light in Kyle's eyes still shone brightly in the darkness, a spark that hadn't been there before.

Kyle rolled to his knees and then got to his feet. He reached a hand down to Noah, who took it and allowed himself to be pulled up. Jake huffed when they started toward the house, but he rolled to his paws and followed. He followed them through the back door, across the kitchen, and then up the stairs. He tried to follow them into the small bedroom, but the door closed in his little doggy face.

This was the room where Noah had figured out he was gay. It was the room where he'd learned how his body worked. It was the room where he didn't feel his father's watchful eye. Kyle dropped onto the bed while Noah checked the boxes Yeira had sent. He opened the one marked *bedside table* and pulled out the bottle he found. Leave it to Yeira to simply dump the contents into a box without caring what they were.

He set it on the table next to the bed and stood looking down at Kyle. Kyle wrapped his arms around Noah and nuzzled his stomach. He'd have been kissing Noah's skin if Noah had been shirtless. But that would come soon enough. For now, he wanted to take things as slowly as Kyle needed to.

"Are you sure?" Noah whispered and leaned down to kiss Kyle's hair.

In answer, Kyle scooted to the back of the bed, pulling Noah's hand until he climbed on top of the covers too. They lay down, side by side, facing each other, saying nothing, doing nothing except holding hands.

"Yes," Kyle whispered back.

Noah pulled Kyle into his arms, resting his head atop Kyle's, holding him gently in his childhood bed. He kissed Kyle's hair and lay still for a long moment. It had taken him most of his life, but Noah understood in that moment what love was.

Kyle disentangled himself enough to look up and catch Noah's lips in a slow, sweet kiss. It wasn't the burning, needful thing they'd shared in the grass, not yet. Instead it was a moment brimming with hope and quiet expectation.

"I don't know what to do," Kyle confessed between the tender meeting of their lips.

Noah ran a hand over his back, and the tension knotted under his fingertips. "You're gonna kiss me," he whispered against the shell of Kyle's ear, his chin resting against the rapid staccato of Kyle's pulse. "We're going to get tangled up in each other, naked and hot." Kyle's fluttering heart slammed against his skin. "I'm going to touch you everywhere, and you'll touch me. Then I'm going to make love to you. Just the two of us, heart, mind, body, and soul."

Kyle sucked in a breath and turned his head, coming off the bed to kiss Noah hard.

"There's no going back," Kyle said, pulling back. "I've been brought up my whole life to believe God will hate me for this."

"We don't have to." Noah sat up, pulling Kyle's hand into his. "We have all the time in the world."

"No, it's time to live my own life. I just have to trust that God made me this way for a reason." He pushed Noah back on the bed, positioning his body above.

"He did. To be with me." Noah met Kyle's lips as they came down toward his. Kyle cradled his cheek even as Noah twined his fingers in Kyle's shaggy hair. The kiss started soft, sweet—a promise. Noah strained to take things slow, but the fire inside him raged. He pushed up, insistent, though the kiss stayed soft. Their bodies rubbed together like tinder, igniting sparks. Kyle's kisses became more urgent, almost needy, their teeth bumping, limbs tangling, desperate to get closer.

Noah didn't want to make that first move to undress. Everything needed to happen at Kyle's pace. Tonight meant everything to him, and he didn't want to screw up. Even though the store wouldn't make it, he'd found in Aster what he didn't even know he was looking for.

Kyle's fingers tugged the hem of his T-shirt, pulling it up just a bit so he could run his fingers over the scant hair of Noah's abs. He tickled and teased, barely touching, stoking that fire they'd lit as they kissed. When Noah tried to mimic Kyle's touches, Kyle broke the kiss and pulled off his own shirt, giving Noah free rein to run trembling hands over his back and chest. The touch of Kyle's naked skin was a gift. The very best gift he'd ever received.

He started with long, slow strokes over Kyle's back, and their bodies settled together as if they were built to be that way. Kyle left one arm under Noah to hold himself up, but the other roamed ceaselessly across Noah's hip, the back of his thigh, up his spine. He shivered.

"Are you cold?" Kyle whispered against his lips.

Noah laughed and sat halfway up to do the awkward dance of removing his shirt. "Not even a little."

Noah's phone rang, but he ignored it. He didn't care about anything but Kyle.

He never knew that sex could be like this. Noah had always done it because it was fun and it got him off, but this—the power of it stole his breath, and they'd barely begun. Love took that feeling to exponential heights.

Noah rubbed a thumb over one of Kyle's nipples and felt a puff against his lips, a quiet "oh" of surprise. Kyle jerked his hips forward, pressing his hard cock into Noah's hip. Dear God. And when Kyle began to move in a subtle, unconscious rhythm against him, he ached.

Kyle fumbled at the button of Noah's shorts, and they broke apart for the moment it took them both to lose the last of their clothes. When they came together again, time moved slower, and Kyle was more hesitant. Almost like a kid who wants to ride his bike without training wheels but is terrified of the consequences.

He wouldn't ask again if Kyle was ready. Instead, he simply opened his arms and brought Kyle in, loved him without words, calmed him with his own surety. They kissed again, the heat building more quickly this time. Noah reached between them and touched Kyle's hard cock, circling it with his fingers, and Kyle gasped against his lips.

"Feels so different," he whispered between kisses.

"Than touching yourself?" Noah asked with quiet amusement. "It's worlds different."

Kyle's breath got heavy and harsh against his mouth while Noah stroked him. They stopped kissing for a moment, their foreheads touching, Kyle's eyes screwed tightly shut. Noah gave him some time to breathe and rolled his balls instead, palming them, caressing them with his fingers. He touched that secret spot behind them and relished the way Kyle writhed.

His own dick pulsed at the guttural sounds coming from Kyle's throat. Kyle had thrown his head back, surrendering utterly to Noah's touch. Like clay. They were about to sculpt something beautiful together.

"Please." That single word encompassed every bit of Kyle's need. Noah wanted to keep going, to pleasure Kyle in every way he could imagine, but Kyle's hand trembled atop his. This first time was about crossing that line. It was about embracing himself. Noah understood. He drizzled the lube into his hand and coated his dick.

"Do you want to—" he started to ask, but Kyle pulled Noah on top of him in clear instruction. He kissed Kyle, slow and easy, trying to quell the trembles in Kyle's body. Noah nestled himself between his lover's legs and let their bodies touch everywhere, skin to skin.

"I love you," Kyle murmured against his neck as he found the entrance to Kyle's body with his fingers, rubbing with the residual lube.

"I love you too." Noah slid his dick back and forth across the tiny hole as Kyle's hips began to rock against his. Noah reached down and used two fingers to stretch Kyle open and slide the tip of his cock inside. The warmth caused a shiver down his spine. He opened his fingers a little farther and pushed in a little deeper. Then he stroked Kyle's cock between them, urging Kyle on. The tight grip of Kyle's body took his breath away when he slid halfway inside him.

A sharp cry escaped Kyle's lips.

"Are you okay?" Noah asked, pulling back to see his face.

"Hurts some, but…."

Noah held himself up on one forearm and used his free hand to coax Kyle's limpening dick hard again. Kyle moaned as Noah's palm slid over the head. He shivered as Noah went just a bit deeper. Then he jerked faster, and Kyle's hips bucked.

He captured Kyle's lips in a kiss and started to move.

They came together again and again, lips, tongues, hips, hands—everything in a perfect, timeless rhythm.

His breaths came sharper, faster as the knot in the pit of his stomach tightened and coiled. But he needed to wait. Kyle had to—

"Fuck," he cried and buried his face in the crook of Kyle's neck, embarrassed a bit at his own lack of control. He came hard and deep, with a cry equal parts jubilation and frustration. He could feel Kyle's breath against the back of his neck, harsh but quiet.

Noah took just a moment of respite in Kyle's arms, kissing his neck, whispering breathlessly. He slid down the bed, kissing his way down Kyle's body. Kyle writhed under his mouth, his tongue on his nipples, first one and then the other. Noah felt his moan as he moved down across his chest and abs. As he rounded Kyle's hip, he took his lover's cock in his hand and stroked. He used rich, long strokes, like an artist of Kyle's pleasure.

Kyle's back arched, his fingers tangled in Noah's hair.

"Noah," he moaned, long and loud, so that Noah's name was nearly indistinguishable from his need. His hips came up from the bed to meet Noah's hand, and Noah tightened his grip. Noah rubbed his dick from root to tip, twisting his fist over the head, and Kyle nearly begged. Noah could hear the plea in the pitch of his voice.

Noah jerked him faster, unrelenting.

The wetness hit his hand just as Kyle cried out his name. Stickiness splattered over his stomach, and his body stiffened, jerked, as his breaths grew harsh.

"Stop, okay, okay," Kyle laughed and pulled back from Noah's touch. Noah laughed and wiped his hand on the sheets. He leaned down and placed a gentle kiss on Kyle's sweaty brow. Kyle pulled him down and hid his face in Noah's shoulder.

"That was…."

"Amazing."

CHAPTER THIRTY-TWO

NOAH LAY in the bed his parents once shared and played with Kyle's hair as he slept. He was on his side facing Noah with a slack, dreamy expression. They'd moved after making love because Noah's old twin wasn't big enough for them to sleep together, and Noah wasn't going to sleep apart from Kyle again. Even now, Noah wanted to kiss him, but he waited. He'd been having nightmares since the break-in, and Noah didn't want to wake him for a kiss they had their entire lives to share. He watched Kyle sleep for another minute or so and had decided to get out of bed and rustle up some breakfast when his phone rang on the bedside table.

He reached for it, trying to get to it before it woke Kyle, and slid the button across the screen on the second ring.

"Hello?" he asked quietly.

"Have you seen it? It's everywhere," Yeira screeched into the phone.

Kyle's eyes flew open at the sound, and he looked around wildly. Noah put a hand on his arm.

"Have I seen what? I'm still in bed." He threaded his fingers through Kyle's and Kyle snuggled closer, laying his head on Noah's chest.

"The story. It's gone viral. It's all over the internet." Her voice held the excitement of a kid whose Christmas had come a month early.

Noah sat up in bed. "When did it air?"

"Last night during the nine o'clock news. You didn't watch it?"

"You didn't tell me!" he cried.

"I didn't have cell service, so I called from a land phone. You didn't answer, so I left you a voicemail!" she cried back.

"You filmed Kyle's interview. He's in it, isn't he?"

"Yes, of course he is, but—"

"They're going to come for him now, Yeira. You needed to warn us. I have to go, I have to call Cooper." He hung up on her without another

194

word and googled the phone number for Aster's police department. It went straight to Cooper.

"Cooper Thompson."

"Cooper, it's Noah," he choked out, climbing out of bed.

"Are you okay? Did something happen?"

Noah jogged a couple feet down the hall back to his childhood room, where all of his clothes were. They hadn't gotten around to moving them. "My reporter friend called. She said that the thing with Kyle aired last night." He pulled open a drawer, looking for a shirt.

"I know, I saw it."

"Did everyone fucking know it was on but me?" Noah growled, ripping an NYU T-shirt from the stack.

"There were commercials for it during the game."

"Yeah, 'cause I watch a lot of football. Anyway, do you think he's in danger?" Noah asked, searching frantically for pants.

"I think he's been in danger since his sister showed up looking for him," Cooper said. "Did you have the new locks installed at the store?"

"Yeah, not that it's going to make much difference when the bank comes to take it."

"How many days do you have left?"

"Two, and the circus that's about to hit us because of this story isn't going to help. Yeira said that it's gone viral."

"Fantastic. That means gawkers coming to town. I'll make sure we have extra guys in the rotation for a few weeks. What a mess." Cooper sighed.

"Yeah, but he's worth it," Noah said simply.

"We'll keep him safe, Noah. I failed you when you were a kid. It won't happen again." Noah could hear the shame in his voice, and then the call disconnected.

"What does that mean?" Kyle asked from the doorway.

"It means that millions of people are watching the story Yeira put together, which includes your interview. Your face is all over the internet." Noah took his clothes and headed for the bathroom.

Kyle followed. "What are we going to do?"

"First we're going to take a shower, and then we're going to work. We'll just take everything as it comes, but I'm going to ask Miss Edna and one of her rifles to hang out with us today." Noah grabbed his hand and pulled him into the bathroom.

An hour later they were showered, fed, and piled into the truck with Jake, Miss Edna, and two of her handgun friends. Miss Edna said that rifles were good from a distance, but they weren't practical for close-up defense. Noah nodded at her, wide-eyed.

"My Frank, rest his soul"—she crossed herself—"taught me how to defend myself. 'You never know what could happen,' he'd say. I had a kid or two try to break in over the years, but I've never had to use a gun on a person. Doesn't mean I can't."

"Thank you for coming with us. God knows what we're in for today if Kyle's cult shows up. After Hope and her friend couldn't grab him, they could already be on their way. We haven't heard from them since the break-in. They may be hiding, but the news story could exacerbate a confrontation."

"I know. Miss Norma has a couple of guys from the church comin' to keep an eye out in shifts too. She cares a lot about you both."

"This is a good little town," Noah said, pulling up in front of the store, which was already crowded with people.

"What in the world?" Miss Edna asked, leaning forward in her seat.

"Maybe they're here to buy books," Noah offered.

"They're here to see the freak," Kyle said, finally joining the conversation.

Noah turned to look at him. He was facing the window with Jake half in his lap. The old dog snuggled against him, taking the brunt of Kyle's frustration and anxiety in rubs and pets along his back. Such a trooper.

"You're not a freak," Noah said sharply, but Kyle just shrugged, his eyes still on the crowd.

"Make 'em pay for the privilege," Miss Edna said. "Paying customers only."

Noah laughed.

"I'm dead serious, Noah. I'll man the register. I can keep my guns under the counter within reach. You tell anyone who wants to come in that they have to buy something. Coffee from Kyle, or a book. If they're going to be stupid about gawking, use it as an opportunity to make some money to help save the store. Hell, we could even put up Save the Store signs and take donations at the door for entry."

"You want me to charge a cover to get into a bookstore." Noah's eyebrows were nearly in his hairline.

"Look at them, Noah. They're already lined up outside."

Noah glanced over, and sure enough, for the first time in the bookstore's long history, it had a line for entry down to the end of the block. He put his head down on the steering wheel.

"Dad would hate that," he said.

"Your daddy ain't here, son," Miss Edna reminded him.

"I'm sorry," Kyle said quietly. "I never meant for any of this to happen. I can leave—"

"No. We do this as a family," Noah said firmly. Jake woofed in agreement, or because he wanted to go out and play with the people, it was hard to tell.

"I'm going to go unlock the door, relock it, and then head around back. Miss Edna, why don't you pull the truck around to the alley and you guys come in the back. I don't want you to have to deal with this mob, and if they're focused on me, maybe they won't go to the alley until y'all are inside," Noah said, watching the milling people as they all stared at the truck. It was weird, like watching a zombie movie where they're all after you.

"You ready?" Miss Edna asked.

Noah sighed. "As I'll ever be." He climbed down out of the truck, and Miss Edna did the same. After she came around the back, he took her hand and helped her into the driver's seat. She used the lever to pull it forward and took a glance back at Kyle.

"I'll be right there," she said.

"Kyle, go ahead and stay in the office until I come back for you. Miss Edna's right. If these people are going to be stupid about it, let's make them pay for it. There's got to be at least a hundred people, and those are just the ones waiting at the door."

"Okay."

Noah leaned in. "Hey, if you don't want to do this, Miss Edna can take you home. There's absolutely no reason for you to go in there. None at all."

"No, I can't run from it. It's going to happen one way or another."

"I love you," Noah said. "If it turns into a thing, we can always leave. Just grab Jake and leave."

"Leave the bookstore? But you've worked so hard to—" Kyle sat forward, and Miss Edna ducked to get out of the way of their heated conversation.

"You are my priority now. Being in love, being in a relationship, sometimes that means making choices," he said quietly just above the din of the milling crowd. He didn't mention the pending foreclosure—he couldn't. It caught in his throat like a dead frog.

Okay, ew.

"That's right, son. No matter what, family comes first," Miss Edna chimed in. "Now, if you two are done, let's get this shit show started."

"Miss Edna!" Noah said with feigned shock.

"What else would you call it?"

Noah laughed and stepped onto the sidewalk as the big truck rolled backward. Then he turned toward the store and the people gathered in front of it. Steeling himself, he pulled the I Heart New York keychain from his pocket.

"I know why you are all here," he said, stepping up onto the sidewalk, level with the gawkers. "And I'm sure that you all want to help him get back on his feet after such a terrible ordeal." Noah saw a few heads bobbing up and down. "He sells coffee inside. If you want to help, grab a book and a cup. Are we clear?"

A few people nodded. Others said, "Yeah." Some just looked at him like aliens were climbing out of his ears. God, he wished Henry were here.

Noah turned his back on them, praying none of them were there with weapons. He didn't think to scan for them. What if someone had come to hurt Kyle? Miss Edna should work the coffee station with Kyle, he decided as he turned the key. People pressed in behind him, and he pushed them back with a step.

"We open at nine," he called sharply, slipped in the door, and slammed it in their faces. He relocked it and disarmed the alarm. "Jesus," he muttered.

The books welcomed him as he wandered down the first aisle. He ran his fingers along their spines. God, he'd miss this place. His whole life had been spent surrounded by books. It hurt in ways he didn't even know he could hurt. They'd come up with half the money, but it still wasn't enough. Noah laid his palm on the counter and took a centering breath.

Maybe he shouldn't open the door.

Noah looked up at the crowd of people just past the glass. The bank had given him until the end of the month, which was the day after tomorrow. He was still over twenty-five thousand away from his goal with no way to make that kind of cash. The people outside wanted to stare at Kyle like he was an animal in a zoo. Noah thought of Henry, stuffed in his attic like garbage for over fifty years. Maybe he shouldn't open. They should walk away.

He glanced at the door again and blanched. Hope was framed in the glass. Noah almost ran to the back to get Kyle and run, but when she stepped aside, he saw Yeira standing behind her. Surprise warred with fear—he thought she'd gone back to New York. The clock above the door said it was still a quarter of nine. If he opened the door, he might not be able to let them in without everyone else swarming through the door, and to be honest, he wasn't sure he wanted to let them in at all.

Go around back to the alley, he told Yeira in a text.

As he watched, she glanced down at her phone and then took Hope by the arm. They disappeared into the small mass of humanity. Noah ran then, getting through the office to the back door. It nearly came off the hinges as he ripped it open. Miss Edna's hand flew to her throat.

"Hurry," he said as Jake bounded in through the door.

"What is it?" Kyle asked as Noah shut the door quickly.

"Your sister is here. She's with Yeira. They're coming around to the back now."

Kyle paled. Miss Edna took his hand and led him into the office just as they heard a knock at the back door.

What the hell else?

Noah gave Jake's head a quick rub and sent him off into the office before opening the door. Hope and Yeira scrambled inside, and Noah saw a couple of people running toward them from the mouth of the alley. Once they were over the threshold, he slammed the door behind them and locked it.

"What is she doing here?" Noah demanded of Yeira, who straightened and stood slightly in front of Hope as if shielding her from Noah's accusations. She stretched to every bit of her five-foot-seven-inch height, her black hair pulled back into a hair tie and her flawless olive skin scrubbed clean.

"I was on my way here from the airport and found her on the side of the road next to a broken-down truck. A teenaged girl alone on the side of the road, of course I stopped to help. When I saw the truck had Montana plates, I figured out who she was. She recognized me from the news and was none too glad to see me but really didn't have any better options. I told her I'd take her to her brother." Yeira glanced at Hope, whose dark eyes were petulant. Her hair was like out of control flames on her head, clothes unkempt, and Noah couldn't even guess the last time she'd eaten.

"So she could finish the job her and her friend started?" Noah took a step between them and the office.

"He's not my friend," Hope growled at him. "He's my husband. Has been since I was twelve years old and my brother deserted me. Now, bookstore man, where is he?"

Noah watched the rage building in her and considered sending them both away, but Kyle and Hope needed to get past this. They were family. Whether they stayed family after today was another question.

"Let me ask him if he wants to see you. Stay right there," he warned. "If you try to hurt anyone, Miss Edna has a gun."

"The old woman?" Hope scoffed.

"I wouldn't mess with gun-toting Southern women," Yeira advised with eyebrows raised.

Damn straight.

Noah slipped into the office and wrapped his arms around Kyle. "She wants to see you. Do you want me to send her away?"

"No. I want to see her. I have to know." Kyle's anxiety spread to Noah, and his hands tingled from it. More than he didn't want the misery in his own life right then, he didn't want Kyle to be hurt by his sister or anyone else. He kissed Kyle gently to give him strength.

"You're a sodomite?"

Noah turned to see Hope standing at the edge of the room with Yeira's restraining hand on her arm. Kyle stiffened and stepped away, his face as red as his hair. Miss Edna rested a hand in her pocket, and Noah stepped back to stand next to her.

The siblings faced off in the middle of the room. Jake went to stand in front of Kyle. He didn't growl or bare his teeth. He simply sat there to protect his new friend. Hope's hands were fisted at her sides and her face was red as well, but for her, it seemed to be rage. She threw off Yeira's hand.

They didn't speak for a long moment but simply watched each other. Kyle regarded her warily but with a soft affection in his eyes. Hope stared back with pure hatred, and Noah knew it would not end well.

"Hey, little bit. Guess you're not so little anymore," Kyle said and tried to smile. His hands were clenched around the back of one of the dinette chairs, like he didn't trust himself to stand on his own.

"You have no right to call me that anymore, Samuel," Hope spat back. "You lost that right when you abandoned our family and stole those papers from mother!" Her voice had risen to a yell. Jake stood up and moved closer to Kyle.

"Mother put me on the bus with a box. She sent me to Aunt Mary's in Chicago. I didn't steal anything," he said, like stealing was a cardinal sin. He rested a hand on Jake's head to calm the old dog, let him know that everything was okay. Noah decided not to take the chance that it would be and slipped his phone out of his pocket.

"Where you gave yourself a systemite name and betrayed us," she said, her voice like ice.

"I was fifteen and our mother told me to run. I didn't know what to do. What was I supposed to do?" Kyle pleaded.

"You could have taken me with you, Samuel," she cried. "You knew what would happen to me. You knew, and you did nothing."

Kyle stayed quiet, and Noah saw the shame fill his face.

"Do you want to know what they did, Samuel? To me? To her?" She took a step forward, and Jake let out a low growl.

Hope just glared at the dog, then at her brother.

"No," Kyle whispered.

"They knew she'd sent you with something that could hurt them. They didn't know exactly what, not at first. Not until they tortured her. The entire camp heard her screaming. I covered my ears and Uncle Clive pulled me against him, into his lap, and held my hands so I had to hear. He said it was instructive. His member was hard against my back the whole time. He liked it when she screamed. He liked it when I struggled." Tears ran down her cheeks, and she wiped them away angrily.

Kyle's face was white, like the skin had come away and it was nothing but polished bone. He didn't say anything and Noah wasn't sure he even breathed. Noah finished typing the text to Cooper with slow movements that he hoped no one would notice. Then he hit Send.

Yeira closed her eyes and bowed her head. She'd told Noah of her own experiences in Syria before her mother had taken her and ran. They escaped to the United States, but not before paying their own price. Noah's hands trembled on the phone. The world was a cruel place.

"And now I come to find that the brother who abandoned me to soulless men is now a sodomite whore."

"Hope," Yeira said, trying to deflect the girl's rage.

"Don't you speak to me. You and my heathen brother destroyed everything. I saw the news. I saw the government raided the camp. They have probably taken Father and locked him up somewhere. I have no home. I have no family. I have nothing." She'd stopped crying, and the emptiness in her voice chilled Noah.

"You could stay here, with—" Kyle started, but she spat a laugh at him.

"What, with you? After everything you've done? I never want to see you again."

"Then why are you here?"

"Because I hate you. You're a sinner. A child of Satan. A blasphemer, and now a sodomite. I wanted to look upon you just once to remind myself what evil is."

Kyle choked back a sob. Her cruelty was swift and sharp like a blade to the heart. Noah wondered if, out of that tirade, it was the *sodomite* that hurt him worst.

No one moved or spoke. Even Jake stood quietly between them, his growl dying in their silence.

It made the pounding on the back door even louder when it came.

They jumped, and Hope scrambled into a corner, cowering and throwing her arms up in defense. Yeira stared at her with dawning horror, recognizing the ingrained response. Noah turned for the door.

"Back away from this door now, or I swear to God, I'll take you all to jail and let you sit there until you have some damn sense."

Noah relaxed at the sound of Cooper's angry voice through the door and unlocked it. He didn't open it—he let Cooper decide that timing so the people who'd found the back door wouldn't rush them all.

He stepped in and slammed the door behind him. The man was in uniform, but it looked disheveled, like someone had been grabbing at him.

"Jesus Christ," he said.

"Cooper Thompson!" Miss Edna cried from her place next to Kyle. She hadn't spoken through Hope's tirade, but she'd moved to take Kyle's hand in hers.

Hope had both hands over her mouth and her eyes were wide. "Blasphemer," she whispered when her hands fell away.

"I'm sorry," he said sheepishly. "But these people out here are crazy. Literally insane. I have never seen anything like this. What the he—" He glanced at Miss Edna and caught himself. "What is happening?"

"It was the news last night. Those people are here to see Kyle," Noah explained.

"Gawk at him," Miss Edna said as Hope muttered the word *Samuel*.

"You have some things to answer for, Miss...." Cooper let it trail off so she could fill in the blank.

"Hope," she said. "Just Hope."

"Please be gentle with her," Kyle pleaded. "She's been through so much, and it was the man with her who set the fire. I guarantee it. Hope loves animals."

"You don't know anything about me," Hope spat at him.

"So you set the fire?" Cooper asked.

"Don't say anything," Yeira told her. "We need to get you a lawyer."

"I didn't set any fire. I didn't know he'd set a fire. We just came to get Samuel and bring him home," Hope said, and then a truly frightening smile lit up her face, her eyes—even her hair—seemed to be set aglow from it. "Father wanted to... speak with him."

Kyle blanched and then turned a little green. Noah crossed the room and took his hand before he could fall.

"Noah, is this one of the individuals who broke into your store?" Cooper asked with a hard look at Hope.

"Yes, Officer Thompson, she is. I saw her trying to take Kyle, and then she fled."

"You need to come with me," Cooper told her and tried to take her arm. She jerked away violently.

"Officer, please. We'll both come with you quietly. Just don't touch her, and I wouldn't try to restrain her either. She's a traumatized victim of severe violence. She won't try to run, will you, Hope?" Yeira asked gently.

"Where would I go?" Hope asked, all of the defiance and glee from the moment before draining from her like sewage on the floor.

"Hope," Kyle said, and she didn't even look at him.

"Can we go?" she asked Cooper, who nodded.

"The car is right outside. I'll open the back door and you can both slide in. I'll keep the people back." Then he turned to Noah. "Fred and Jonas are out front. They're going to help you with the people."

"Thank you."

"I sent that box over to the FBI. They raided the camp last night just before the story broke," Cooper told Kyle. "Your father is in custody."

Hope choked back a sob.

"Thank you, sir," Kyle said and turned into Noah's arms.

"I'm going with her. She needs a lawyer, and I have a friend who might be able to help." Yeira and Hope followed Cooper to the door. Before he could pull it open, Hope turned on Kyle.

"I hope you're proud of yourself, brother. You've destroyed us."

Cooper opened the door and pushed them both through before she could say another word.

"I don't know what to say," Noah whispered.

Miss Edna whistled and took Jake out to the front of the store. Jake looked up at Noah and Kyle first and then followed.

"There's nothing anyone can say. She's right. I destroyed them."

"But think of all the kids in that place you saved from what happened to you and Hope? Think about—" Noah stopped when Kyle put a finger to his lips.

"God wasn't in that place. I understand that now. I don't regret doing it. My pain is Hope's pain. I should have done something for her sooner. I should have gone to the police." Kyle jerked his body out of Noah's arms and bent over the sink and dry heaved.

Noah took a breath, trying to not to cry. He needed to be strong for Kyle. He needed to be a grown-up. "You were a teenage boy. There was nothing you could do. Your aunt Mary could have called the police, but she didn't. Please don't take this on yourself," Noah finished in a whisper.

"Noah, we need to open before they come through the glass," Miss Edna called from the counter. "It's getting kind of ugly out there."

"We're not going to open," Noah told Kyle. "I don't care what else happens now. I'm not going to let those people near you." He turned for the main part of the store, but Kyle grabbed his arm.

"No, let's just do it. I have to face it. Better to get it out of the way now." Kyle grabbed a paper towel and wet it down in the sink. He washed his face with it, and then the back of his neck.

"Better?"

"A little."

Noah leaned forward and kissed him gently. "Whatever happens, we're in it together."

"Together," Kyle agreed.

They held hands as they shuffled from the office to the main part of the bookstore, neither excited about opening the doors. But Kyle was right. People would just keep coming back if they didn't get their train-wreck kind of look. At the junction of the rooms, Kyle turned left and headed for the coffee bar while Noah kept on toward the door. He heard Jake pattering behind him, and he turned to see Miss Edna take her place behind the counter.

They were ready.

The chimes rang as he opened the door. They kept ringing over and over as each person came through, letting the door close just enough to hit them in the spaces between. A few decided to be inconspicuous and headed for different sections of the store, but most decided they were going to die without a cup of coffee and made a beeline for Kyle. Noah followed and stationed himself behind the counter, taking money and keeping Kyle stocked with cups and lids.

"What was it like?" A teenaged boy not much younger than Hope had made his way to the counter. He was the first to break the silence with Kyle. Others were bubbling excitedly at one another in line, but no one wanted to be the first to be intrusive. Southern manners, God forbid.

"What was what like?" Kyle asked, filling his order of iced coffee. He didn't look up, just concentrated on loading ice into the cup like he knew what was coming and didn't want to see it hurled at him.

"What was it like being in a cult?" the boy asked, like it should have been obvious to anyone with half a brain what he wanted to know, what he presumed he was entitled to ask. A hush fell over the waiting patrons, a blanket of silence thrown over the crackle of embers.

"I imagine it was like growing up in prison," he said, pouring coffee into the cup. "People told you what to do, you did it, and you couldn't leave. What more can I tell you? I have nothing to compare it to. We didn't play video games or eat junk food. We worked. We prayed."

"Next," Noah called, bringing the next wide-eyed tourist. He didn't recognize any of these people. Aster folk already knew Kyle—they had more tact.

At nine o'clock that night, Noah locked the door with a low moan of exhaustion. People had been filing in and out all day. Kyle had run out of coffee at midday, but the flow of humanity didn't stop. When Noah reminded them that it was a retail establishment, they simply bought magazines instead.

He'd ushered the last two out after they'd been "browsing" for nearly three hours. However, they did buy nine books between them, so he couldn't really complain about that.

Noah had brought down a stool for Miss Edna from Henry's apartment upstairs. He didn't really think the old guy would mind—especially not now. She perched on the edge of it, balancing the register.

When he walked back through the store, he saw Kyle counting out the money from his stand. It wouldn't be enough, so it didn't matter. The foreclosure notice had already come. They'd start packing up the inventory tomorrow. Maybe he could sell the stock on Amazon or eBay. There were a lot of antiques throughout the store too, stuff his dad had probably bartered with Thad to get.

His dad.

The memory of him sitting there in that big chair by the fire, reading to Noah, came unbidden, along with tears that he didn't feel worthy to shed. He'd lost his father's store. Ebenezer would have been appalled at his abject poverty.

"Noah...."

Noah turned to see Miss Edna smiling at him. "We brought in six thousand today."

He gaped at her. He didn't think they'd done six thousand in any of the weeks he'd been there. "Are you serious?"

"Yep. What about you, Kyle?" she called into the room. The sound echoed off the rows of shelves. Noah heard something from the other room, and they waited.

"Kyle?" she called again.

"Hold on, please. I'm almost done." He sounded studious, like he was concentrating hard on the task at hand. It took another full two minutes for him to answer.

"I have four thousand," he said, coming into the room and holding up a box. He sidled over to the counter and put it carefully next to the register.

"That's ten thousand, Noah. Is that enough?" Miss Edna asked, hope plain in her expression. He hated to snuff it out. He hated it almost more than losing the store.

"No. They're going to call the loan soon. The payoff amount was a little over fifty thousand dollars. That money on the counter, plus everything we've made over the last six weeks, plus the rare books and first editions we sold, plus what was left over from Dad's insurance and stuff makes almost thirty-five thousand. We aren't going to make it." His voice hitched, and he looked away. "Kyle and I will start packing up the stock tomorrow. We can store it at the house until I can sell it. The notice said we have fourteen days to pay in full, plus penalties and interest, or vacate. That's not a lot of time."

"I'm sorry, Noah," Miss Edna said, her eyes sparkling with tears. "What will you do?"

"I have no idea."

CHAPTER THIRTY-THREE

"HOW ABOUT this, Noah?" Kyle asked, holding up some Christmas decorations he'd found in one of the storerooms: pine garland with red bows, candles, and a host of little Santas, reindeer, and gingerbread men.

"Uhm. I don't know, maybe Ananda or Thad want some of it. Just put it in the front corner. We'll have them come over later and check it out." He went back to packing up the last of the children's shelves. He'd planned to donate those books to the local school. No point trying to compete with Amazon and sell them. Maybe he'd donate the rest to the library after he declared bankruptcy.

James had rescinded his offer when he found out they weren't going to make it. A building in foreclosure was a steal, he'd told Noah with a horrible chuckle. Handley was ready to sell it to him for the balance on the loan. Noah didn't even know how that was legal.

He sighed, stood up, and stretched. His back popped painfully, and he grabbed another empty box from the pile Thad had brought over from his last few shipments. Hopeful but pragmatic, he had started saving boxes in anticipation of packing up the store. Noah was grateful. He headed over to the classics section and started with the books on the bottom of the first shelf. Then the next, and the next.

"Noah, I found some of Granddaddy's records upstairs. I think… would you mind—" Ellie called from the bottom of the stairs.

"Take them, Miss Ellie. He would have wanted you to have them."

"Noah, there's some personal papers and stuff back here in the office. What do you want me to do with those?" Miss Edna called from the back.

Noah sighed. It was just too many decisions. "Put them in a box. I'll go through them later," he called, weariness evident in his voice.

The top shelf was one of the glass-fronted sections where he'd found the first editions. They were all empty now except this one. He'd gone through each one, pulling the first editions, selling his father's precious books one by one. In the end, it was for nothing.

He used the I Heart New York keys to open the glass. Only one book remained, lying on its side on the bare shelf. Noah wrapped his fingers around it and pulled it down carefully, lovingly. It was the copy of *A Christmas Carol* he and his father read every year at Christmas, sitting in front of that electric fireplace. They'd done it for as long as he could remember. It was their thing. A tear slipped down his cheek as he looked at the book's cover. The novel appeared old but in great condition because his father had kept it that way, because it was theirs.

Noah opened the book and slid his finger down the title page. He noticed the writing there and cocked his head to look at it. The book appeared to be signed, but by whom he couldn't imagine. He might just be imagining that it said *Charles Dickens*. The pages flipped back easily. Noah checked the republication date and gasped. There wasn't a republication date.

It was a first edition.

His father had spent every Christmas reading to him out of a first-edition Charles Dickens novel.

"Oh my God," Noah said. Miss Edna stood up from where she'd been cleaning under the front counter and looked at him. He could only imagine how his face looked, because she came running over.

"Son, what is it?" She put a hand on his arm.

"Dad read this book to me every Christmas. It was our tradition. We sat right over there," he said, indicating the leather chair now stacked with books and knickknacks waiting to be packed.

"I remember. He looked forward to it," she said fondly. "So what's wrong?"

"This book is a signed first edition. He read to me from a signed first edition, and he kept it when things got bad financially. Because it was our thing."

"Okay…." The word came out more as a question than a conclusion.

"If this is authentic, it could be worth a fortune. An absolute fortune," he finished in a whisper.

"How would we know?"

"Well, it looks like it was signed to an Edward Stirling. Kyle!" he called. Kyle looked up from the Christmas lights he'd managed to wrestle into a box. "Could you get my laptop and google Edward Stirling for me?"

Kyle dropped the lights and headed for the counter.

"Let's check my dad's office. Maybe there's something authenticating this book." He grabbed Miss Edna's hand, and together they hurried into the back office.

"I put all his papers in this box. Wait—" She started digging through, searching. "There was an envelope here with your name on it. I didn't think anything—here it is." She pulled out a sealed business-size envelope and handed it to him. He hefted it, and it felt like more than a sheet of paper.

When he opened it, a small key fell into his palm. Noah set it on the desk and pulled out the piece of paper. He opened it with trembling fingers.

Hey, kiddo—

We just finished our annual Christmas Carol *reading, and you're curled up asleep at the end of the sofa. I look at you and I see my little five-year-old boy instead of the twenty-five-year-old man you are now. You're wearing a T-shirt and sweats instead of your reindeer pajamas, and you need a shave, but I still see my little boy. You're older and smarter and more sophisticated, but you still quoted the line at the end of the story just the way you have since you were five. You've changed—but you haven't. And that makes me so proud of you. You're still good.*

I was worried for a long time. That I wouldn't be a good parent, that you needed more motherly influence than Miss Edna and the church ladies could give you, that you'd get screwed up by my failures. And when I realized you were gay—it didn't change how I loved you, but it did scare me to my toes. As hard as most people had it, you were going to have it that much harder. I didn't want that for you. I never wanted things to be hard, let alone that hard.

I want you to have whatever you want, to be able to do whatever you love to do. I couldn't give you much growing up except attention and love, and I hope that was enough. The fact that no matter what was going on in your life, you always—always—managed to get home for Christmas told me your heart was in the right place. You've never done anything to make me ashamed of you. I hope that's reciprocal.

Old Doc Simmons told me today that I have a bad ticker. A time bomb is actually what he said. So if something happens to me, and it must have if you've found this, you'll inherit the bookstore. I DO NOT want you to keep it if you don't want it. I know you love New York and your life there. Don't stay here unless it's something you really, really want. Of course, it would make me happy if you decided to make Stardust part of your life, but it will make me equally happy if you were to sell the store and use the money to buy a condo or something. Ditto with the house. It's a nice house, but it's just a house. Don't feel like you'd be tarnishing my memory or something if you decide to sell.

Aster's a good place, with good people, and I've been happy here. But there are other good places, and other good people, and wherever you're happy is where home is. I won't be insulted if you walked away from here.

Speaking of walking away... please don't hate your mom too much. I know she isn't a part of your life any more than she is of mine, but I did love her once. And I like to think that maybe, if things had been different, she would have found a reason to stay. But she needed something other than you and me and Aster.

The key is for a safe deposit box at Handley's bank. The box number is 33812. It's the authentication documents for our copy of A Christmas Carol. *I never told you how valuable it was, but it's a first print first edition. I never told you because I didn't want you to think*

*anything of us reading it together. I didn't want it to be
a thing. Don't sell it in a misguided attempt to save the
bookstore or, God forbid, extend my life if I'm on support
somewhere. You use it for yourself, what you want. I got
it at auction so many years ago. I don't know how it got
missed—I can't believe how lucky I was to find it. The
seller must not have known what he had.*

*But then again, it was also the day your mom told
me she was pregnant. So it was a doubly lucky day.*

*By the way, Dickens signed the book to Edward
Stirling. He was the man who first adapted the story for
the stage. There's a copy of the playbill in the box—it's a
facsimile, not real, so don't get excited about it.*

*And Alastair Sim was the best Scrooge. Don't even
talk to me about Bill Murray.*

Love you always,
Dad

A sob caught in his throat, and he dropped the letter to the desk next
to the key. Miss Edna picked it up and read through it, her fingers at her
throat. A quiet "oh" escaped her parted lips, and he started crying in earnest.

"Noah?" Kyle asked from the door. His mouth had fallen open, and
he still clutched the laptop with both hands.

"It's a letter from my dad," Noah said, waving vaguely at the paper
in Miss Edna's hands.

"Why wasn't this with all of his other paperwork?" Miss Edna
asked as she handed the note back to Noah.

"Maybe he only meant for me to find it if I wanted to keep the
store. So he left it here." Noah shrugged. "I have no idea."

"What does it say?"

"That he loves me, that he's proud of me." Noah hiccupped back
the tears. "He had a book that we could have sold to save the store, but
it's so important to both of us. I just… I don't know. I don't know what
to do anymore. I'm sick of all this being put on me. I can't…."

Kyle dropped the laptop onto the desk and wrapped his arms
around Noah.

"It's not on you, Noah. It's on all of us. We all want to help," he whispered. "What can we do?" He rubbed Noah's back and Miss Edna put a hand on his arm.

"I don't know," he whispered back.

CHAPTER THIRTY-FOUR

"THAT'S IT, then." Noah tossed the thick envelope he'd just received onto the counter and rubbed his eyes. "It's game over. That's the final notice. We have to be out tomorrow."

"What about the book?" Kyle asked. "If you showed it to them and told them what it's worth...."

"I'd have to get it appraised, and we've run out of time. If I'd found it two weeks ago, maybe. God, I wish Henry was still around. He was always so good at talking around things."

"Well, what would he have said?"

"I don't know." Noah pinched the bridge of his nose. He was going to start crying again any minute, and he didn't know if it was from grief or frustration.

"Maybe that lawyer guy would know if the book would help."

"Steve? Maybe."

"Call him. What's the worst he can say?"

"Um, 'Brother, you're screwed'?"

"So then you're no worse off than you are now."

Noah nodded and picked up his phone.

IT TOOK a while and a couple of missed callbacks, but he finally connected with Steve. "Sorry," the lawyer said. "I was presenting a webinar. What can I do you out of, Noah?"

"Well, it's about the mortgages? They're due tomorrow, and while I haven't got the money, I did find a first edition of a book that I think is valuable. I just don't have the time to get it authenticated, but I'm pretty sure it's worth more than the mortgages are."

"Hang on, kiddo. The mortgages are due tomorrow? I thought you had until the end of the year to get them caught up."

"Well, I got them current right after I saw you—you said I should. And yeah, I thought I had till the end of December too, but a couple of weeks ago I got a letter from the bank telling me they'd be due November 30. And then today I got the final letter saying they're due tomorrow. I have some of the money, but not all of it, but I thought if they'd take the book on security maybe they'd give me a couple more months. At least enough time to get it appraised or whatever."

"Okay. I'm confused. You got the accounts caught up."

"Yeah."

"And the estate's still in probate."

"Yeah. But Matt said that the bank, as a primary lienholder, can foreclose even if the estate's not out yet."

"Technically, yes, but that usually only goes if the account is still in arrears. Which you tell me it's not."

"Right."

"Well, I don't know about the book—it's something you should talk to the bank directly about. But I do know that a deed in lieu should give you enough time to get the book appraised and even sold."

"What's a deed in lieu?"

There was silence on the other end. "They didn't offer you the deed in lieu of foreclosure option?"

"I don't think so. Kyle, can you hand me that letter? Thanks. Okay. No. It's a 'pay up' letter. There wasn't anything in the other notice either, except for a Post-it from Matt saying 'tried, sorry' and a smiley face."

Again, a couple of moments of silence. Then, "Let me check into something and get back to you, okay?"

"Sure. Whatever you can do. I mean, we're packing up the books, but we won't be done with that by tomorrow either. I'm hoping they don't want us to clear out immediately."

"No, I'm sure not. Give me a few, okay?"

"Sure. Thanks for your help."

"Uh-huh." Steve sounded distracted. Noah assumed someone else was demanding his attention until Steve came back and said, "Put together everything—and I do mean everything—you have on the mortgages."

"Will do." Noah clicked off and looked at Kyle. "Is it my imagination, or do you think he's onto something?"

"I hope he is. He seemed pretty taken back by what you told him."

"Well, guess we'd better get those papers together."

Kyle nodded. "On it."

WHEN THE phone rang a little while later, it wasn't Steve's number that came up but a local Aster exchange. "Hello?" Noah asked curiously.

"Hi, is this Noah Hitchens?"

"It is."

"This is Bob Washington over at First National. I just got off the phone with Steve Gorwin, and he's got me confused about the terms of the mortgage and the foreclosure. Would it be possible for you to come by the bank this afternoon and bring all the paperwork you have for both mortgages?"

"Sure." He glanced over at Kyle, who was watching him with hope in his gray-green eyes. "What time?"

"How about in an hour? That'll give me time to go through our records as well."

"Sure."

"Okay, see you then. Just let the receptionist know you're here to see me, not Matt."

"Okay... sure. See you in a bit." He clicked off the phone.

"Was that Steve?"

"No. That was Bob Washington at the bank. He's the VP of the loan department. Fucking Matt Handley's boss."

"One of these days you're going to slip and call him that to his face." Kyle grinned. "I want to be there. So, the boss, huh?"

"Yep. And we need everything we can possibly find for the bank. I'm not trusting just the mortgage paperwork. I want everything. Can you help?"

"Is the sky blue?"

THEY TRIED to organize everything as it went into Noah's messenger bag, but it was still a thick wad of paper he carried into the bank, right on time. Bob was standing outside his office, talking to a teller, but when he saw Noah, he waved him over and into the office.

"Thanks for coming, Noah. Things have been crazy for you lately, haven't they? What with the cult and your friend and all—on top of losing your dad."

"Yeah, pretty much. Thanks for coming to Dad's funeral. It was nice to see so many people cared about him."

"Charlie was good folks. He'll be missed. And Aster wouldn't be the same without Stardust Books."

Then why are you guys trying to shut us down? He didn't speak the words out loud, just gave him a thin smile and pulled the stack of file folders out of his bag.

Bob took the pile and went through the first few, which were the mortgage papers for both the twenty-year-old mortgage on the house and the newer loan against the store. Then he went through them again. He made some notes on the computer, then sat back, pinching the bridge of his nose. "Noah, would you mind waiting outside a few minutes? I need to go over something with another employee. Leave the papers—I'll take care of them."

"Sure." Noah got up and picked up his empty messenger bag.

"There's coffee on the sideboard. Help yourself." Bob was already picking up the phone as Noah left the office.

He sat on the leather couch just outside Bob's office. He'd gotten spoiled for good coffee and didn't have any interest in the stuff that had been probably sitting there since the bank opened. Thinking of coffee made him think of Kyle—but then, practically everything made him think of Kyle—and he allowed himself a little smile.

Matt's door opened and he came out, and Noah's smile vanished. When he saw Noah, though, Matt's lips curled in a smug grin. "Begging for mercy, book boy?"

"Not yours," Noah said dryly and pulled his cell phone from his back pocket to avoid any more interaction with him.

Matt snorted and went into the office.

"Close the door," Bob said curtly, and Matt obeyed.

Noah couldn't hear anything at first, but apparently Bob was building up a good head of steam, because eventually he could make out phrases, if not actual sentences. Phrases like "customer service" and "bank reputation" and "I don't care if it's technically legal, we don't do business like that!" Then it was on to "foreclosure costs" and "bad decisions."

Matt said, "But there won't be any costs! One of our bigger clients has already made a bid for the store!"

Dead silence. Then Bob snapped, "You are not telling me you shared confidential information regarding a client with another client?"

Muttering from Matt.

"And we do not differentiate between our clients. I expect you to treat every client—from six-year-olds depositing their allowance to the biggest multimillionaires—with exactly the same courtesy and confidentiality."

Noah glanced over at the teller Bob had been talking to. She was grinning widely, and when she met his eyes, she gave him a thumbs-up.

Another door opened and Mike Handley, president of the bank, emerged. He paused when he saw Noah and gave him a nod. "Noah."

"Mr. Handley."

The bank president went into Bob's office, and there was quiet conversation for a quarter hour. Then the door opened again and both Handleys came out. There was no smug smirk on Matt's face; he didn't look at Noah at all.

"Thanks for waiting, Noah. Come in."

KYLE POUNCED as soon as Noah floated in the door. "What happened?"

"Fucking Matt Handley got his fucking ass handed to him. In pieces. It was glorious." Noah dropped the messenger bag on the counter and grabbed Kyle, hauling him into a passionate kiss. "The store mortgage was all fucked-up from the get-go, and the foreclosure shit was as well. The bank doesn't take any action on current accounts that are in probate, like Steve said. It's standard procedure. And even if they did, there were options we had that Matt didn't tell us about. The store mortgage is being converted into a business loan at better terms, which is how it should have been to begin with. And—the authentication and appraisals for the book that Dad had done a few years ago were in the safe deposit box. Steve told me that increased my assets tremendously since it's worth way more than fifty grand. Best yet? It's in my name, not Dad's, so we don't have to wait for probate. They're going to refinance the loans at a lower interest rate based on my new circumstances, namely that I came into possession of a very valuable asset." Noah dropped onto the stool behind the counter. "After probate's completed, the bank is going to convert the mortgage on the house into my name, but Bob said there wouldn't be any trouble doing it, even with the school loans."

"And you won't have to sell your dad's book." Kyle put his arms around Noah. "Oh, boy. I feel like a weight is lifted off us."

"A fifty-thousand-pound weight," Noah said. "Yeah."

"It's like we both get to start our lives all over again," Kyle said, and Noah could see in his face that he was thinking about his family.

"Only this time, we get to start them together." Noah wrapped his arms around Kyle and kissed him lightly.

"Together," Kyle agreed.

CHAPTER THIRTY-FIVE

DECEMBER BEGAN with a chill not often seen in Georgia. Even Jake was reluctant to leave the warmth and comfort of their house, and he wore a full-time fur coat. Noah pulled his heavy winter coat out of the New York stuff he still hadn't gone through yet. He had another, dressier one that he gave to Kyle. Together they climbed into the truck and headed out to Calhoun Baptist, where generations of Henry's family had been buried. The church was a small white building laid back against the countryside just outside Aster. The day might have been cool, but the sun shone bright and strong against the church steeple high above them. It had a one-room-schoolhouse kind of feel to it with four low windows along its side. An American flag waved at them from a pole out front, and sparse well-kept greenery lined the entrance. Those were the only colors against a cloudless blue sky.

They parked in a small gravel lot next to the church and headed for the wrought iron gate peeking out from behind the building. Rust dotted the surface of the fence, but the space within was well maintained. There were few leaves between the modest markers as they peeked up out of the ground in bunches. Miss Berenice said that the old church cemetery had nearly hit its capacity, but old Reverend Lincoln remembered her daddy and opened up its gates. She hadn't held a service because all of Henry's friends were long dead. Instead she simply asked them to lay him to rest.

Noah lifted the latch on the gate, and it moved with surprising ease. He held the gate open for Kyle, and together they walked directly to the only grave covered in dying flowers and a mound of dirt that hadn't had a chance to settle. They read the tombstones along the way and found Renee McDaniel, Henry's wife. Then, just a few markers up, Estelle and Jonah McDaniel, which judging by their dates must have been Henry's parents. They found a few others who might have been siblings, though

Henry had never mentioned any. But soon they stood above the new markerless grave, and Noah's curiosity turned to sorrow.

"Hi, Henry," he said, his voice barely above a whisper. It felt sillier than it should talking to a mound of dirt after spending a month with a ghost. "We were able to save the store. My dad had a first edition you would have loved." Noah smiled then, thinking about how excited Henry would have been to see the rare Dickens book.

Kyle reached down and held his hand, cold in the icy December morning, and a tear slid down his cheek.

"The coffee bar is doing well, and the cult has been broken up. Yeira said that most of them are in jail. Hope went into protective custody, and it looks like she'll be okay. Berenice is good. I think finding you and talking with you brought her some peace. I think she's got the church to host a dinner for all of the county firemen. She's a force," he said with a chuckle. He was quiet for a long moment after, letting his eyes roam the landscape. They landed on a tree in the corner of the cemetery, the fence bulging up out of the ground around it. It stood old and strong like a sentinel watching over the dead.

"I miss you, Henry, but I'm glad you're at peace now. Maybe you and my dad can become friends. Maybe he can thank you for helping his son save his store. Because I'm very grateful to you. You made such a difference in my life, even in just that one month, and I'll never forget what you've done for us." The tears came faster now, and Kyle squeezed his hand a little harder.

They stood there for several minutes, hands clasped, looking down at the mound of dirt. Noah wasn't sure what he expected to happen, but nothing happened except a soft breeze and the rustling of leaves against the fence. The tree swayed soundlessly above them.

"Let's go home," Kyle said and pulled him close. He kissed Noah's hair and led him back to the truck.

Kyle drove carefully. Since the cult had been disbanded, Kyle was free to get government registrations, IDs, and his driver's permit. He'd planned to do those things after they'd cleared out the bookstore. The whole world lay before them now.

They parked in front of the store and had just stepped up on the curb when Noah glanced up and noticed movement in the store. He put a hand over his eyes and peered through the window. Miss Edna flitted across the aisle, carrying a tray. With the shadows, he couldn't make out what she carried, but she disappeared into the coffee bar. He glanced at Kyle, who shrugged and turned the knob on the door. It opened easily even though the Closed sign showed through the door.

"Hello!" Noah called and heard a bit of murmuring on the other side of the room. "Miss Edna?"

"I'm back here making coffee," she called.

"Why are you making coffee, we aren't even op—" He stopped abruptly as he came around the corner to see half the town squeezed into the coffee bar. A handmade banner that read "Congratulations" hung on the back wall with balloons.

"Surprise!" she cried with a smile. Her voice seemed to break the milling crowd from their silence, and they surrounded Noah with handshakes, smiles, and half hugs. Miss Berenice and Miss Ellie gave him the hardest hugs of all.

Noah stood quietly, dumbfounded by their support, looking around at their familiar faces, and knew he was home.

JP BARNABY, an award-winning gay romance novelist, is the author of over two dozen books, including *Aaron* and the Little Boy Lost Series. She recently moved from Chicago to Atlanta to appease her Camaro, who didn't like the blustery winters. JP specializes in recovery romance, but slips in a few erotic or comedic stories to spice things up. When she's not hanging out with hot guys in leather, she binge-watches superheroes and crime dramas on Netflix. A physics geek, she likes the science side of sci-fi and wants to grow up to be Reed Richards.

Want to keep up with JP's latest releases?

Follow her on Amazon, Facebook, Twitter, or on her website.

Amazon: www.amazon.com/J.P.-Barnaby/e/B003ZL3J9A
Facebook: www.facebook.com/profile.php?id=780094684
Twitter: @JPBarnaby
Website: www.JPBarnaby.com

ROWAN SPEEDWELL is a cynic who believes in romance, an obsessive-compulsive who lives in chaos, and an introvert who loves to start conversations with strangers. Everything is fodder for a story, so be careful what you say to her.

While not plotting either a novel or world domination (which will never happen because she's far too lazy, but the world would be run so much better if she was in charge), she can be found reading, watching superhero movies, reading, and trying to avoid being bitten by her cat, Psycho. (Just kidding—her cat's name is Pandora. Not kidding about the biting, though.) And reading. She loves history but hates historical novels, because people never get them right. Historical romances are okay because no one expects them to be remotely accurate. Her other hobby is buying craft supplies. Not doing crafts, just buying the supplies.

Her favorite activity is untangling yarn snarls.

She is a longtime member of the Society for Creative Anachronism.

She has a website, www.rowanspeedwell.com, but is terrible about